# *Ruthless Vows*

## Sutton Kay

**Sutton Kay Books**

# Also by Sutton Kay

**The Ruthless Love Series**

*Ruthless Vows*

*Ruthless Temptations* – Coming Summer 2026

ISBN-13: 979-8-9953617-01

Cover design by: GermanCreative - Lesia
Library of Congress Control Number: 2026907389
Printed in the United States of America

*For those who want to be chosen, no matter the cost.*

# Playlist

"The Summoning" – Sleep Token

"Control" – Halsey

"In the Woods Somewhere" – Hozier

"Go to War" – Nothing More

"Way Down We Go" – Kaleo

"Granite" – Sleep Token

"Blood // Water" – grandson

"Take Me to Church" – Hozier

"Hurricane" – Fleurie

"Lovely" – Billie Eilish

"Taken Me Back to Eden" – Sleep Token

"I Will Follow You into the Dark " – Death Cab for Cutie

# Content Warning

This is a dark romance intended for mature readers (18+)

Ruthless Temptation is a dark contemporary romance that contains mature themes, including violence, attempted assault, grief, organized crime elements, and complex family dynamics. This story features morally gray characters and protective, possessive dynamics that may not be considered "soft" romance.

Reader discretion is advised.

# Chapter 1

*Sierra*

Bass pulsed through *Last Call*, thick and relentless, but it reached the back bar softened, muffled by walls and distance. I moved behind the counter unhurried, pouring measured drinks for men who didn't like to wait but hated being rushed. Friday nights always packed the place; back here, the noise gave way to low conversations and watchful eyes, the air heavy with expectation, and with a kind of freedom I hadn't tasted in months.

A few strands of my black hair kept slipping loose, brushing my cheek every time I leaned forward. I shoved them back with my wrist, already annoyed. I should've clipped it up, but Jenna had insisted I wear it down, and I hadn't felt like arguing.

The jacket stayed, though. Oversized denim, sleeves shoved up where they always ended up, tattoos finally healed enough that I didn't worry about bumping them on glassware. My old band tee hung long over my leggings, the hem tugged crooked from moving all night. The Docs felt solid against the floor—good traction, good weight. I wasn't trading that for heels, no matter how much Jenna pushed.

I'd met Jenna my first week at the bar, and we'd clicked instantly. Giovanni Marcello, the bar's owner, had a soft spot for strays with shadowed pasts, and both of us carried more than we admitted. Jenna, with her honey-blonde hair and sunshine smile, hid a sadness in her eyes I recognized too well. Even with separate apartments, we rarely spent nights apart. Our friendship filled cracks the world didn't bother looking for.

Tonight shouldn't have been any different, but despite walking to work together, I hadn't seen her once since the rush hit. Jenna usually worked the main bar, where her charm practically glowed. *Last Call* had a way of feeling like two bars stitched together.

The front bar was all exposed brick and borrowed glamour, packed shoulder to shoulder with fresh twenty-ones chasing neon, bass, and the idea of danger without its teeth. Jenna thrived there. She worked the room like she was doing everyone a favor, bright smile, easy laugh, pouring drinks fast enough to keep the night light.

The back bar was something else entirely.

It stayed dim even on busy nights. Leather chairs replaced stools. Conversations dropped an octave. The men who sat back here didn't dance or shout over the music. They wore tailored suits and spoke softly, talking business no one asked about and nobody interrupted.

This was my territory.

I didn't smile unless I meant it. I didn't flirt unless there was leverage in it. Behind the back bar, I set the tone—measured pours, steady eye contact, an unspoken expectation that anyone sitting there knew how to behave. Antique photographs lined the walls: sharp-suited men, some holding guns, others just looking like they didn't need to. Rumor said *Last Call* used to be a mafia haunt. The back bar didn't bother denying it.

A few hours into the shift, I smelled her before I saw her—something light and fruity that didn't belong back here.

"SIERRRAAAAA!" Jenna's sing-song voice cut straight through the noise.

A few of the young men at the back bar glanced up, irritation flickering across their faces. Not startled. These weren't frat boys—still young, but polished. Tailored trousers, crisp button-ups with sleeves rolled to the forearms, ink visible where cuffs should've been. Watches that probably cost more than my rent caught the low light. Their eyes were glassy but sharp, riding that precise edge where judgment dulled and confidence sharpened. Dangerous, not drunk.

I clocked it automatically. Men like that always noticed Jenna.

She pushed through anyway, all sparkle and momentum. I understood the stares—honey-blonde hair piled into a messy bun, bright makeup framing blue-green eyes, pink shirt-dress unbuttoned just enough to be intentional, white thigh-high boots making her legs look endless.

She slid across the bar like it belonged to her and nearly collapsed into my side, breath coming in exaggerated, ragged huffs. "You will never guess—"

Another voice cut her off.

"So this is where you disappeared to."
It used to give me butterflies.
Now it froze my blood mid-pulse.

The bar slipped out of focus, like the glass sliding from my hand.

Bright lights. Crystal glasses. Laughter warm against my ear.

An arm heavy around my waist, breath sweet with wine as he whispered, *You are mine now, little dove.*

It had felt protective then.
Now the memory made my stomach roll.

I blinked, but the room blurred again. He stepped closer—slow, deliberate. Like a cat stalking something cornered. My heart slammed in time with the bass.

Silverware clinking in another room. Another penthouse. Another party I didn't belong at. Laughter floating too far away to help. His hand closing around my arm, hard enough to bruise. The dress clinging to me like a cage.

His pupils blown wide with cocaine, smile too sharp.
"You embarrassed me," he hissed—

**SMACK.**

White light. Cold floor. Silence.

The sharp crack of pool balls echoed from the corner table, bouncing off the low walls. I flinched, gripping the bar, only halfway present. Jenna's voice called my name somewhere past the counter, muffled by the low hum of conversation. I smelled cologne and sweat, sharp and familiar, mixing with the faint sweetness that always clung to her.

Cold metal biting into my wrists. A chair beneath me. The slow drip… drip… drip of water in the dark.

Matteo stepped into view. Hair wild like fire. That once-sweet smile curling cruel at the edges.

His knife tapped my cheek—slow, patient.
"You don't walk away from me, *little dove*."

A twitch.
The blade pressed into my skin.

"Sierra!" I could hear Jenna calling my name, my head felt like it was going to explode. A deep voice said something about blood, I looked down at my hand but all I could see was blood on the concrete steps.

My blood.

I watched the taillights of the car that dropped me speed away.

My mother's scream, someone picking me up.

I could hear their voices, arguing.

*Oh my god. They were still going to make me marry him.*

I ran that night. Packed everything I could shove into a duffle, hailed a taxi, and disappeared. I thought I was free.

But the monster I'd been running from had found me.

The sounds of the bar rushed back—glasses clinking, muted laughter, ice rattling in a shaker. And there he was, draped across the bar like he owned it, every inch of him predatory. His dark auburn hair caught the dim light just enough to make him look careless—and dangerous. The young men who'd been daring enough to sit at the back had scattered. They liked living on the edge, but crossing him was a line they didn't dare test.

At 6', broad-shouldered, moving with that slow, deliberate weight that screamed control, he looked like a panther ready to strike. The room seemed to shrink around him even before he'd moved. He leaned toward me, elbows on the bar, voice low and deliberate.

"I told you I'd find you," he said. "Daddy gave you up when he was… persuaded." A laugh, sharp and empty, cut through the noise. There was nothing warm in it—only danger.

Eight months ago, my parents tracked me down. They showed up at Giovanni's, my mother's face a mask of desperate hope and my father's a storm of forced patience. They thought a few months of freedom would be a rebellious phase, that I'd have come to my senses.

My mother played her part, talking of family, of duty, of the life I was throwing away. My father cut to the chase, his voice low and cold. He threatened to disinherit me, to cut me off from every cent of the Blackwell fortune. It was the only card he had left to play.

I just laughed. I told them they couldn't threaten me with a life I'd already run from, and they certainly couldn't pay me enough to go back to the monster they'd chosen for me. After a few more choice words, they finally got the message. I wasn't their bargaining chip anymore. They left, and I hadn't heard from them since.

Until now.

"Matteo, you need to leave," I said, forcing the words past a throat tight with fear. I tried to keep my voice steady, but his gaze terrified me. I knew what he was capable of. My scars, physical and mental, were a cold reminder of what money and power could do, how easily it could twist love into ownership.

My hand was stinging. I looked down. The rocks glass I'd been holding had shattered, and adrenaline I hadn't even realized was flooding me surged through my veins. Before I could register the pain, his hand shot across the bar, fast and hard. He flipped my hand over, palm up. A shard of glass was embedded in my skin, and blood was already welling up, dripping onto the polished wood.

"Oh," he clicked his tongue, his eyes fixed on the cut with a disturbing fascination. "I'm not leaving without you. *You are mine*." His voice dipped into that darker, proprietary tone I recognized all too well. He pulled the glass out and I winced at the pain.

I tried to pull my hand back, but his grip tightened, a steel band around my wrist. "You're hurting me," my voice was barely a whisper, a pathetic sound I hated.

Suddenly, the bar around us came into sharp, terrifying focus. The clinking of ice and low murmur of conversation had died. The young men by the pool tables had stopped their game, trading tense glances. The older men nursing their whiskeys were suddenly intent on their napkins, doing their best not to see what was happening. Even Jenna was frozen beside me, clinging to my other arm like a life preserver, her face a mask of horror and disgust.

"Am I?" Matteo practically growled, and yanked my palm to his lips. He slowly, deliberately licked the blood trickling from the cut. Bile rose hot and acidic in my throat. I tried to yank my arm back again, but he just pulled harder, the sharp edge of the bar slamming into my hips, pinning me in place.

"Matteo."

The voice wasn't mine. It was calm, deep, and cut through the suffocating tension like a shard of ice. Giovanni stood at the end of the bar, a polished rag in his hand, his eyes hard and unflinching. He wasn't looking at me or Jenna. He was looking only at Matteo.

"You're done here," Giovanni said. It wasn't a question. It was a statement of fact, delivered with the quiet certainty of a man who had seen far worse and knew exactly how to handle it. "Get out."

"Relax, old man, I'll go." He released my hand, but the gleam in his eye sent a shiver down my spine. "Don't worry, little dove, I know how to find you now."

He winked at Jenna, probably enjoying her terror, as he walked to the door. He took his time, making sure everyone was paying attention. Once the door shut behind him, the tension relaxed immediately, like a balloon had popped.

"Jax, take over," Gio nodded at the dark-eyed bartender, Jax Vitelli, who seemed to have materialized next to him.

"You got it boss," Jax nodded, his steel gray eyes immediately zeroing in on the scene in front of him. He glanced from my hand to Jenna's grip on my arm. "I got you," he whispered as we passed him, moving out from behind the bar. I knew it was meant for just Jenna so I pretended I didn't hear. We followed Gio toward the front bar, past the entrance Matteo had left through. A narrow hallway joined the front and back bars with Gio's office and the bathrooms leading off in opposite directions.

The office door closed behind me with a soft click, sealing me away from the music and chaos outside. I barely noticed Giovanni gesturing toward the chairs as he retrieved a first-aid kit from his desk drawer, my mind still spinning.

"GIRL. WHAT. THE. FUCK." Jenna practically yelled at me. *Yeah… what the fuck?* My thoughts bounced like a pinball, each one colliding with the next. I closed my eyes, forcing myself to breathe evenly. Eight months. I thought it was enough. I thought I was finally free.

"How could they tell him where I am?" I whispered, the words barely leaving my lips. I sank into one of Giovanni's plush chairs, leather soft enough to swallow secrets whole, the kind of seat that made it feel like whatever I said would never leave the room.

Jenna's hand found mine, gripping it gently. Blood still seeped from where the glass had cut my palm. "We need to get that cleaned up," she said softly, worry flickering in her eyes.

Giovanni crouched beside me, opening the first aid kit he'd grabbed with deliberate care. I watched him work: antiseptic swab, careful cleaning, then the soft wrap of gauze around my hand. His hands were steady, sure, and I realized my pulse was finally starting to slow.

"There," he said quietly when he finished, tucking the end of the tape neatly. "That should hold for now. Keep it elevated if you can."

I flexed my fingers gingerly, testing the bandage. Jenna squeezed my other hand and gave a small nod, but I could still feel the tension in my shoulders. Matteo had found me, and nothing in the room—no soft leather, no antiseptic bandage, no whispered reassurances—was going to make that reality any less dangerous.

"So… are you going to explain all that?" Gio's voice was gravelly from years of smoking the pipe he was lighting, but somehow it was still comforting. Hints of sweet vanilla and tobacco drifted through the office as he puffed.

I knew eventually I would have to, but I wanted it to be on my terms. No one else's. I owed him an explanation—after all, it was my fault a psycho like Matteo had made such a scene at his bar.

I took a deep breath. "Do you have any wine in here?"

His eyes crinkled at the edges, betraying a small, amused smile. Without a word, he pulled a bottle from the cabinet: *Notturna Moretti Riserva*, dark, sweet, perfectly mine. Growing up in the more elite side of town had its perks, and yes—I had acquired elite tastes along the way. Maybe a little spoiled, but I didn't care. I liked my wine.

Jenna uncorked the bottle using the little corkscrew on her wristband and poured. The first sip warmed me, and I let myself relax just enough to start talking.

I told them about Matteo, the expectations, the engagement I'd been forced into to save face after a deal gone sideways. I explained how he charmed me at first, how the parties seemed like nothing more than wealthy sons trying to outdo one another, and how I had thought the rumors were just that—rumors. I tried to rein him in, and it backfired.

I told them about the little things first—the too-tight handholds, the moments he held me in place, caging me, testing boundaries. How I had started planning an exit, but had no idea how to get out safely. How I'd watched him lose it over some random slight, the blood, the chaos. How I had witnessed things I wasn't supposed to see—and he made me regret it.

Then there was the last party. A docked yacht, extravagant and suffocating. He wanted me to test a product he was buying, to be his guinea pig. I refused. He knocked me out and dragged me to the dock house. That's where he cut me with his damn switchblade for the last time.

By the time I finished, Jenna and I had almost drained the bottle. My hand still throbbed slightly where the glass had cut me, but I let the wine burn away some of the panic, the fear, and the memory. Gio puffed on his pipe, face a deadly combination of calm and anger.

"He will not be allowed back in here." His statement was final, solid. I wanted to believe him, but I knew better.

"Gio, can we go home early tonight?" Jenna was using her sweet voice. I rolled my eyes, this is how she charmed everyone. "Its just been a long night and it might be good to get out of here, you know? Sierra can stay with me tonight!" Even though we were both 27, we hadn't outgrown sleepovers and I definitely didn't want to spend tonight alone.

"That's a good idea, make sure you clock out first." Gio nodded, waving us out of his office. Jenna pulled me up from the chair and linked her arm in mine.

"We will!" she chirped, flashing him a wolfish grin.

******

Jenna's place hit me the moment we stepped inside. I'd been here before, but only rarely overnight—usually we crashed at my apartment. Despite living by herself, her parents didn't like the idea of her having friends over at odd hours, especially ones who could be… unpredictable. Our families ran in similar circles so they of course had heard about my "digression." And besides, my place was closer to our favorite hangouts, easier to disappear into the night.

Still, stepping through the door now, I had to admit it felt different. The doorman gave her a familiar nod and let us through without a word. The lobby smelled faintly of polished marble and vanilla candles—everything neat, controlled, and perfectly curated. Swanky, yes, the kind of place her parents adored: high ceilings, floor-to-ceiling windows, a view of the city that glimmered like it existed to impress.

Inside, the apartment was just as polished. Minimalist furniture, glossy surfaces, expensive art, and warm, ambient lighting. The kind of place where a socialite could host cocktails and convince everyone her life was effortless. And yet, Jenna's personality cut through it all—plush rugs over hard floors, cozy throws on sleek couches, little signs that someone actually lived there.

Her parents would have been thrilled for her to stay here forever: marry someone rich, handsome, impeccably polite, and live exactly the life they'd mapped out. But Jenna wasn't built for that, and neither was I. We wanted something real, something we chose. Someone who loved us, not our names or the inheritance that came with them.

I sank into the couch, letting the leather mold to me, and tried to breathe. For one night, at least, I could forget Matteo, forget the past, forget all the rules shoved down our throats. Here, in Jenna's world of curated perfection, I could just be me—edges rough, scars hidden, and maybe, for a little while, that was enough.

By the time we'd ordered enough junk food to shame a small convenience store, we were sprawled across the couch in Jenna's living room, laughing like idiots at reruns and each other. Crumbs and empty soda cans littered the coffee table, and I couldn't remember the last time I'd felt this… normal.

Then her phone rang. Late. Who the hell could be calling now?

Jenna groaned, snatching it up. "Hello?" Her voice started light and cheerful, the usual sing-song tone I'd come to depend on. Then the sound of her words shifted, sharp edges creeping in. My ears tuned automatically. "No, I told you—… I don't care what the dress code says!........ Fine!.......I said I'd be there, but…."

I sank further into the couch, pretending to focus on the TV, but the tension in her voice sliced through everything. She hung up after a few more harsh words, muttering something under her breath before sliding back next to me.

Her energy had changed. The lightness that filled the apartment moments ago was gone. She didn't say it out loud, but I could feel it; the way her shoulders slumped, the way her smile was tighter, forced.

"There's an art gallery opening in a couple nights-big to do about it ," she said finally, trying to push the cheer back into her voice. "And… you're coming with me."

I didn't answer immediately. My throat felt tight. I hated those kind of events. They felt more like a social trial by fire, a world I wasn't ready to step back into. Jenna hadn't reached my no-contact point yet—she was still trying to please, still trying to smooth over the edges that our parents and the city's elite demanded of her. She had tried a few other times to get me to go; a garden party, charity auction. She was staring at me afraid I'd say no, I could feel it in the way she fussed with her hair, the subtle bite at her lip.

"…Okay," I said reluctantly. My voice barely above a whisper.

Her face lit up instantly, all sparkle and momentum again, and she grabbed my hand. "Yes! Dress shopping first thing! You're going to love it—I promise."

I allowed myself a small smile, watching her excitement ripple through the room. Even when the world pressed in, Jenna carried this ability to make it feel lighter, just for a little while. And tonight, after everything, I could use that.

******

We started the day at one of those sunlit cafés Jenna loved, the kind with marble tables and perfectly frosted pastries. She chattered nonstop, dragging me along while I nursed my coffee, half-listening and half-watching the city wake up around us. For a little while, it was normal—laughing over spilled syrup and toast crumbs, talking about anything except Matteo, the gallery, or our parents.

By mid-morning, we were at the boutique, the smell of new fabric and polished wood greeting us as we stepped inside. Racks of dresses stretched in every color and texture imaginable, the soft jazz overhead somehow making the place feel smaller, intimate. Jenna immediately started digging through the racks, and we split up, each disappearing into separate dressing rooms.

I pulled on the dress I'd had my eye on—deep red, off-the-shoulder straps, a plunging neckline, and a high slit. It hugged my curves, the slit grazing my leg with every move, and the neckline left my collarbone scar bare. It wasn't subtle, but it was exactly the kind of bold statement I wanted tonight. I took a deep breath, steeling myself, then stepped out of the dressing room to show Jenna.

And immediately, I crashed into someone.

"Oh—I'm so sorry!" I blurted, stumbling back slightly.

He was impossibly tall, broad-shouldered, and perfectly Italian. Dark hair fell in just the right waves over his forehead, and stormy eyes locked on mine like he had been waiting. The faint scent of leather and something richer, darker, hit me, and I froze, caught in the heat of him without even knowing why. He held me steady by the elbows, his touch calm, deliberate, predatory without being threatening.

"Careful," he said, his accent making the word feel teasing, dangerous, and intimate all at once.

"Sierra! Oh my god, you look amazing!" Jenna's voice squeaked behind me, but it wasn't oblivious this time. Her gaze darted from me to the man, her smile faltering as she took in the intensity of his stare, the way he was still holding me.

I could only stare at him, words trapped somewhere between curiosity, caution, and… something I wasn't ready to name. "I—I wasn't looking," I managed, trying to pull my hand free, but he let go slowly, his gaze still fixed on me.

"Clearly," he said, low, restrained, and utterly mesmerizing. He noticed the bandage still wrapped on my hand. "Apparently you make chaos a habit."

I nodded, heat creeping to my cheeks. Jenna, now standing beside me, subtly nudged my arm, her eyes wide with a silent question. "I just pulled like four more dresses to try! Let's go!" she said, her voice a little too bright, trying to break the spell, tugging at my arm.

I followed her mechanically, but my eyes kept drifting back to him. Even standing still, he radiated a kind of calm power that made the air feel heavier, the world smaller. I could feel his gaze, intent on my back. And I had the sinking, thrilling suspicion that this wasn't an accident at all.

Jenna was holding up a blush-pink cocktail dress, long, flowing, with just the right hint of shimmer to look effortlessly elegant. "What do you think? Too much?" she asked, twirling lightly.

I circled her, my hands hovering over the fabric, smoothing out imaginary wrinkles. "No," I said softly. "It's perfect. Sophisticated, elegant… and it'll totally turn heads without screaming it."

She grinned, clearly pleased with my approval. "I knew you'd get it. You have that… eye," she said, brushing a strand of hair behind her ear.

I nodded, glancing toward the entrance again. My pulse ticked up every time a shadow of movement crossed my peripheral vision. We'd already noticed him—the tall, dark stranger from earlier—leaning against a rack, scanning the boutique as though the whole place belonged to him.

Jenna's voice dropped to a whisper. "Do you think…?"

I shook my head subtly. "Shh. Don't stare too obviously, but yeah… definitely him. That guy. Something about him…"

She leaned closer, lowering her voice even more. "He's… intense."

"Yeah. Dangerous-looking intense," I murmured, eyes flicking back to him. Even at a distance, I could feel it—the way he carried himself, measured, like everything and everyone was part of his calculation.

Jenna grinned despite the caution in her tone. "Well… he's certainly making this dress shopping feel more exciting."

I allowed a small smirk. "Just don't let him see you notice too much."

We continued whispering back and forth, critiquing fabrics, lengths, and sleeve styles, all while glancing at him through the racks. Even as we finished up at the checkouts, the air between us and him thrummed with that silent, predatory energy I couldn't ignore. I glanced around for him one last time before we left, but he had disappeared.

Jenna teased me as we got into the car, the driver asking where we wanted to go. "Oh home please, we've had enough fun for today!" She waggled her brows making me laugh harder than I had since Matteo showed up.

"You're incorrigible," I swatted at her, but I couldn't keep the smile off my face.

She just laughed, bright and easy, and I had to admit—she wasn't wrong. Running into our mystery man in the boutique had been… exhilarating. My pulse had picked up, my heart had thudded a little faster than it should have.

But I forced myself to let go of his face, his presence, the way he'd loomed over me like a storm waiting to break. I was done with the bad-boy type. Hell, I might be done with all boys at this point.

Jenna nudged me with her elbow, sensing my brooding. "You're going to think about him all night, aren't you?"

I groaned, leaning back against the seat. "Probably," I admitted, my hands tightening on the edge of the car door. "But I'll forget about him in a couple days."

She grinned, unbothered by my stubbornness. "Oh, sure. That's exactly what's going to happen."

I rolled my eyes but laughed anyway. Maybe letting go wasn't going to be as easy as I'd hoped, his dark eyes still searing into me.

******

The boutique doors closed behind me with that soft click of perfection, the scent of new fabric and leather fading as I stepped onto the street. Tailored suit zipped up safely in a simple black garment bag, the fabric cut just right—something the curator of that gallery would notice. My family's vineyard was providing the centerpiece for tomorrow night's opening, a favor for the curator. Favors were the currency that mattered, more than money ever could. A gesture here, a whispered acknowledgment there, and suddenly doors opened where none should exist.

I watched from across the street as the blonde and her raven-haired friend slipped into a car, laughing like they owned the world. License plate committed to memory. My mind burned with the image of the woman in the wine-red dress—her bold stride, the way the fabric clung just right, the flash of collarbone scar under the plunging neckline. I wanted to know who gave it to her. I wanted to know her name. I wanted to see her again.

The Maserati growled under my hands as I slammed it into gear. A few blocks later, the driver dropped them off in front of some swanky apartment building, the kind of place built to impress and cage at the same time. Another mental note. I let the engine purr as I watched them disappear inside before I drove off, patience already burning beneath the surface.

******

Back at the family office, my older brother Marco's voice cut through the low hum of my thoughts like a blade.

"Lorenzo," he said sharply. "Are you even listening?"

I lifted my gaze. Marco sat at the head of the table, immaculate as ever, fingers steepled, expression carved from discipline and expectation. Dario lounged near the window, polishing a glass he didn't need to polish, watching the room like it amused him.

"I'm listening," I said evenly.

"No," Marco replied. "You're somewhere else. Tomorrow night isn't a party. It's leverage. Favors. Connections. Currency. Money means nothing if the right doors don't open."

I resisted the urge to scoff. "I know how this works."

"Then act like it," he snapped. "We're supplying the wine as a favor to the curator. That's the public face. The real reason we're there is Gabriel Bellandi."

Dario's mouth curved. "Matteo Rinaldi's cousin. Cleans money through art sales. Likes attention. Likes to feel important, brother."

"Which makes him useful," Marco said. "We observe. We isolate. We don't make noise."

I leaned back in my chair, jaw tight. These events always felt the same, perfume, polished smiles, shallow conversations pretending to matter. Silk and lies, served with good wine.

Dario glanced at me, amused. "Careful, brother. Not everything can be solved with fists and blood. Sometimes the knife stays hidden."

I didn't answer. My mind had already drifted—uninvited—to dark eyes, dark hair, the deep red of a dress that had clung like it belonged to her. The way she'd moved through the boutique as if the world adjusted around her.

Marco noticed the silence. He always did. "Whatever you're distracted by," he warned, "it waits. Tomorrow, you show up. You smile. You play your part."

"I will," I said, though my fingers curled against the desk.

The meeting ended shortly after. Dario left first, whistling under his breath. Marco lingered just long enough to level me with a look that said *don't fuck this up*, then disappeared down the hall.

I retreated to my office and shut the door.

I didn't hesitate before calling Emil.

He picked up on the second ring. "Lorenzo," he drawled. "Miss me already?"

"I need two things," I said, cutting him off. "First—a license plate. Black sedan. Tinted windows." I recited the number from memory.

A pause. Then a low chuckle. "Interesting."

"Don't," I warned.

"Relax. I'll have a name by morning."

"Good. Second—Bellandi will be at the gallery tomorrow night."

Emil's tone shifted instantly. "The Rinaldi cousin."

"Yes. I want everything he knows. Money movement. Art sales. Shipping lanes. Quietly."

"And the plane crash?" Emil asked. "You still chasing that?"

My grip tightened on the phone. "I want to know if it was an accident or if Alessio Rinaldi decided to clear the board."

Silence stretched between us, heavy.

"Understood," Emil said finally, his voice stripped of humor. "You want me there?"

"No," I said immediately. "You make people nervous. I need Bellandi comfortable. I'll handle him."

A beat. Then Emil laughed softly. "As you wish, brother. Try not to get sentimental."

I ended the call and leaned back, staring out at the city lights.

Tomorrow night wasn't just about favors anymore.

It was about a woman in a red dress.
A scar at her collarbone.
A fresh cut on her hand.

And the sudden, dangerous certainty that whoever had hurt her had just made himself my problem. After tomorrow night, I was going to find her.

# Chapter 2



After dress shopping, Jenna's driver took us back to her apartment. We gossiped about the handsome stranger from the dress shop almost the entire way.

"He was just so intense," she breathed lightly. "I wish someone would look at me that way."

I rolled my eyes, swatting at her. "He wasn't looking at me in some special way. I think that's just his face."

Still, I sank a little deeper into the couch, thinking about that face—stormy eyes that felt like they could burn straight through me, dark hair I wanted to run my fingers through, an accent that made my knees go weak.

"Oh my god, you're blushing!" Jenna squealed.

I threw a pillow at her from across the room, but she dodged it, laughing.

"You know," she said more gently, "it's okay to get excited about someone again."

She meant Matteo. I'd told her how I'd sworn off men and relationships after the hell he'd put me through. I wanted no part of love if it came with conditions.

"He was a handsome stranger in a shop," I laughed, the sound almost bitter. "I doubt we'll ever see each other again."

Maybe later, when I was alone. Just for me—a fantasy man who could keep me warm without ever hurting me.

My phone buzzed on the table. I glanced at the screen and groaned. "Gio needs me to cover Marcus' shift tonight."

As much as I wanted to stay, I needed the money. While I hadn't officially been cut off yet, I refused to touch my bank card or AmEx. My parents needed to see that I didn't need them.

I sent a quick reply to Giovanni, letting him know I'd be there—but that I wasn't closing.

"You know you'll end up closing," Jenna teased. "When Marcus calls off, everyone suddenly finds a reason to leave early."

"I'm not," I said, shaking my head as I forced myself off the couch. "Can your driver take me to work? I don't exactly have my car."

Since we'd left together the night before, my car was still at Last Call.

"I'll come with!" she said, a little too quickly.

I glanced at her. Now it was my turn to smirk.
Jax.

"Oh? Is Jax working tonight?" I asked lightly.

She stuttered—still not used to me calling her out.
After a quick lunch, we got dressed and headed out.

Late summer evenings were my favorite. I loved
the way the soft breeze lifted my wavy hair. I swapped
my usual black leggings for bike shorts and an oversized,
faded band tee, paired with my trusty Docs. Jenna,
aiming to impress, opted for her signature pink summer
dress, tight in all the right places, effortless as always.

We piled into the black sedan and disappeared
into the night.

We entered through the back, heading straight for
the bar. Gio feigned surprise when he saw Jenna perched
on one of the leather stools, then shot me a knowing look.

It wasn't overly busy, but there was a steady flow.
Music from the dance floor bled through the walls,
muffled but rhythmic. A few guys were playing pool—
one of them leaning against the table with what he clearly
thought was a sexy look plastered across his face.

I rolled my eyes after dropping off their drinks.
They always tried their luck, harmless and predictable. I
played my role, indulging the fantasy that one night

they'd charm their way into my pants. We both knew it would never happen.

When they tried flirting with Jenna at the bar, Jax shot them a look, clear, territorial. A warning she was taken, even if she technically wasn't. Thankfully, they got the hint.

The night settled into its familiar rhythm. Easy work, inside jokes, the comfortable hum I'd been chasing for months. My thoughts drifted back to the man from the dress shop. The memory of his piercing, almost hungry eyes made me shiver.

As if summoned, the door opened—and the mood shifted.

Two men walked in.

They were both dangerously handsome, dressed in fitted black jeans and rolled-sleeve henleys. Similar chiseled jaws, high cheekbones. Brothers.

The shorter one carried more flair, his styled hair and polished movements suggesting confidence born from charm. The taller had dark, messy hair that begged to be touched—and something colder behind his eyes.

He scanned the room like he was looking for something.

Then his gaze locked on me.

The same stormy eyes from the shop.

His lips twitched, almost a smile. The shorter brother followed his line of sight, murmured something under his breath.

They sidled up to the bar. The younger brother immediately struck up a conversation with Jenna. The man from the shop leaned against the bartop, his attention never leaving me.

My body stuttered under that look. Heat crept up my neck, my face flushing. Someone cleared their throat.

"Uh, can I get a refill?" The sandy-haired guy from the pool table shook his empty glass at me.

I arched a brow. He was usually better than that. I turned toward him, hand settling on my hip as I reached for the glass.

"Not with that attitude, babe," I said, leaning into the overfamiliar cadence I usually reserved for tourists, assholes, rich boys.

The man at the bar shifted. His heavy gaze slid from me to the guy, sharp and unmistakably displeased— as if the interruption were a personal offense.

I refilled the glass with bottom-shelf liquor and ice.

"On your tab?" I asked, all practiced professionalism.

He nodded once before retreating to his friends, shoulders tucked, tail between his legs.

I turned back to the man at the bar and sighed. "Now that you've successfully scared away my customers, what do you want?"

"What do you think?"

His voice was deep, accented the same way it had been yesterday. There was a challenge threaded through it.

Normally, I'd shut this down. Instead, I found myself leaning in.

"Hm." I lowered myself to his eye level, letting his hazel eyes hold mine. "Definitely not beer. Not a cocktail. Not a margarita."

I straightened, arms folding as I tapped my chin thoughtfully. His mouth twitched again.

"Wine," I decided. "Something vintage. Something Italian."

I knelt and pulled my favorite bottle from the rack—Notturna Moretti Reserva. I didn't ask permission. I uncorked it.

Jax slid behind the bar and handed me a glass, casting a warning glance toward Jenna's would-be suitor.

"This one's my…" I stopped, unsure why I felt the sudden need to explain myself. "… this one's actually my favorite." I poured his glass carefully.

Jenna glanced over at the shift in my tone. Her attention slid past the younger man still trying far too hard and landed on the one in front of me. Both her brows shot up as she fixed him with a pointed look.

*It's him.*

She didn't say a word, but the message rang loud and clear. So much for never seeing him again.

"A Moretti red." Amusement threaded his voice as he accepted the glass, his fingers grazing mine and staying there, deliberate and unhurried. The man next to him swiveled around suddenly interested in our conversation.

"Ah, a good choice, *bella*." His voice softened—less sharp, though the accent stayed.

"Forgive my brother," he added, giving the man beside him a firm slap on the back. "We've tried to teach him manners, but Enzo here…" He tapped his own temple, circling his finger. "Thick head. Some screws loose."

"Dario-" a warning in his voice, "It's actually Lorenzo," his brother snapped, irritation cutting cleanly through the bar noise.

I bit back a laugh, enjoying the flash of frustration on his face.

"Well, Enzo, let me know what else I can do for you." I lingered on his nickname, clearly one he didn't like people using. I just wanted to push his buttons. He shifted in his seat, his eyes brushing over me, lingering just long enough on the scar along my jaw to make me feel self conscious.

I slipped to the other end of the bar, taking care of new customers. Closing time was approaching, and the bar was winding down. Jenna had left already, but not before making sure I really wanted to go home tonight. She gave me a quick hug before slipping out, giving Jax a wink. Lorenzo and his brother, Dario, were still there, but had moved to play darts, hitting the targets with deadly accuracy. Throughout the rest of the night, I felt his eyes on me—whether someone flirted a little too much or I passed him.

I called out the last round of drinks and started closing tabs. Jax was wiping down the bar when Lorenzo approached to pay.

"I figured out what you can do for me," he murmured, keeping his voice low, almost a secret. Our fingers brushed as I took his card, and he held it firm, prolonging the contact. My breath caught.

"And what's that?" I asked, forcing my voice even. His hazel eyes locked onto mine.

"Give me your number." It wasn't a request, it was an order, the kind he clearly knew how to give. I could have given it, but in that instant, I bristled under his gaze. I was not a girl who took orders anymore.

I wrenched his card away and laughed, deliberate. I swiped it, the weight heavy in my hand. A black AmEx—an invite-only card. I glanced at the name as I handed it back.

"I hate to disappoint you… Mr. Moretti." My voice caught slightly, and I paused. Moretti—the Moretti's. The multi-millionaire in the wine industry. The maker of my favorite wine, the one I had just admitted to liking. I flicked my eyes up at him. The smirk lingering on his lips made my stomach twist.

"But there are some things even your money can't buy." His brother's low, dark laughter cut through, like an inside joke I didn't understand. Jax appeared behind me, realizing it was just the four of us now and I had just insulted a man who looked like he could snap someone in half.

"Time for you to go, gentlemen," Jax said, voice level but tinged with warning.

Lorenzo's brother draped a lazy arm around him. "Thick head." He tapped his temple again, amused. "Come, frate." He tugged gently, but Lorenzo didn't budge.

"Till we meet again." Lorenzo's honeyed voice carried an edge, not mean, but final. Like he meant it. I should have been mad, annoyed, maybe even scared. I'd seen the dark and deadly before, but this… this was different. Despite the intensity, his words didn't frighten me. They made me feel alive.

******

### Lorenzo

Despite being midnight, the city still felt alive, quieter, but still humming with energy. The breeze was warm against my face as we stepped out of the bar.

"So, this girl, eh?" Dario nodded toward the bar behind us. "She's your mystery girl from yesterday?"

I nodded silently. Emil had already gotten details about the car the girls had taken from the dress shop. It was registered to a subsidiary of an equities marketing group under Benedict Cole. A few quick searches later, he had identified their daughter, Jenna Cole. He sent me a snapshot from her social media: she was smiling, cheek to cheek with the same girl from the shop, probably at some recent concert. Thank God these social media types photograph everything—but there was no tag.

Another scan revealed she worked at Giovanni's. Dario and Emil had been there a few times, but they preferred the front bar where the dance floor was full of gorgeous women. Another photo popped up showing Jenna, her friend, and a male bartender with blue-green eyes, all smiling behind the bar. The dots connected easily.

Marco had been irritated that we were using company resources to dig into my mystery girl, insisting there were more important matters; shipments, vintage release schedules, the Bellandi situation. Dario waved him off, said everything was handled, reminded him it had been years since I'd shown interest in a woman for more than a convenient distraction.

I'd bristled at that—but he wasn't wrong.

Tomorrow night, we'd corner the little rat and find out what really happened to our parents' plane. Tonight, though—tonight was still mine.

Dario ground out the cigarette beneath his heel. He only smoked when he drank. "Don't get caught." He shot me a knowing look. "And if you do—leave."

The last word landed heavy. Not a suggestion. A line.

I didn't answer. I didn't need to.

He clapped my shoulder once, then turned and disappeared down the sidewalk, already pulling his phone from his pocket, already elsewhere.

I stayed.

The Maserati purred to life under me, familiar, expensive, obedient. I rolled the windows down and cut the engine, letting the night seep in—music bleeding faintly from inside Last Call, laughter drifting out in loose, careless bursts. The city breathed around me.

I wasn't following her.

That was the word people liked to use when they wanted something to sound dirtier than it felt. *Stalking.* It implied desperation. Hunger without discipline.

This was…observation..

Still, the word hovered, unwelcome, because I knew myself well enough to recognize the pull. When something caught my attention, I didn't half-step. I latched on. Always had.

The memory of the dress shop surfaced uninvited—her colliding into me, solid and warm, like she'd crashed straight through whatever careful structure I'd built around my life. The way she'd looked up, eyes sharp and unapologetic, mouth already forming a challenge. Confident. Carefree. Capable.

Not fragile.

That was the part that mattered. The faint scar along her collarbone I'd noticed when she moved, pale against her skin—not something decorative, not something accidental. And tonight, another one at her jaw, half-hidden unless you knew to look for it.

Marks of impact. Of survival. Her eyes hid secrets I wanted to uncover.

I wanted her—yes, physically, there was no point lying to myself—but it went deeper than that. She was interesting. And I had always been drawn to interesting things, even when they cut.

Especially when they cut.

Several years ago, I'd been softer. Younger. Foolish enough to believe that wanting someone meant trusting them.

I could still see it when I closed my eyes—the door to the apartment slightly ajar, the wrong shoes by the entryway. Red hair tangled in my sheets. One of the Rinaldi boys, smug even naked, like he thought his name would save him.

It hadn't.

I remembered fists, bone on bone, the copper taste of blood in my mouth. His face swelling under my knuckles. A few good punches landing on me too—enough to remind me I wasn't invincible. We'd both ended up broken that night. Him physically.

Me… elsewhere.

I hadn't been the same since. Harder. More careful. Less inclined to confuse possession with vulnerability.

Which was why this—sitting in my car, watching the bar she worked in—irritated me.

Because it felt familiar.

The doors of Last Call opened again as the other bartender took the trash out. A shadow moved near the entrance, not hers. Someone else lingering. Waiting.

My attention sharpened instantly.

Interesting, indeed.

I stayed where I was, engine silent, eyes tracking movement through the dark. Waiting. Watching.

******

She came out laughing.

Not guarded. Not careful. Loose in a way that snagged something low in my chest.

The bartender walked beside her, saying something under his breath that made her tilt her head back, dark hair catching the streetlight. I leaned forward slightly in my seat without realizing it, the Maserati still dark, still quiet.

"Give Jenna a goodnight kiss for me, Jax," she called, playful, wicked. She winked, blew an exaggerated kiss in his direction.

The kid flushed instantly. "Watch out for your new shadow, Sierra."

Her name landed like a strike. *Sierra.*

It fit her. Sharp. Untamed. Beautiful in a way that suggested danger if mishandled.

She rolled her eyes, but heat climbed her neck anyway, blooming up into her cheeks. She was thinking about me. I knew it in the way her steps slowed just a fraction, the way her gaze flicked—quick, searching— down the street.

Jax laughed, backed toward his car, gave her a mock salute, and drove off.

Sierra turned toward the lot, digging into her bag. That's when I noticed her car.

A sleek black Audi, older model. Well-kept but not precious. The kind of thing you hold onto because it's yours, not because it's impressive. It fit her more than I expected.

She fumbled with her keys.

And then the shadow moved.

Not mine.

He came out of the alley beside the bar—big, all muscle and intent, moving too quietly for someone his size. Before my brain fully caught up, he had her by the arm, slammed her back against the Audi hard enough to rattle metal.

"Get the fuck off me!" she shouted—not screaming. Furious. Fighting.

She twisted, fast, drove her boot straight down onto his foot.

He howled, staggered back—

—and lunged again.

This time he caught her wrists, pinned them above her head with brutal efficiency.

I was out of the car before I realized I'd opened the door.

I crossed the lot in seconds. My fist connected with his face in a dull, wet *crunch*—bone giving way beneath knuckles. His head snapped sideways. Blood sprayed. His nose was ruined.

I hit him again. And again. Controlled. Precise. Not rage—*purpose*.

He swung back, wild and angry. One punch clipped my jaw, bright pain flashing white, but it barely slowed me.

I drove my shoulder into his chest, wrapped an arm around his neck, dragged him back into a crushing headlock. He clawed uselessly at my forearm, gasping.

"Why," I said into his ear, tightening my grip, "were you watching her?"

He choked, panicked. "Just—just doing a job—"

My arm tightened another fraction.

"Who sent you?"

His struggle weakened. I leaned closer, voice low and lethal.

"Answer me."

His hands clawed at my arm, breath coming apart in wet, broken sounds.
"M… m—"

He went limp before the word could form.

"*Merda.*" I released him, and he hit the pavement with a dull, final thump.

I dragged a hand through my hair, pulse still loud in my ears, thoughts colliding too fast to sort.

"Excuse me—what the absolute *fuck* was that?"

Her voice cut straight through the haze, sharp enough to reset me instantly.

So much for not being seen.

"The correct response," I said calmly, pulling my phone from my pocket, "is *thank you*."

I snapped a photo of the unconscious man at our feet. Emil would know how to find a name. He always did.

I lowered the phone and finally looked at her.

Alive. Furious. Unbroken.

Good.

"What is *wrong* with you?" she snapped, closing the distance between us in three furious strides. "Do you just lurk in parking lots now? Is that your thing, watching women like some kind of psycho?"

I huffed a breath that might've been a laugh if the adrenaline hadn't started draining out of me. My face throbbed where the bastard had clipped me, a dull ache blooming into something sharper. Warmth slid down my temple, I reached up and came away with blood.

Before I could form a decent lie, she barreled straight through it.

"You followed me. You watched me inside. You were out here waiting." Her eyes were bright, furious, *alive*. "Don't even try to deny it."

I paused—long enough to breathe, long enough to choose control over instinct.

"You've been reading too many romance novels," I said evenly. "And you shouldn't flatter yourself."

Her hand moved before my brain caught up.

*Crack.*

Pain flared hot and sudden as her palm connected with my jaw. Not hard enough to break anything—but hard enough to stun me. Hard enough to steal the air from my lungs.

I stood there, utterly unprepared, staring at her as if she'd just rewritten the rules of the world.

She didn't wait for a response.

She spun on her heel, yanked open the door of her Audi, and peeled out of the lot, tires screaming as she disappeared into the night.

I stayed where I was, blood drying on my skin, pulse still thudding.

And for the first time in a very long while—

I smiled.

# Chapter 3

*Sierra*

"…and then he said *don't flatter yourself*—can you believe that?" I threw my hands up as I finished recounting the night.

We were at Jenna's apartment getting ready for the gallery opening. She spun away from the vanity, where she'd been applying perfectly matched eyeshadow and lipstick, her brows shooting up.

"What the *fuck*?" she said incredulously. Then, after a beat, she tilted her head. "I mean… he *is* hot, though." She nodded as if that alone justified everything. "And rich. A black AmEx?" She met my eyes through the mirror.

I let out an exasperated sigh. Of course she'd romanticize the whole thing; some white-knight nonsense wrapped in good bone structure and money.

"Can you zip me up?" I asked, turning around.

The zipper slid smoothly, the dress fitting me like a glove.

"Ow—*ow*," Jenna whistled appreciatively.

I laughed as I zipped her into her blush-pink dress. "We're going to kill tonight. No one's even going to be looking at the art."

As much as I hated to admit it, she was right. My dress hugged my curves, the high slit making my legs look longer than they were. My hair fell in long, soft curls. Jenna looked like exactly what her parents wanted her to be tonight—an heiress in pale pink, her hair swept up with loose ringlets framing her face.

She snapped a selfie before we headed downstairs.

I groaned the second I saw the vehicle waiting for us.

A blacked-out SUV.

The Coles had arranged it—courtesy of Blackwell Enterprises, one of my parents' companies. Luxury vehicles had been their bread and butter, but they'd recently expanded into hotels and resorts. With my engagement to Matteo, they'd hoped to secure me a seat on the board, leverage my vote, and seal deals that would put Blackwell chauffeurs at every Rinaldi hotel and resort, even hoping to build joint-resorts.

When I disappeared, the contracts already signed became a noose around my father's neck. He was indebted to the Rinaldis.

After they found me—and the life I'd been carving out—they moved fast. Jenna had pulled strings with her parents, convincing them to intervene, to get mine to back off. I'd thought, after the last disaster, they might finally listen to someone.

But once Matteo admitted they'd given him my location, I should've known this was coming.

"You don't *know* they'll be here," Jenna pleaded as we climbed into the SUV, trying to lift my mood.

I already hadn't wanted to come. It was far too late to back out now.

"We both know they will," I said quietly. "Just promise you won't leave me alone with them."

"As long as you don't leave *me*," she shot back. "You know they're going to try to introduce me to some dumb son who thinks he's God's gift to women." She mimed gagging.

I laughed, nerves buzzing beneath it.

"Pinky promise," I said, lifting my finger.

She hooked hers with mine. "Into the den of lions we go."

The art gallery rose ahead of us—glass and steel softened by ornate carvings. Modern, but not cold. Low lights guided guests toward a set of open double doors.

Blacked-out SUVs, sports cars, even limos lined the street. Everyone arriving was dressed to impress.

This wasn't about art. It was about proximity. Power. Being seen.

A blacked-out sports car purred past us, the sound tugging at something familiar. For a moment, I frowned, but couldn't place it.

We linked arms and stepped inside.

The space opened wide—paintings lining the walls, sculptures positioned like quiet sentinels. Servers drifted through the crowd with trays of wine and hors d'oeuvres. Socialites and CEOs mingled beneath low light and polite laughter, all of them circling one another, hungry for whatever came next.

We managed the correct nods, smiles, and waves for nearly an hour;bjust enough to avoid being pulled in any one direction. Despite the glitter and glam, I kept my head on a swivel, unsure who—or what—I was watching for.

My parents.
Matteo.
*Lorenzo.*

Heat pooled low in my stomach.

He was co-chair of Moretti Wine Holdings. Jenna and I had scoured every digital source we could find. His parents had died in a plane crash six months ago, en route to Sicily. Tragic. Public. Conveniently vague. Lorenzo and his older brother, Marco, had stepped in immediately. Dario worked for the company in some undefined role. There was also a younger brother, Emil—barely mentioned anywhere except in grainy tabloid shots that made my stomach twist.

He had the same hollow look in his eyes Matteo used to get when he was high.

Between them, the brothers controlled hundreds of millions in assets—more money than anyone I'd ever been close to. And when you had that kind of money, you could bury a lot of problems. People like them belonged at events like this.

The thought of seeing Lorenzo again made my pulse trip. Uneasy didn't even begin to cover it.

Whether he meant to or not, it was clear he'd been sitting in his car after leaving the bar. I hadn't walked out for another thirty minutes—so he was absolutely doing *something*. Watching. Waiting.

And still—I couldn't lie to myself.

I was glad he'd been there.

His words echoed uncomfortably in my head. When he had demanded to know why the creep was watching me, he'd said it was a *job*. The idea settled wrong. Had my parents hired someone to scare me? To push me back into line? Had Matteo?

I touched my wrist absently, fingers brushing the faint bruising still visible there. The memory of the man's grip flashed hot and unwelcome. Some guys waited until the bartender was alone. Some guys thought they could take what they wanted. Either way, it made my stomach churn.

Jax had felt awful for leaving before I did. I'd told him it wasn't his fault—and it wasn't.

Jenna and I looped through the crowd again, stopping in front of a painting neither of us cared about. A white canvas splattered violently with red.

"A kid could do that," she scoffed.

I laughed, but my mind wasn't there.

All I could see was Lorenzo's face.

Hazel eyes gone dark, burning with fury. Blood sprayed across his cheek from the impact of his fist, more seeping from the cut above his eye. The way he moved—fluid, efficient. Trained.

It should've terrified me.

Instead, a shiver ran through me, sharp and undeniable.

Before we could even think about moving, Jenna's mother materialized like a hawk.

"Jenna, darling, you simply must meet Edward Whitmore—heir to the Everton Group," she said, voice honeyed but firm.

Jenna froze, and our eyes met —silent panic passing between us. *Not him. Not now.*

Her mother's hand nudged her gently but insistently forward. Jenna gave me one last pleading look, a mix of *please don't make this worse* and *help me out here*, before she allowed herself to be swept away.

I stayed rooted in place, watching the pink swirl of her dress disappear into the crowd, disappearing behind her mother's iron-clad escort.

Left alone, I turned back to the painting. White canvas. Red splatter. Sharp lines, chaos contained in a frame.

And all I could feel was the echo of her absence— and the heat of my own pulse, thinking about the eyes that had haunted me from the bar, the ones that could be anywhere in this crowd.

No one knew. Not yet.

I touched the faint scar on my wrist again, the memory of the other man flashing too quickly to process.

The gallery hummed around me, voices blending into low murmurs, glasses clinking, laughter curling over polished marble. I had to stay calm, but every instinct screamed that *he*—Lorenzo—was here somewhere.

I felt exposed, but I wasn't going anywhere.

******

***Lorenzo***

I spotted her the second I pulled up. Sierra. Standing on the curb, framed by the low gallery lights, oblivious to everything but the crowd she floated through. My jaw throbbed faintly from the punch I'd taken back at the car—sharp when I moved too fast—but another, hotter sensation crept in as I remembered her palm snapping against me.

*Why the hell did I like that?*

I parked the Maserati and let the valet take over, stepping out into the warm night. The city smelled faintly of late summer, exhaust, and something sweet I couldn't place. I ran a hand over my face, tasting the ghost of adrenaline, heart pinging with anticipation and irritation in equal measure.

Dario and Marco were already waiting outside the gallery, leaning casually, checking the arriving crowd with practiced eyes.

"Everything set?" Marco asked, voice low and precise.

I nodded, taking a deep breath, ignoring the dull ache along my jaw.

Marco outlined the plan once more. "I'll handle the introductions for the wine. Lorenzo," his eyes met mine, steel and calm, "you'll circle the shadows, look for Bellandi. Mid-forties, auburn hair, clean-shaven. We've got one shot at this—don't get sloppy."

Dario gave me a grin. "And I'll be the charming Moretti brother in the crowd. Smile, shake hands, make it easy for him to trust me. Once you spot him, I'll lead him to the closed-off section. Tell him it's a preview of a new piece—unfinished, private. Bellandi shouldn't recognize me. Not now."

Marco's gaze sharpened. "Then it's on you, Lorenzo. Extract what you need. Threats, intimidation. Violence if necessary, but control it. We only need information."

I let the plan settle in my mind. Each piece aligned. Each role precise. The gallery would be crowded enough to hide us, quiet enough for me to move unseen. We nodded to each other, silent acknowledgement passing between us.

"Same entrances?" Dario asked.

"Separate," Marco said. "No unnecessary attention. Walk in like everyone else."

The doors opened. I felt the pulse of the crowd behind them, the hum of conversation, the clinking of glasses. Every instinct I had was wired to her—Sierra. But I couldn't let her see me—not yet. I stepped inside, letting the crowd swallow me, circling the shadows, waiting, watching, every nerve stretched taut.

The night had begun.

I moved through the gallery like a shadow, keeping a careful distance but never losing sight of them. Jenna laughed, tilting her head at something Sierra had said, the sound soft and light. I caught every detail—the sway of her hips in that tight dress, the curve of her neck, the way her hair fell just so over her shoulders. I wanted her, more than I had any right to want anyone.

The thing that unsettled me, the thing that made her magnetic, was how unafraid she was. She'd faced the creep outside the bar without hesitation. No panic. No hesitation. Just fire and control. She wasn't fragile. She was everything I wanted to break through, and everything I wanted to protect at the same time.

They passed just a few feet from me, unaware of my presence. She moved with confidence, glancing around, pretending casual, but I knew the way her eyes swept the room. Searching. *Looking for someone.*

A few minutes more and I spotted him—Bellandi. Mid-forties, auburn hair, clean-shaven. Exactly as the intel had said. He was sipping wine, leaning into a younger woman far too young for him, the kind of careless flirtation that screamed privilege. Not his wife.

I slipped my phone from my pocket and sent a quick message to Dario. Almost immediately, I saw him across the room, moving in with ease, clapping Bellandi on the back like an old friend. The gleam in his eye was subtle, but unmistakable, laying seeds without giving away the plan. Bellandi had no idea.

They shook hands and went separate ways. Dario passed me smoothly, murmuring, "East hall. Thirty minutes."

I checked my watch. Half an hour. Just enough to get close.

I melted back into the crowd, glass in hand, then grabbed another for good measure. Both hands steady as I navigated closer. My pulse picked up when I finally positioned myself behind her. Too close, perhaps, but I didn't care. I leaned just slightly toward Sierra, low enough so only she could hear.

"Interesting painting," I murmured. Her perfume hit me—vanilla, soft at first, then something darker lurking beneath. Not too sweet. Perfect.

She barely reacted. Just the faintest tilt of her head. Like she had been expecting someone. "It looks like blood," she said softly, glancing at the canvas without looking at me.

I smirked just a fraction, letting the heat of her calm, deliberate words sink in. "A little violent don't you think?"

"I didn't take you for someone so afraid of blood, Mr. Moretti."

"That title was for my father. You can just call me Lorenzo." I let the words hang for a moment, measuring her reaction.

"I'm sorry for your family's loss," she said softly, her gaze steady. "But it's okay… I prefer Enzo."

She knew. She had looked me up. But the way she said it—the familiarity, the casual claim of a nickname— lit a fire in me I couldn't describe. We were so close, the warmth of her body pressing into mine that it felt like we shared the same air.

"For you." I handed her the glass. She took it with a slight nod, those dark eyes of hers never leaving mine.

"My, my… what a gentleman you actually are," she said, her words soft, laced with deliberate sarcasm. I watched comprehension flicker across her face. I'd specifically requested bottles of the *Notturna Riserva* tonight—her favorite. Despite my best efforts, the corners of my mouth curled up.

She turned back toward the painting, sipping her wine thoughtfully. "So… you are still *stalking* me, I take it?" She shifted, pressing her body subtly against mine.

"*Observing*," I corrected, finishing my own glass. I checked my watch—still time. Signaling a waiter to take my glass, I leaned forward, pressing the rest of the way into her. "I've been *observing* you." My voice dropped to a whisper, my lips brushing against her ear. A shiver traced through her.

"Why?" she barely breathed.

I toyed with the easy lies on my tongue. Instead, I gave her the truth—the kind I didn't hand out lightly.

"Because…" I let my words linger, drawling slightly. "From the moment you ran into me, I haven't been able to stop thinking about you." I slid my arm over hers, our fingers interlocking. "Because you intrigue me, Sierra." Her name tasted like temptation on my lips.

My attention snapped. Dario was leading Bellandi toward the east wing. Inwardly, I sighed. Time to move.

"Because your face haunts me," I murmured, turning her gently toward me, bringing her hand to my lips. I brushed a soft kiss across her knuckles, though every fiber of me wanted more. "I have to go, *tesoro mio*," I whispered, "but I will see you again."

I let her hand go and melted back into the crowd, heading toward the east wing, anticipation and duty coiling through me like a live wire.

******

### Sierra

For a moment, I wanted to follow him. To see whatever had stolen his attention. He was like a ghost, already disappearing through the crowd, a dark suit melting into the sea of them. I turned and placed my empty glass on the tray of a passing waiter. Of course he had remembered my favorite wine; it was easy when he was the one who made it.

A flash of pink caught my eye across the room. Jenna. She was laughing politely at something a generically handsome, ashy blonde man was saying. His suit didn't seem to fit quite right and his body was tense. He must be the Everton heir. He looked almost as miserable as she did. Our eyes locked and she held out her pinky, reminding me of our promise. I smiled at her and nodded. I was on my way to save her.

I started moving through the crowd, which was starting to thin as the main event drew closer. The curator would speak soon, then unveil the new piece that would be on display once the east wing was finished. Really, it was just a way to show off who had donated the most money. Just another game for the ultra-wealthy.

Just as I was about to pull Jenna aside, an excuse on my lips, a hand reached out and grabbed my wrist. I winced. It was the one with the bruise from Matteo's grip. I was getting really tired of people grabbing at me. I turned on my heel, ready to tear into whoever it was, but as I saw who was on the other end, the insult died before it made its way out.

My mother. Vivian Blackwell.

Now, she, she looked like she belonged—her emerald green evening gown flawless, black hair slicked into a severe updo that hadn't shifted all night. Her expression was the same one I'd grown up under: cool, appraising, perpetually dissatisfied.

"And exactly who was *that* wrapped around you?"

The words sliced clean and precise. Even at twenty-seven, her tone still landed the way it had when I was seventeen—sharp, corrective. She said it like we'd been fucking against a canvas for everyone to see.

"Well, hello to you too, Mother." I kept my voice light, though irritation buzzed beneath it. If she wanted to get straight to the point, I wouldn't stop her.

Her mouth tightened when she said *that*. Like he was something she'd stepped in. Someone beneath her. It made my skin crawl.

She hadn't grown up with much, but once my father's business took off, money had rewritten her entire personality. By the time I was ten, everything revolved around optics—image, whispers, leverage. Love had been replaced with strategy. I was still shocked I'd escaped mostly intact.

"Oh? Did you notice something?" I played dumb, though my mind was already several moves ahead.

Her gaze sharpened as she pulled me closer, fingers clamping around my bruised wrist like a reminder of ownership. "Someone could see that and get the wrong idea," she hissed. "You're still engaged, and you need to start acting like it before someone gets hurt."

She scanned the room, eyes darting like she was waiting for a scandal to detonate.

"I am most certainly *not* still engaged." My voice rose despite myself. "Listen to me very carefully—I will *never* marry Matteo. If he comes near me again, I will file a restraining order. Frankly, I may do that anyway."

She scoffed softly. "Do you have any idea what your little stunt has done to your father's deals?"

I leaned in, prying her fingers off my wrist one by one. "Do *you* have any idea what *his* stunt did to me?" I shot back, my voice low and venomous. "Or did you forget the part where your perfect, handpicked son-in-law enjoys using his fiancée as a punching bag?"

She didn't answer. Her silence told me everything.

"And for your information," I added calmly, "that man was Lorenzo Moretti."

I waited.

Three.
Two.
One.

Recognition slid into place with chilling speed.

Her posture shifted—just slightly. Her eyes flicked, calculating, not panicked. Not angry. Even worse, interested. "The Moretti's?" she murmured, almost to herself. "Wine. Shipping. European holdings…"

She looked past me, scanning the room now with purpose. Measuring. Weighing.

"Lorenzo," she repeated, tasting the name. Suddenly, I felt protective of him, like I needed to keep her claws from sinking into him.

Her gaze lingered on me for a beat too long, something cold settling behind her eyes. The calculation finished.

"Be very careful, Sierra," she said softly, the warning wrapped in silk. "Men like Lorenzo Moretti don't involve themselves with bartenders by accident."

I stiffened.

"And women who attach themselves to them," she continued, "tend to forget how exposed they are."

There it was. Not a threat. Not yet. A reminder.

She adjusted the fall of my sleeve, fingers brushing my wrist again—this time deliberately. "You're still using the Blackwell name whether you like it or not. That means your choices reflect on us."

I laughed under my breath. "You mean they reflect on *you*."

Her smile sharpened. "I mean your father still controls your trust."

The words landed heavy. Calculated. Precise.

"Your apartment," she went on, voice low, almost conversational. "The one you're so proud of paying for yourself? It's still tied to a Blackwell guarantor."

My chest tightened.

"And that charming little bar you work at," she added, eyes flicking briefly toward the gallery entrance as if she could already see Giovanni's neon sign in her mind. "Its liquor license renewal is up next quarter, isn't it?"

Ice slid straight down my spine.

"I don't know what game you think you're playing," she said, finally meeting my eyes again, "but if you embarrass this family, if you entangle yourself with men who complicate our position, I *will* clean it up."

I stepped closer, refusing to give her the satisfaction of watching me flinch. "And if I don't fall back into line?"

Her lips curved—not cruel, not kind. Certain.

"Then you will discover," she said quietly, "how very easy it is to take everything away from someone who insists on being difficult."

The music swelled nearby. Laughter chimed. Champagne glasses clinked.

No one watching us would have guessed a threat had just been delivered.

She smoothed my hair once, maternal, performative. "Enjoy the rest of the evening, darling."

Then she turned and vanished into the crowd— leaving me shaking, furious, and suddenly very aware that the most dangerous predator in my life might not be Matteo…

but my mother.

The moment my mother disappeared into the crowd, the air rushed back into my lungs like I'd been underwater too long. My hands trembled despite my best effort to steady them.

"Sierra."

Jenna's voice cut through the noise, soft but urgent. She was already there, fingers closing around my elbow, anchoring me before I could even turn.

"What did she say?"

I swallowed, blinking hard. "Nothing new."

Jenna didn't buy it for a second. Her gaze flicked in the direction my mother had gone, then back to me, sharp and assessing. "That's not how you look after 'nothing new.'"

I let out a shaky breath, forcing my shoulders to relax. "She just… reminded me how conditional her love is. She threatened Giovanni's liquor license renewal."

Jenna's jaw tightened. "God, I hate her."

I huffed a weak laugh. "You're not supposed to say that about someone's mother."

"She's not acting like one," Jenna shot back immediately. "She cornered you, didn't she?"

I nodded. Her grip on my arm tightened, protective. "Do you want to leave?"

The offer alone nearly undid me. I shook my head slowly. "No. If I leave now, she wins."

Jenna studied my face, reading everything I wasn't saying. "Okay," she said finally. "Then we stay. Together." She linked her arm through mine, solid and unapologetic, a quiet statement to anyone watching. "But you don't get pulled away again. Not by her. Not by anyone."

My throat burned. "You don't have to—"

"Yes, I do," she cut in gently. "You're not doing this alone."

I exhaled, leaning just a fraction into her side. Jenna scanned the room once more, her gaze snagging on something over my shoulder. Her brows knit slightly. "Is that the Moretti guy from the bar?"

My pulse spiked. I followed her line of sight—and there he was.

Lorenzo.

His suit jacket sat slightly askew, like he'd put it on in a hurry, and the cut above his eye looked freshly reopened, a thin line of red against his skin. Dario stood beside him, his hair messier than it had been at the boutique, his usual easy confidence dulled around the edges. Something had happened. They leaned casually against the frame leading into the unfinished east wing, shadows clinging to them like they belonged there.

And Lorenzo— He was watching me. Not smiling. Not hiding. Just waiting.

Jenna leaned closer, her voice barely a whisper. "Do I need to spill wine on someone?"

Despite everything, a real laugh escaped me. "Not yet," I murmured. "But… stay close."

She squeezed my arm. "Always."

And across the room, I felt it—the shift. The moment Lorenzo's gaze flicked from me to the spot where my mother had just stood, and back again. He saw the confrontation. He saw Jenna's arm linked through mine. He saw that I hadn't run. A muscle in his jaw tightened, a subtle, almost imperceptible acknowledgment. He realized my mother had just drawn a line… and that I hadn't stepped back from it. He just didn't realize the role he had played in it.

Jenna tugged me gently forward, steering us back into the flow of the gallery before I could freeze in place. We moved slowly, deliberately, like we belonged—heels clicking softly against polished concrete, wine glasses refilled by a passing server without either of us needing to ask.

"So," I murmured, keeping my eyes on a large abstract hanging near the west wall, "who was the ashy-blonde your mother ambushed you with earlier?"

Jenna snorted quietly. "Edward Whitmore. Legacy hedge fund money. Personality of a wet napkin."

"That bad?"

"Worse. He kept calling me *darling* like we were already engaged." She shuddered.

I smiled faintly. "You slipped away fast."

She lifted one shoulder. "We both knew it was a setup." Her voice dropped, casual but clear. "I played my part. Smiled. Listened. Let them think I was being agreeable."

"Strategic compliance," I said.

"Exactly." She flashed me a sideways grin. "You did great too, by the way. Minimal scandal. Very controlled."

I exhaled. "High praise."

We drifted toward the center of the room where the crowd thickened, stopping briefly as another waiter offered a tray. Jenna took a fresh glass of red without hesitation. I followed suit, the familiar weight of the stem grounding me.

"What are you actually excited to see?" I asked.

Her eyes lit instantly, the tension easing from her shoulders. "The new piece. The unfinished one they've been whispering about all night. Apparently it's controversial."

"Of course it is."

She leaned closer. "Word is, they kept it off the main floor on purpose. Makes people feel like they're being let in on a secret."

I took a slow sip of wine. "Manufactured intimacy."

"Works every time."

We shared a look—knowing, practiced—before continuing on, glasses in hand, slipping through the gallery like we weren't carrying threats, expectations, and very dangerous men, or mothers on our heels.

# Chapter 4

*Lorenzo*

I woke before the sun, my penthouse still wrapped in that quiet hour where even the city seemed to hold its breath.

For a moment, I stayed still, staring at the ceiling, cataloging sensations the way I always did after a night like that. The faint ache in my knuckles. The tight pull along my shoulder where I'd used too much force. The dull, simmering anger that hadn't burned off with sleep.

I exhaled slowly and swung my legs over the side of the bed. In the kitchen, I moved on instinct—water into the moka pot, coffee grounds leveled with practiced precision. The familiar rhythm steadied me. When the espresso began to bubble up, rich and dark, the memory followed it.

The gallery.
The unfinished east wing.
Concrete dust and exposed beams swallowing sound.
Bellandi hadn't even seen it coming.

Dario had played his part beautifully, smiling, charming, steering him away from the crowd with the ease of a man leading someone toward a private joke. A lamb to slaughter. He'd had been laughing when I stepped out of the shadows.

A quick punch to the gut dropped him.

A kick for emphasis.

I hauled him up by the neck and shoulders and slammed him back against the wall, my forearm pinning his throat just enough to make breathing a suggestion. Dario chuckled softly as he lit a cigarette, like we were killing time.

"It's been a while," Dario said pleasantly, smoke curling upward. "Since anyone's needed the old-fashioned approach."

Dario asked the questions.

I enforced the answers.

Bellandi was cooperative at first, too cooperative. He confirmed what we already knew.

Yes, he was connected to the Rinaldi group.

Yes, Matteo was his cousin.

Yes, he sat on the board.

Yes, he cleaned money through art galleries—this one included. Others too. Offshore accounts. Shell collectors. Inflated valuations. The less legitimate arms of the Rinaldi empire needed washing, and Bellandi was very good with soap.

Dario nodded along politely, like this was all perfectly reasonable.

"You didn't order the hit," Dario said mildly. Bellandi sagged in relief, mistaking acknowledgment for mercy. "But," Dario continued, "you helped make it disappear." The relief vanished.

Money. Logistics. Paperwork. Insurance claims. A bribe slipped quietly to the right official so the final report would read *mechanical failure*. Tragic. Unavoidable. My grip tightened.

"We want a name," I said evenly. "Who ordered it. Who carried it out. And why."

Bellandi swore he didn't know. I twisted his arm. Bone protested. He screamed.

He talked faster then—too fast. Said he hadn't known it would be a plane crash. Said he thought it would be subtler. Falsified maintenance logs. Skipped safety procedures. Something slipped into the pilot's water. Enough chaos to make an accident inevitable without blood directly on anyone's hands.

Still no name. That was when I broke his arm.

The sound echoed sharply through the unfinished wing. Bellandi collapsed, howling, but we were deep enough that it didn't matter. No one was coming.

I crouched, gripping him by the collar and hauling him eye level.

"Give me a name," I said quietly, my voice lethal. "Or you spend the rest of your life wondering when I decide to finish this."

Dario leaned against the wall, watching, cigarette glowing softly in the dark.

Bellandi sobbed. "Matteo," he choked.

I knocked him unconscious without hesitation. I wiped the blood from my hands onto his shirt and stood.

Dario checked his phone, tapped once. Let it ring. Hung up.

"Time to go," he said. "Cleaners will be here soon."

We straightened our jackets, adjusted cuffs, became civilized men again.

The espresso finished gurgling. I poured it, the scent sharp and grounding, and took a slow sip, my jaw tightening. Matteo Rinaldi.

Back at the gallery, everything had looked the same, but I saw it differently now. I spotted her instantly.

Sierra stood near the edge of the room, prying a woman's fingers off her wrist with controlled precision. The woman, elegant, severe, leaned in close, saying something I couldn't hear.

Sierra's face paled. She didn't step back.

The woman—her mother, unmistakably—smoothed Sierra's hair in a gesture so patronizing it made my teeth grind, then turned and disappeared into the crowd.

Jenna was there in the next heartbeat, latching onto Sierra like a shield. Then she had looked up.

Our eyes locked across the room. And in that moment, I understood two things with brutal clarity:

Matteo Rinaldi had signed his own death warrant.

And whatever war was coming next, Sierra Blackwell was already standing in the middle of it—whether she knew it or not.

I finished the last sip of my espresso, savoring the bitterness. My phone buzzed on the table. Emil's text brought the final clarity, the last pieces slipping into place. Sierra Blackwell's phone number. She was going to help me break Matteo.

A little digging by Marco last night had revealed another weak point in the Rinaldi empire. Nearly a year ago, an engagement had been announced between the daughter of Charles Blackwell, up-and-coming luxury magnate. On paper, Blackwell Enterprises was all sleek SUVs and glittering hotels. In practice, they dealt in leverage—board seats, property guarantees, liquor licenses, favors that could move mountains or shut them down.

The Blackwells had quickly ingrained themselves with the Rinaldis, every handshake and dinner a calculated step in a larger strategy. To solidify the deal, Sierra had been engaged to Matteo. Every move was designed to ensure their name carried weight—and that anyone who crossed them felt the consequences. It was easy to see that Alessio, the senior Rinaldi, had hoped an engagement would keep his son's feet on the ground. Instead, it seemed to have unleashed a monster.

I programmed her number into my phone. Somehow, I still paused before hitting send, the text making me feel like I was sixteen texting a girl for the first time. But she wasn't a girl. She was a woman. A woman who had been nearly killed by the man who killed my parents. Now I had to find a way to convince her to face him again so I could return the favor.

I set the phone down, letting the message sit for a second longer than necessary. Then I moved on. The shower was quick, hot, purposeful, washing off distraction and leaving only focus. Dressing was the next step—calculated, deliberate. I went with a crisp white shirt, unbuttoned at the collar just enough to hint at ease, slim dark trousers, polished leather shoes. Sharp, clean, unmistakably me.

I pulled up to the cafe early, parked, and stepped inside, choosing a semi-private table with a clear view of the entrance. Confident she would show, I settled in, letting my gaze sweep the street.

And then she appeared.

Summer sunlight caught her as she walked, light and deliberate, every step measured yet effortless. A flowy, pale blue sundress swirled around her knees, strappy sandals brushing the pavement. Her hair was down, loose in the warm morning breeze, catching the light, brushing her shoulders in soft waves. The tilt of her head, the faint sway of her hips… my chest tightened. She looked delicate not like a flower in the wind, but like a grenade, and I wanted to pull the pin.

For a moment, control slipped, just enough to make her presence dangerous in the best way. Confident, purposeful, alive—she had no idea the effect she had on me, or the game we were about to play.

******

### Sierra

The text had come through an hour ago: *The Gilded Spoon. 11:00*. No please, no question. Just a command. I'd stared at the unknown number, my stomach doing a slow, nervous flip, before I'd recognized the tone. Lorenzo. I still had no idea how he'd gotten my number, and the violation of it should have sent me running. Instead, I'd found myself pulling on a blue sundress and leaving my hair down, a silent act of defiance against my own better judgment.

He was already there when I arrived, looking like he owned the place. He sat at a small table in the corner, a crisp white shirt on, the top two buttons undone, revealing a hint of dark chest hair and the sharp line of his collarbones. Black fitted pants stretched across powerful thighs. He looked up as I approached, and his stormy eyes tracked my every move.

I slid into the chair opposite him, placing my purse on the table like a shield. "Let me guess," I started, my voice tight. "You 'observed' my schedule and just happened to be in the neighborhood?"

A slow, dangerous smile touched his lips. "Third time, Sierra. You keep accusing me of stalking. I'm simply observing."

"Observing," I repeated, the word tasting like ash. "Is that what you call it when you show up at a woman's work, then an invite-only event, and now text her out of the blue? Because from where I'm sitting, it looks a lot like stalking considering I never gave you my number."

His gaze didn't waver. "And from where I'm sitting, you look beautiful in that dress." The compliment was a direct hit, disarming me completely. The air between us crackled, thick with unspoken things. I hated how my body responded, a slow warmth spreading through my veins. I cleared my throat, trying to regain control.

"You disappeared last night," I said, changing the subject. "One minute you were there, the next you were gone. What happened?"

He picked up his coffee cup, his movements unhurried. "I had to take care of something."

"Something?" I pressed. "Or someone?"

He deflected with practiced ease. "Your mother seemed upset. Did she enjoy the rest of her evening?"

I bristled, huffy and annoyed that he'd seen that, seen her corner me. "She was fine. Just being herself. Reminding me that my value is tied to who I marry and what deals I can secure." I looked away, staring out the window. "She threatened Giovanni's liquor license." *Why was I telling him that?*

When I looked back, his expression was unreadable, but his eyes had hardened. "I see."

"Secret for a secret, *Enzo*," I challenged, leaning forward slightly. "You tell me where you went and I'll tell you all the pathetic details of my maternal dysfunction."

He considered me for a long moment, the silence stretching between us. "I took care of a problem," he said finally, his voice low and final. "That's all."

My gaze drifted up to the cut above his eye. It was still healing, a thin, pink line against his tanned skin. Without thinking, I reached across the table, my fingers gently tracing the edge of it. He flinched, just barely, his eyes darkening as he watched me touch him. The air grew thick, heavy. My thumb brushed his temple, and I felt his sharp intake of breath.

"Is this what 'taking care of a problem' looks like?" I whispered, my voice softer than I intended.

He didn't answer. He just watched me, his gaze so intense it felt like a physical touch. I pulled my hand back, suddenly feeling exposed. I needed to regain the upper hand.

"So, I told my mother we were involved," I said, letting the words linger between us. "Exclusive." I sipped my mimosa, like I'd told him what the weather was.

The predatory gleam returned to his eyes, sharp and hungry. He leaned forward, resting his forearms on the table, closing the distance between us. "Is that what we are?" he murmured, his voice a low rumble that vibrated straight through me. "Exclusive?"

I didn't hesitate. "Just a warning shot. She should learn I make my own rules and I don't bend for anyone."

His eyes flickered, sharp, like he'd caught the spark behind my words—the part meant for her, not him. I saw it there: that smirk tugging at the corner of his mouth. *He gets it. He knows exactly what I'm doing.*

"Then we are," he said, the agreement coming so easily it was more terrifying than any refusal. It wasn't a question. It was a statement of fact. "I can be whatever you want me to be."

He leaned across the table, gently pulling my hand into his, turning it over, his finger gently brushing against the faint bruise refusing to disappear. "So, *tesoro mio,* what do you want?"

I was surprised at how quickly he agreed, a knot of anxiety tightening in my stomach. Beneath it, though, a secret, thrilling current of pleasure ran through me. "You're sure?" I asked, eyes locked on his. It felt like we were teetering on the edge of something dangerous, about to fall into an endless ocean of unknowns.

"What. do. you. want." His voice was low, soft, but firm, each word deliberate, less a threat than a promise. Like whatever I said, he would make it happen. His lips brushed the inside of my wrist, and heat flared through me.

I wanted to use him as a shield against my mother, a barricade against Matteo, a way to stake my claim. But sitting there under his possessive gaze, I realized with a sickening, exhilarating certainty: I also wanted him, every single piece. And the terrifying part? I was sure he already knew.

Just as I was about to answer, a bright flash exploded behind him. Fuck. A tabloid photographer. My stomach dropped, nerves tightening like wires ready to snap.

Lorenzo didn't hesitate. He stood, dragging me up with him as if we were the only two people in the world. "Time to shine, *carina,*" he murmured, voice low, deliberate, dangerous. His arm slid around my waist, pulling me impossibly close, pressing me into the solid heat of him.

And then his lips were on mine. Rough, claiming, and utterly consuming. His stubble scraped against my skin, his hand tangled in my hair, anchoring me to him as if he could make the world fall away. I could feel the flashes from the corner of my eye—hundreds of eyes trying to capture us—but it was like they weren't there. Only him. Only the way his body molded against mine, the way his mouth devoured mine, the way he *owned* this moment.

I should have panicked. I should have pulled away. Instead, a part of me—the reckless, desperate part—welcomed it. Every brush of his lips, every press of his chest, every heated inhale made the danger pulse through me, thrilling me. I wasn't just being seen. I was letting myself be seen with him, letting him claim me in public, letting the risk make me ache in ways I didn't fully understand.

And the terrifying part? I knew he knew. Knew exactly what he was doing to me, knew how much I wanted it, and he didn't care. He just deepened the kiss, pressed closer, and whispered against my lips in a way that made my knees weaken. When I finally pulled away, the air between us still crackling, I realized we had crossed that imaginary edge—and a selfish part of me didn't want to come back. People were staring, but I didn't care.

My hand slid down his arm, fingers interlocking with his as if claiming a private piece of him in public. "I want to make people talk," I murmured, letting my gaze linger, drinking in every sharp line, every dangerous curve.

His laugh rumbled low, warm, and something wild flickered inside me.

"Then let's be seen."

We walked through the cafe toward the exit. The hostess stopped us, eyes narrowing on me with something like jealousy. "Mr. Moretti, I'm so sorry—I'm not sure how—"

Lorenzo cut her off. The shift was instantaneous—every trace of heat and playfulness gone, replaced by cold, sharp authority. My body reacted before my brain could. Heat rushed through me, thick and unfamiliar. "Do not let it happen again," he said, voice hard, controlled, slicing through the chatter. "My fiancée and I do not take kindly to being photographed without consent."

*Fiancée*. The word hit me like a punch. Not what we had agreed on. My chest tightened, a flicker of alarm surging through me.

He caught the moment, the way my pupils dilated, and smirked—just a fraction, but enough to promise trouble. *Oh, we would absolutely be fucking talking about this.*

### *Lorenzo*

I pulled out of the cafe, windows up, the city blurring past. My hand tapped the steering wheel almost unconsciously with the music, and I glanced at her out of the corner of my eye. She was glaring. Not subtle. Not even close. Perfect.

"I still can't believe you called me your fiancée," she said, voice sharp, a little clipped—but I caught the faint curl of something amused underneath. "That is *NOT* what we talked about."

I smirked, leaning back in the seat, letting her simmer. "Couldn't resist," I said smoothly, though I didn't bother explaining why. Truth was, *I wasn't entirely sure why I'd said it*. Maybe I wanted to see her rattle. Maybe I liked the way *fiancée* rolled off my tongue better. Maybe… I was becoming unhinged.

Her jaw ticked, that little flare of temper she tried to hide but never could. "You do realize that makes people think—"

"I know exactly what it makes people think," I interrupted, voice low, playful, deliberate.

She blinked at me, caught off guard. A small, almost unintentional flash of heat crossed her face, and I could feel the tension coil between us, thick and sharp.

She crossed her arms, leaning slightly into her own glare. "You're impossible."

I laughed softly, a low rumble that seemed to vibrate in the space between us. "I know," I said, watching her with intent. "But you… you look…*selvaggia* when you're mad."

Her eyes narrowed again, and I could tell she wasn't sure whether to scowl or smile. And I didn't care which. Because right now, the fight—the fire—the absolute chaos of her—was mine to watch, mine to provoke, and mine to enjoy.

"My car is still there." She refused to look at me, eyes fixed on the passing street, but I caught the tiniest hint of a smile tug at her lips.

"Sì, sì. I'll have someone pick it up and bring it to the house," I said, nodding, mentally filing away yet another detail.

"Uh… to my house, you mean?" Her head whipped around, arms crossed, fire in her gaze. *Merda*. She could be my undoing.

"Our house, *tesoro*," I said, letting the words hang between us. I reached for her hand, brushing my fingers over hers, letting them settle in mine. Not hard, just enough to make the claim clear.

"Why shouldn't you move in?" I murmured, voice low, teasing, but carrying a dangerous edge. "Everything's easier if you're here. Safer. More… ours."

"No no, you don't get to just decide," she snapped, trying to pull away. I tightened my grip just a fraction.

Her eyes narrowed, and then her voice cut sharply through the tension: "Let go of me—Matteo!"

The word hit me like a punch. Rage and something darker coiled inside me, but I couldn't ignore the flicker of fear in her eyes. She hadn't meant it, and yet, *merda*, I'd pushed her too far.

"My… I'm not him," I said, voice low, tight. A growl lurked beneath the calm I forced into my tone. Her slip, the fear, the comparison—it made my stomach turn, and my blood burn in equal measure. *How could she even think to compare me to him?*

I loosened my grip, though not entirely. She flinched at first, then hesitated, caught in the heat between us. Her shoulders tensed, arms crossed, as she pulled her hand away. I let her go this time.

"Look at me," I said, trying to reclaim the moment without letting my anger break the fragile thread between us. "I'm not Matteo."

She didn't answer at first, just glared, a mix of fury and residual fear. My chest tightened, part of me wanting to pull her closer, part of me wanting to strangle the very thought of him in my head. But mostly… I wanted her to understand, to feel the difference. To know this—*us*—was mine.

# Chapter 5

Sierra

We pulled up to his building, and I couldn't stop my eyes from sweeping over it. A sleek, glass-and-steel high-rise that gleamed in the late afternoon sun, modern lines and polished luxury bleeding sophistication. It was intimidating, yes—but also a little alluring, like it belonged to someone who *knew* exactly how to own everything in sight.

We drove down to the underground garage, the fluorescent lights casting harsh shadows that seemed to highlight every curve and edge of the car. I gripped the door handle, my chest still tight from the ride, my pulse still hammering in my ears.

Lorenzo stepped out of the car, closing door firmly, not a slam like I had expected. He came around and opened my door, waiting.

Before stepping out, I finally found my voice. "Lorenzo… I—I'm sorry. For calling you… Matteo," I admitted, hating how my words stumbled out. "I was just… overwhelmed and when you didn't let go…"

He gave a slow, measured exhale, leaning against the open door. "You're right," he said, voice low. "I shouldn't have. I… I'm sorry." This moment, his apology felt more intimate than it should have.

"I knew about the engagement," he said, his tone even, but I could feel the sharp edge underneath. "That much, at least. The rest… not so much."

I laughed softly, shaking my head. "Most people didn't." Most people either didn't see it—or chose not to. That was the way it always was when money was involved. "My parents used me to secure voting power on the Rinaldi board. If I'd married Matteo, I would've automatically had it."

I didn't know why I was telling him this, but it felt good to finally get it off my chest. Not that I needed—or even wanted—to protect any of them anymore. Lorenzo didn't say anything. His gaze stayed fixed on me, steady, unreadable.

"Matteo started out as exactly what you'd expect," I went on, my laugh hollow. "Charming. Polished. Perfect in public." I swallowed. "But behind closed doors?"

I shook my head. "He was a monster. He carried this switchblade everywhere. Always flipping it open, closing it again—like it was a game." My hands curled in my lap. "He'd hold me down and trace it along my skin."

I shivered.

"He used it," Lorenzo said. Not a question. His voice had gone dark, dangerous.

I brushed my fingers along the faint scar on my jaw, then tugged the neckline of my dress down just enough to expose the matching mark on my collarbone. "He didn't like it when I said no." A humorless smile tugged at my mouth. "He'd get high on God knows what and start demanding… things."

I didn't elaborate. I didn't need to.

"After the last time, I knew I had to get out," I said quietly. "My parents weren't going to help me. In fact—" My voice tightened. "While I was bleeding on their doorstep, they were already talking about sending me back."

Lorenzo's hand reached for mine, firm but gentle. His gaze met mine, unwavering. "No one will ever do that to you again," he said, low, almost a growl. "Not anyone."

I swallowed, the words settling in my chest, strange and grounding. There was no theatrics, no pity— just the quiet, absolute certainty in his voice. For the first time in a long time, I wanted to believe it.

I pushed down the tears threatening to spill. I was not doing that in front of him.

"So," I said lightly, forcing a crooked smile, looking up at him, "are you going to take me inside, or do

you live in the creepy garage?" I hoped the sarcasm
would chase the darkness from his eyes.

"We don't have to…," he said carefully, too
carefully, giving me space. An out. A choice.

Practically, it made sense. We both knew my
parents had told Matteo where I worked. He could've
sent that guy to do… anything. Staying with Lorenzo
would, *should*, keep him away. It would also get me out
of my building, which, as my mother had been quick to
point out, was technically tied to my father's company. A
not-so-subtle threat of eviction wrapped in concern.

And then there was the situation he'd pushed us into.
Publicly pushed us into.

*Fiancée.*

The thought of living together terrified me—but
not in a way that felt wrong. More like standing on the
edge of something vast and dangerous, knowing one step
forward would change everything. Being that close.
Sharing space. Mornings. Nights. This tension between
us was already electric.

My mind betrayed me, replaying the café—his
mouth on mine, his fingers threading through my hair, the
heat of his breath against my skin. The way it had felt like
he was trying to consume me, like restraint was
something he wore rather than possessed.

We'd already crossed an invisible line. But this felt different. Like following him inside meant crossing a threshold I couldn't uncross. Like once I stepped into his world, there would be no pretending this was temporary. No going back to *before*.

I looked at him—really looked at him—and realized the fear wasn't about actually moving in. It was about how badly I wanted to say yes. About the choice itself. Knowing it was mine to make.

I swung my legs out of the car and reached for his hand. He pulled me up effortlessly, his grip firm as he shifted us together and shut the door behind me with his free hand.

"Yes, we do," I said, stepping back just enough to reclaim my balance. Then, because honesty felt dangerous but right, I added, "Besides—I want to."

I turned and stepped into the elevator alone, pressing the button before I could second-guess myself. When I glanced back, the smirk on his face was the perfect balance of danger and desire—like he'd just been handed permission and was deciding how carefully to use it.

"As you wish, *tesoro mio*."

******

The polished steel doors slid shut, sealing us in a tomb of silent tension. Her perfume—something sharp and floral, like defiance itself—hit me the second I stepped in after her. She'd walked ahead, a challenge in the click of her heels on the concrete garage floor. Now she was trapped against the back wall, and the beast I'd been caging since the dress shop rattled its chains.

My hand shot out, palm flat against the cool metal beside her head, before the elevator even began to move. The other followed, caging her in. She didn't flinch. Those dark brown eyes just burned up at me, a storm of fury and something else… something that made my blood thicken.

*I need to taste that fury.*

I dropped my head, my nose skimming the line of her jaw. Her breath hitched. A tiny, victorious sound. My lips found the soft skin beneath her ear. She was all heat and silk. I inhaled, dragging the scent of her deep into my lungs. *Mine.* The thought was primal, unwelcome, and utterly undeniable.

"Enzo," she breathed, and my name on her lips was a brand.

My mouth traveled down the column of her throat, teeth grazing, not biting. *Yet.* I felt the fine tremor that ran through her. Not fear. Anticipation. Her head tilted back, granting me more access, even as her hands came up to brace against my chest. She pushed. I didn't budge. It was a challenge.

*God, she's perfect.*

My lips moved lower, to the hollow of her throat. The wide neckline of her dress gave way. And there it was. The ridge of scar tissue just above her collarbone, pale against her skin. Matteo's signature. Rage, white-hot and blinding, flashed behind my eyes. My mouth hovered a breath away from it. I wanted to trace every millimeter with my tongue, to kiss it until the memory of his touch was erased and replaced only with mine. To worship it and curse it at once.

*I can't.*

Touching it felt like claiming his damage. Acknowledging his prior claim. My jaw clenched so tight it ached. I pressed my open mouth to the unmarred skin just beside it instead, sucking lightly. She gasped, her fingers curling into the fabric of my shirt. A mark. My mark.

*Let him see that.*

My hips pinned hers to the wall. The hard ridge of my erection pressed against her stomach, through every layer of fabric separating us. The friction was agony. Bliss. Her little gasp turned into a moan, swallowed by the hum of the ascending elevator.

*This is a mistake. She's leverage. A pawn.*

But she was also warm and yielding against me, her body arching subtly, seeking more pressure. One of her legs shifted, her thigh brushing against mine. My control was a frayed wire, sparking.

I dragged my lips back up to her ear. "Tell me to stop," I growled, the words rough, barely recognizable.

Her only answer was to turn her face, her lips finding my jaw. The contact was electric. Soft. Deliberate. A kiss that wasn't a kiss, just a searing brand of permission.

*I should stop. I have to stop.*

My hand left the wall, my fingers splaying across her ribcage, thumb brushing the underside of her breast. The lace of her bra was a faint texture under my palm. I ached to fill my hand with her, to hear the sounds she'd make.

But that scar… it was a ghost between us. A reminder. If I touched it, I'd lose the last shred of my purpose. This wasn't just about wanting her. It was about ruining him. Using her. The two desires were a tangled, vicious knot in my gut.

With a raw, gut-deep sound of frustration, I tore myself back. My hands fell to my sides, fists clenched. I took two stumbling steps until my back hit the opposite wall of the elevator, putting the entire small space between us. The cold steel shocked my overheated skin. I stared at her, chest heaving, the war inside me a silent scream.

******

*Sierra*

He looked… wrecked. Lorenzo, the billionaire with the world on a string, was braced against the elevator wall like it was the only thing holding him up. His hazel eyes were pure fire, locked on me, tracking every shaky breath I took. The air between us was thick enough to choke on, charged with everything we hadn't done.

My lips tingled. My skin felt too tight, everywhere his mouth had been singing a desperate, hungry song. The damp spot on my dress from his mouth near my collarbone felt like a brand. *He didn't touch the scar.*

That was the game, wasn't it? He'd pushed us both to the edge of a cliff, looked over, and pulled back. To see if I'd jump? To prove he was the one in control?

*A challenge.*

The realization washed over me, cold and clear. This man, who'd declared me his fiancé to a room full of strangers, who'd all but kidnapped me from the curb, who was hiding in every corner, was testing me. He created the storm and stood in the eye to see if I'd beg for rain.

Fury, hot and bright, burned away the last of the haze he'd left me in. *No.* He didn't get to set the rules and then forfeit. He didn't get to make me feel this… this *needy* and then walk away first.

The power shifted. It was a physical sensation, like a settling in my spine. My own breathing began to steady. I let my gaze travel down his body, lingering on the obvious, straining bulge in his tailored trousers. A slow, deliberate smile touched my lips. I saw his abdomen clench.

Pushing off from the wall, I took the two steps he'd put between us. He went utterly still, a predator unsure if the prey was approaching or attacking. I stopped inches from him. The heat radiating from his body was immense.

I leaned in, my lips a hair's breadth from his ear. I could smell the faint, expensive scent of his cologne, and underneath it, the pure, salty scent of *him*. Of his sweat and his restraint. My voice came out low, a whisper of silk over stone.

"And Dario had told me you had manners," I breathed, letting my words feather across his skin. I felt the shudder that racked him. "Guess I'll have to teach you some."

I didn't wait for a reaction. I didn't touch him. I simply sidestepped him as the elevator chimed, its doors sliding open to the muted opulence of his penthouse foyer. I walked out, my heels sounding sure and steady on the marble, leaving him alone in the charged, aching silence of the elevator.

I didn't look back.

# Chapter 6

***Lorenzo***

*Fuck. Me.* She walked into my home like she owned the place. Matteo had tried to grind her into dust, and for a while, he'd almost managed it. He left fissures in her soul, hairline fractures that caught the light in the most unnerving ways. Her parents saw those cracks and tried to plaster them over with threats and polite society, treating her like a porcelain doll. They saw weakness. They were fucking fools.

This version of her wasn't weak. She was delicate in the way a tripwire is. In the way a coiled snake is. A shiver, sharp and visceral, ripped through me. The world wouldn't just burn when she finally snapped; it would be flayed, piece by piece, and she would be the one holding the blade. I just hoped when the dust settled, it wouldn't be at my throat.

I took a deep breath, settling my thoughts and followed her inside. My gaze was a physical weight as she moved through each room, her eyes taking a slow, predatory inventory. She wasn't admiring the decor; she was performing an autopsy on my life, trying to piece together the monster from the bones of his furniture. Five years I'd lived here, and I knew I could have a bag packed and be gone in sixty seconds flat. She moved with a liquid grace, her head tilting just so, like she wasn't just counting exits, but measuring the distance between them and the kill zone.

The penthouse unfurled around her, a cage of glass and shadow, and for a moment, I tried to see it through her eyes. Too silent. Too high. The city a smear of indifferent light below, a world she could fall from. No curtains. I've never needed them before. From her vantage point, the glass wasn't a shield; it was a stage, and she was the only performer. I filed that away: she feels exposed. Good.

Her fingers ghosted over the back of the couch. Black leather. Cold. So heavy it would take two men to move it. I saw her register the finality of it—the weight, the absolute certainty that nothing here moves unless I will it. The furniture wasn't for comfort. It was a statement. A warning.

She drifted into the kitchen, her body coiling tighter. Sterile. The kind of clean that smells of bleach and obsession. Her eyes flicked to the knife block. I knew they would. They always do. Honed to a razor's edge, polished to a mirror shine, aligned with a precision that bordered on psychotic. They weren't for chopping vegetables. They were honest about their purpose. From her side of the granite island, it must have looked less like a kitchen and more like a morgue. A place for preparation, not pleasure. She didn't touch a damn thing. Smart girl.

She pushed deeper, toward the bedroom, and the air grew thick, charged. I didn't rush her. I wanted to savor this. The bed dominated the space, a black monolith, vast and devouring. From where she stood, it wasn't an invitation to sleep. It was an altar. A promise. I let the silence hang, let her imagination do the work.

The art made her stop. A brutal splash of crimson on a stark white canvas. She turned to me, and I could feel the question forming on her lips, a perfect, soft thing in this hard place. I just gave a slow, deliberate nod, letting the smirk play on my mouth. It was the piece from the gallery. Our first real conversation, painted in acrylic. A reminder that violence and beauty can be born in the same breath. I wondered what conclusion she drew from it. I wondered if she knew how right she was.

The light remained low, intimate, casting everything in shadow. I could have flooded the room with light. I didn't. Control. The illusion of it, the reality of it. Mine. Hers. She turned one last time, a slow, deliberate circle, taking in the space, the silence, the complete and utter absence of anything soft. And watching her, I had a revelation. My penthouse didn't feel empty to her. It felt claimed. Occupied. Not by me. By us. It was a hunting ground, and we were the only predators left. I followed her, a shadow in my own domain, and the irony was so sharp it tasted like blood. She wasn't the one in the cage. We both were.

"Are you satisfied with your kingdom?" The sarcasm was a flimsy shield, a question I couldn't quite bring myself to ask directly. A peace offering to make sure she wasn't about to bolt, to confirm she understood the terms of this war we were in.

She dropped onto my bed, a slow, deliberate fall that was anything but clumsy. Her black hair fanned out against the dark sheets, a chaotic crown. That soft blue dress, the one that looked so innocent, hitched up her thighs, revealing a slice of skin that was a promise and a threat all at once. *Merda*. She knew exactly what the fuck she was doing.

"You're a *terrible* decorator." She rolled onto her stomach, propping herself up on her elbows. My gaze, usually so steady, fractured. The soft curves of her breasts strained against the thin fabric of her dress, rising and falling with a breath that seemed to hold all the secrets in the world. My mouth went dry, and every thought of control, of observation, of strategy, evaporated. If she was going to play dirty, then I would stop holding back.

I didn't answer. I slipped my phone from my pocket, my thumb moving with a practiced, lethal calm. The call was picked up on the first ring. "She will be staying," I paused, locking onto her eyes, letting the weight of the words sink in, "-indefinitely." I savored the immediate flare of defiance in her gaze, the way it narrowed from curiosity to combat. "Mhm, yes, box everything…deliver and unpack…7pm." I shot her a wolfish grin, thoroughly enjoying the daggers she was mentally burying in my throat.

"What the hell was that?" she snapped, pushing off the bed and onto her feet. Her movements sharp, angry.

"None of your things are here," I said, layering my voice with a false innocence. "I thought you might like to have your… possessions." The truth was, her apartment had been emptied the moment she'd left it. Alexio, the only man I trusted other than blood, had overseen the operation personally. There was never a chance for another outcome. This was a foregone conclusion.

"You need to start asking before you decide things for me," she stated, her tone almost flippant. It was a dare. A tell. She wasn't angry; she was thrilled. The idea of me taking control, of erasing her past and forcing a future on her, was a goddamn aphrodisiac. She was resistant the way a house cat wanted a warm bed but bolted for the door every time it opened.

"Or what?" I challenged, raising a brow. The game was on.

She ignored me, turning to walk past. Her arm brushed mine, a deliberate, electric touch that screamed *reach for me*. Oh, *Dio*, I wanted to. My fingers ached to grab her wrist, to pull her back against me and show her exactly what "or what" meant. But I wouldn't. Not yet. The hunt was too sweet. I followed her like the loyal hound she wanted me to be, my eyes glued to the sway of her hips.

"I think it needs a woman's touch," she said, gesturing vaguely at the hall, the kitchen, the living room. "My touch… your *fiancée's* touch." She lingered on the words, tasting them, testing them on her tongue. Her admission, that she was accepting the title, that she was *mine*, sent a jolt through me so powerful it was almost painful. It was a dark, possessive satisfaction I couldn't name, but I craved more of it.

"We can go wherever you like," I offered, the words a lie designed to give her the illusion of control.

She headed back toward the hall, toward the elevator, but her gaze snagged on a closed door at the end of the corridor. She looked at me, a silent question in her eyes. I answered before she could give it a voice. "That room is off limits. Even to you." I let the steel show in my tone, a warning I hoped would be enough. My office was the cockpit of my empire, the one part of me that was not for public consumption, not even for her.

Her look was pointed, a demand for an explanation I refused to give. I closed the distance between us, moving with the silence of a predator. I wrapped my arms around her waist, pulling her flush against me, caging her with my body. Her hands flew up, gripping my forearms, a reflexive mix of surprise and surrender. I tilted my head down, my lips brushing against her ear.

"Sometimes, *amore*," I murmured, my voice a low rumble, "you have to learn to accept the word 'no'." I pressed a hard kiss to her temple, breathing in her scent, a mix of vanilla and defiance. "Let's go." My voice came out a growl, rougher than I intended, thick with the effort of holding back.

This time, she listened. We headed for the car.

******

### *Sierra*

Lorenzo barely spoke as we pulled into the store parking lot. The moment I saw the glass cases and casually armed security, I understood—this wasn't about furnishing a space. It was about marking one. "A jewelry store?" I was getting annoyed with his constant mind games.

"You are about to lay claim to my home," he gave a dismissive wave, "I figured, if we're engaged, I should do the same, *amore*." His voice was deep, but held that guarded tone I was beginning to recognize.

"We really need to lay some ground rules with that actually," I said straightening, letting him know I meant business. "I think it would help us keep things from getting twisted since this isn't a *real* engagement." I lingered on the word real, like a reminder to both of us - we had reasons for this. Sure, there was a simmering attraction, but this wasn't real. Just another illusion bought by money and fear.

His gaze narrowed, thoughts running behind his eyes. He moved to get out so I turned to open my door.

"No." his voice was low, like a threat, his arm snaked out to stop me.

"I will be doing that from now on."

"I am perfectly capable -" he cut me off by getting out immediately. He cross to my side in a few short strides, frustration on his face. His lips mumbled words I couldn't hear. I had pushed his buttons. In one brisk motion, he opened the door and reached for my hand. I slid out effortlessly, not taking his hand. I swear he growled.

The security outside stifled a laugh as we walked up but cut it short after what I can only assume was a death stare from the shadow behind me. He opened the door and I flashed him the sweetest smile I could manage. Aurelia's was definitely the kind of place that most people only dreamed of coming into. Even growing up in the higher parts of society, this was the type of store you only window shopped in, but never bought from. It would make sense this is where he would go - somewhere to show off.

Each salesperson had plastered on their perfect customer service smiles. The ladies seemed to revel in his gaze as he swept it over the glass cases.

"Mr. Moretti," an older, distinguished gentleman in a tailored suit met us inside. "Thank you for choosing Aurelia's to help you celebrate this exciting moment." he shook Lorenzo's hand and held mine for a moment, like old money.

"Ms. Blackwell, please take your time, explore each case and let us help you find something that excites you." he gestured to the cases behind him. "You are our only appointment today, so there's no rush." it dawned on me, he planned this. Lorenzo arranged for us to be here, uninterrupted. He was good, I'd give him that.

I shot him a glance. "The pleasure is ours. Everyone knows Aurelia is the best. I would be honored to wear something your master jewelers have crafted." I was laying it, I know, but this was my first chance to create *her* - the perfect fiancée for a Moretti, someone the public would eat up. Like insurance. We each had our own motives, but I learned a long time ago how to shift the public perception and we both knew that was the name of the game - optics, blending truths with lies until the fabric told the story we wanted.

I trailed my fingers long the edges of the cases. These rings were absolutely stunning, I couldn't lie. After a few cases though, they were all similar. Gold and platinum bands lay in precise rows, each one cradling a diamond meant to stop breath and start futures. Round cuts, princess cuts, ovals and cushions, all lifted high in prongs that caught the light and threw it back in obedient flashes.

Some bands were thin and delicate, others thick and engraved, worked with filigree or subtle texture meant to suggest craftsmanship without demanding attention. A few broke from the uniformity—pale sapphires, soft emeralds, a blush of morganite, but even those felt rehearsed, variations on the same promise.

Everything sparkled.
Everything behaved.

I leaned closer, inspecting the offerings, trying them on my finger, waiting for the pull—something right, but felt nothing. The diamonds were too eager, too loud. They begged to be admired, to be chosen, to be worn as proof.

They all said the same thing. Forever. Tradition. Safety. Beautiful, yes. Impeccable. And utterly forgettable.

My sigh was audible though I tried to hide it. The shopkeeper glanced nervously at Lorenzo, a quiet, but imposing figure. He was dressed in his routine black tailored pants and fitted shirt, sleeves rolled just enough to be casual, dark ink melding with his olive skin. He looked almost out of place here.

"Do you have anything in, onyx?" I let a smile play on my lips, keeping my eyes on the case in front of me, like I was bored.

"...For your engagement ring?" The shopkeeper looked nervous. He shot another look to Lorenzo whose eyes I could feel boring into my back. I simply nodded. He snapped his fingers with a small huff, clearly he did not like this.

The lady at my case disappeared through a back hallway reappearing a few moments later with a small velvet tray. There were a few sets with onyx and diamonds, beautiful pairs of black and white set in gold and silver. We were getting closer, but still not there. I shook my head pulling out a slight pout to get the point across.

"I think something with some…spark would best define our relationship," I turned to take his stare head on. I was only focused on him, his reactions, his breathing. A playful smile twitched at the corners of his mouth. "Something that feels….eternal,." Oblivious to the game happening around him, the shopkeeper seemed to have a moment of clarity. He disappeared through the same hall and returned a moment later with a small black leather-covered box.

"I think this will capture your heart's desire," he opened the hinged lid revealing the ring, like a secret inside. It was white gold, cool and luminous, its surface polished to a near-mirror sheen. It caught the light without warmth; controlled, deliberate. Nothing ornamental for ornament's sake.

Black onyx stones formed the spine of it, faceted into sharp, elongated shapes that felt almost predatory, like obsidian blades set in sequence. They weren't soft or round. They didn't sparkle. They absorbed light, drank it in.

Where diamonds should have been, garnets replaced them—deep red, bordering on black at the center. Not bright. Not romantic. The color of dried wine, of blood seen in shadow. They were cut smaller, tucked between the onyx and along the band, glinting only when the light hit just right.

The contrast was striking: white gold against black stone, punctured by restrained flashes of red. A balance of control and threat. Luxury sharpened into something almost violent.

It wasn't delicate. It wasn't meant to be. It looked like a promise you couldn't take back once accepted. And it was - "Perfect," Lorenzo said. His voice was deep and smooth.

I hadn't realized the small gasp I'd taken when I saw it, but he had. He closed the remaining distance, his body stopping just a breath from mine, and took the box from the shopkeeper.

"*Solo per te*," he murmured, the words shaped like a secret.

He removed the ring gently and slid it onto my left hand. Despite its delicate size, it felt heavy on my finger. Like an expectation. Like a chain. The shopkeeper's voice faded into background noise. My breath hitched when Lorenzo lifted my hand and pressed his lips to my knuckles without breaking eye contact.

This was exactly why we needed ground rules.

The shopkeeper cleared his throat, jarring both of us. Lorenzo's expression darkened, murderous, as if the interruption were the gravest offense imaginable.

"So sorry," I said lightly, patting Lorenzo's arm. "My fiancé gets a little caught up. His brothers and I are trying to teach him some manners, but nothing seems to stick."

The shopkeeper's anxious expression softened.

"Yes, well," he said, recovering, "as I was saying, we do have a matching band for you." He handed another box to Lorenzo.

Inside was a rugged design: a single onyx stone set into a wide white-gold band, offset with small blood-red garnets. It was stunning.

But it was not him. I could tell by the rise of his chest—he was about to speak, and it would not be polite.

"Actually," I said smoothly, "he prefers a solid black band. Not too wide." Our eyes met. "Something sleek."

The shopkeeper hesitated, clearly reconsidering every life choice that had led him here. "Something so simple?" he asked then stopped short at the look I gave him.

"I know what my fiancé likes."

He signaled a saleswoman. She returned with several options, laying them out carefully. Lorenzo remained silent. Apparently, this choice was mine. I studied each band in turn until I found it.

A flat band of blackened tungsten, unmarked, unpolished, built to last through whatever battles we would undoubtedly fight. I picked up the ring without asking, and his hand came down on the counter—not to stop me, just to be there, hovering close.

Broad palm. Scarred knuckles. Warm. Steady. Heavy with restraint. The kind of hand that didn't need to threaten to be obeyed—because it already knew exactly how much pressure it took to make someone listen.

I took his hand and slid the ring on his finger. It felt final. Like a lock clicking into place. He had to feel it, too. He flexed his fingers as if letting the weight settle, like he realized that we were bound now.

The shopkeeper fidgeted with his hands nervously, "So glad you have found the perfect set." His words hinged on 'perfect' - clearly he had a different idea of what an ideal engagement set looked like. "How would you like to handle the paperwork? Some couples prefer to go ahead and use the married name otherwise you will have to come back in…?" his voice trailed off, waiting.

I must have looked confused as he gave me a small smile and explained, "At Aurelia's we register every piece sold in order to ensure our beautiful pieces are never separated from the purchaser. Your ring will have a jeweler's signature etched on the underneath side that will be registered to you." He glanced between us. It dawned on me, he was asking if I wanted to register as Sierra *Moretti*.

He didn't realize it but this was now going to be another landmine in the battlefield we were creating. "Forgive me, it's just been such a long day." He smiled in acknowledgement. "Please register them both under Moretti."

Lorenzo's gaze sharpened, not surprised, but intent. As if he understood exactly what I'd just given him. And what it would cost.

The drive back to his penthouse was quiet, but not strained, each of us weighing the reality of what we were doing. Parts of the city felt familiar, but like I was seeing it from a different angle.

I wasn't prepared for how quickly it had happened. The penthouse door closed behind us, the quiet settling the way it always did—but something was different. The air felt… softer. Not warmer. Just altered.

I took a step in and stopped.

A cream throw blanket lay draped over the back of the couch, casual, like it had always belonged there. Under the coffee table, my black-and-red rug anchored the space, its familiar pattern cutting through the stone and steel like a signature. Tall potted plants framed the windows—matching, alive—breaking the hard lines of the city beyond the glass.

Books lined the shelves. Not his. Mine. Stacked neatly, grouped the way I liked without ever realizing I had a system. I crossed the room slowly, as if sudden movement might make it all vanish. My oversized reading chair sat near the window—the one Jenna and I had dragged home from a thrift store months ago, laughing the whole way because it barely fit in her car. It looked impossibly right here. Like it had been waiting.

My chest tightened.

The bathroom confirmed it. My toothbrush stood beside his. Shampoo, body wash, scrubs, lotions lined the counter. My makeup arranged carefully, not rummaged through. His flat, severe bath mats were gone, replaced with the soft memory-foam ones I loved.

The bed stopped me completely. At the foot of it lay a blanket, bigger, heavier, dark red. My favorite one.

I didn't ask how he knew. Or how it had all happened - we'd only been gone for a couple hours.

The closet answered the rest. One section cleared, filled with my clothes. Band tees beside sweaters. Dresses hanging unwrinkled. Leggings and jeans folded into drawers. My Docs and heels lined up on shelves like they'd passed inspection.

In the kitchen, my favorite coffee mug sat on the counter. My coffee maker stood plugged in beside the sleek, unforgiving coffee pod machine. I opened a cabinet and blinked. So many water bottles. More than I remembered owning.

It all should have terrified me. Instead, it felt… inevitable. Like this space had been waiting for me to catch up.

Then Lorenzo noticed the coffee machine. His body went still. His jaw tightened.

"What," he said slowly, in Italian, "is *that* doing here?"

I turned just in time to see him gesturing at my coffee maker like it had personally insulted his bloodline.

"Oh, don't start," I said, already smiling.

"That is not coffee," he snapped. "It is an abomination. A crime. I will have it removed."

I laughed. Not a breath. Not a huff. A real laugh— bright, surprised, loose.

His head snapped toward me. "You are laughing."

"I am," I said, wiping at my eyes. "You're actually offended."

"It isn't funny."

"It's a little funny."

"I will throw it out."

"You absolutely will not."

He stepped toward the island. I mirrored him, stopping on the opposite side. The counter stretched between us like a line drawn on the floor.

"Or else," he said calmly.

My smile sharpened. "Or else what?"

For a moment, neither of us moved.

The air changed—charged, tight. This wasn't about coffee. It never had been. It was about space. About what survived once our two worlds collided. About how much of me he intended to allow—and how much I was willing to surrender.

Then, a knock at the door.

Sharp. Deliberate. The moment shattered, leaving it hanging between us, unresolved. Lorenzo's gaze slid from mine to the door, his expression closing like a vault.

******

### Lorenzo

Her defense of the coffee abomination would be dealt with later. I was certain Alexio had enjoyed every second of installing it, probably laughed himself breathless while doing it.

Marco arrived right on time.

I glanced back at her as I crossed the room, her posture loose, curious, unaware. The door opened, and the moment he stepped inside, the air shifted.

"Brother." Marco's voice was calm. Steady. A reminder of what this was supposed to be. An agreement. A contract.

A flurry of texts earlier that morning had decided it. After a brief, pointed expression of disappointment in me after I changed the terms from "dating" to "engaged", he'd agreed this was necessary.

We had already decided Sierra would be the most effective way to draw Matteo out. Publicly dating her would be salt in an open wound. Matteo would see it as a challenge. He always did.

I hadn't forgotten how his brother—older, clever, patient—had once slid into my bed with the woman I thought I'd marry. Three years together. Long enough for me to believe in things like permanence. Like love.

I knew better now. I hadn't dated publicly since. Lust, yes. Names I didn't bother remembering. But love was a liability I no longer afforded myself.

"Sierra," I said, turning back, "this is my brother, Marco."

Ever the gentleman, Marco took her hand and pressed a brief kiss to her knuckles. She blushed faintly. Something sharp twisted in my chest. Jealousy?

"Charmed, *bella*," Marco said, releasing her hand and gesturing toward the table. "Shall we?"

He set his leather briefcase down carefully, the muted click of the locks sounding louder than it should have. Sierra followed easily, though the confusion on her face made my mouth curve.

I was beginning to enjoy these moments—our small, private standoffs. The way we traded daggers dressed as words.

"What exactly are we doing?" she asked. She addressed Marco, but her eyes stayed on me.

Marco exhaled slowly, pinching the bridge of his nose. He already knew—I hadn't warned her. "We're drafting a contract," he said carefully. "For your engagement to my brother."

I leaned back in my chair, arms crossing loosely. The storm gathering behind her eyes pleased me more than it should have.

"A contract," she repeated. Cold. Sharp.

"I believe you called them *ground rules*, amore."

Color crept up her neck—betraying her despite herself. "So official," she said dryly. "So romantic."

"Romantic my brother is not," Marco said smoothly, cutting in before it escalated. "But this is… prudent."

Her gaze flicked between us. Prudent. That was one word for it.

Marco slid a thin document from the briefcase but didn't open it.

"This isn't *ownership*," he said first. "It's containment."

Sierra's lips parted slightly. "Of what?"

"Of damage," Marco replied calmly. "To you. To Lorenzo. To anyone watching."

I tilted my head. "You're assuming she needs protection."

Marco didn't look at me. "I'm assuming you do." That earned a glance from Sierra. Sharp. Assessing.

"What exactly are you proposing?" she asked.

Marco folded his hands on the table. "Parameters. Public conduct. Privacy. Physical boundaries."

"Boundaries," she echoed. "For him too?"

"Yes."

That surprised her. I saw it in the brief pause, the recalibration. "And if one of us breaks them?" she asked.

"Then there are consequences," Marco said evenly. "On both sides."

She scanned the document again, then looked up. "I choose who's listed under unrestricted contact."

"Agreed," Marco said instantly. I frowned but didn't interrupt.

"No marks that can't be concealed," she continued. "No restraint in public."

Marco nodded. "Already noted."

She turned to me then, chin lifting slightly. "And I don't ask permission to leave."

A slow smile curved my mouth. "Notification," I corrected.

Her gaze didn't waver. "Notification." Marco's pen scratched across the page.

"You don't touch me when I say no," she said quietly. The room went still.

Marco didn't look up. "That is non-negotiable." My jaw tightened, but I said nothing.

"Good," she said, leaning back and folding her arms. "Then we're on the same page. What about termination?"

Marco finally lifted his eyes. "If the engagement ends, it ends cleanly."

"And if it doesn't?" she pressed.

Marco closed the folder. "Then the rules evolve."

Her breath caught—just slightly.

I leaned forward then, resting my forearms on the table. "In public," I said, "we move together."

She arched a brow. "Meaning?"

"No disappearing acts," I replied calmly. "No wandering off to prove a point. If you need space, you say so. I don't search for you." Marco nodded, already writing.

"I don't like being managed," she said.

"I don't like being embarrassed," I countered. "This protects us both."

A pause. "Fine," she said at last. "But you don't steer me."

A corner of my mouth lifted. "I wouldn't dare."

Marco hesitated, then added the note: *mutual proximity— no physical direction.*

"If you leave," I continued, "you leave with notice."

She stiffened. "We already covered that."

"I'm clarifying," I said evenly. "You don't vanish to punish me."

Her jaw set. "And you don't stalk me to intimidate me."

"I only observe," I said mildly. "But agreed." Marco underlined the clause twice.

"And one more," I added quietly.

They both looked at me. "If either of us breaks these rules," I said, "the other is not obligated to forgive it immediately."

Sierra tilted her head. "You're asking for what— grace?"

"I'm asking for time," I replied. "Time to correct behavior before consequences escalate."

Marco studied me for a long moment before nodding. "That's… reasonable."

Sierra's eyes stayed on mine. "You're very confident you'll be the one doing the correcting."

I smiled. "I'm confident," I said, "that I won't be corrected often."

Sierra exhaled slowly, folding her arms. "Let's be clear about the goal here."

Marco looked between us but said nothing.

"This makes me unreachable," she said. "It puts a wall between me and the rest of the Blackwell family. Socially. Physically. Matteo can't touch me if I'm engaged to you."

I didn't correct her.

"It buys time," she continued. "We stay engaged long enough for the attention to die down. For everyone to lose interest. Then we dissolve it when it's convenient."

Her eyes flicked to mine. "Cleanly."

Marco nodded once. "That is the intended outcome."

I leaned back in my chair. "It also sends a message."

She tilted her head. "To Matteo."

"Yes," I said. "And to anyone watching him."

Her jaw tightened. "You want him uncomfortable."

I smiled faintly. "I want him exposed."

She studied me for a moment. "You think he's responsible."

I didn't answer directly. "I think he's not as untouchable as he believes." That was enough for her.

"And this helps your family," she added. "Public stability. One of the Moretti brothers finally settling down." She flicked her eyes to Marco, a small smile on the corners of his mouth.

"Appearances matter," I agreed easily.

She nodded, satisfied—for now.

Marco closed the folder. "Good," he said. "Then we are aligned." He removed a single page and slid it across the table, aligning it carefully with the grain of the wood.

"Final clause," he said. "Non-negotiable."

Sierra picked it up. The language was dense. Precise. Written to leave no room for interpretation. She read it once. Then again.

Her voice, when it came, was steady. "This says that if Lorenzo violates the terms—"

"—then you are withdrawn from the engagement," Marco finished calmly. "Immediately."

Withdrawn. Not released. Not compensated.

"Withdrawn to where?" she asked.

Marco folded his hands. "A secure location. Temporary, unless otherwise deemed necessary."

"And I lose contact," she said, reading. "With family. Friends. Employment."

"Correct," Marco said. "Until the breach is resolved."

Her eyes lifted. "Resolved how?"

"That depends," he replied. "On Lorenzo."

She went very still. "And if I violate the terms?" she asked.

Marco didn't hesitate. "Then the engagement proceeds as planned."

Her fingers tightened on the page. Just slightly. "So there's no scenario where *he* is removed," she said quietly.

Marco met her gaze. "There is no scenario where my brother is the liability."

I watched the understanding settle in her eyes. This wasn't a punishment clause. It was a failsafe.

I had known—intellectually—that Marco would protect me at any cost. That this document was never about fairness. But seeing it written, clean and clinical, did something sharp to my chest. Because this clause didn't exist to restrain me. It existed to preserve the arrangement.

To preserve *me*.

If I broke the rules, she disappeared—not because she was at fault, but because she was movable. Containable. I felt something cold coil low in my gut.

Not guilt. Recognition.

This contract didn't assume I would fail. It assumed that if I did, the world would bend to absorb the impact. And she would be the one removed from its path.

Marco slid a pen across the table. "When you're ready," he said.

I didn't look at Sierra. I didn't need to. The rules were no longer about what we were allowed to do. They were about what would survive.

I signed first. My name moved quickly across the page—clean, efficient, without flourish. No hesitation. No wasted motion. The signature of someone accustomed to binding things permanently.

Sierra stared at my name for a moment longer than necessary. Then she took the pen, our fingers brushing slightly.

Her signature bloomed across the paper—looped, deliberate, unmistakably hers. Full. A little defiant. As if she believed there was still room to shape what came next. When she finished, the ink gleamed wet and dark against the page.

Red. Too red. I watched the ink dry. Watched the space between our names disappear.

Marco slid the last page into the folder without ceremony. "That's it," he said. "It's done."

Her eyes, still dark and raging met mine. It was like we both finally understood that this wasn't a contract we had signed. It was a line we had crossed.

# *Chapter 7*



I watched the two brothers embrace. Marco was slightly taller, his hair a shade lighter, but they were unmistakably the same—strong jawlines, tanned skin, hazel eyes that missed very little. They spoke in low whispers by the door. Marco glanced at me once, a faint, almost pleading look, before he slipped into the night.

The door closed. Lorenzo turned back toward me, hands in his pockets, that infuriating smirk already in place.

Gods, I wanted to smack it off his face. I was quickly realizing just how much of this he had orchestrated behind my back. I wanted to be angry. I *was* angry. I wanted to be furious—righteous, volcanic, uncontained.

Instead, I felt like I could breathe. Like all my enemies had finally been locked away. My gaze dropped to the ring on my left hand. Cruelly beautiful. Heavy. I turned it slightly, watching the garnets catch the light, wondering what the cost of that breath would be.

"You have work tonight." His voice was quiet. Not a question.

"Yes." I answered cautiously. We hadn't discussed our work in the contract—not really. I knew he helped run his family's wine business, but I had no idea what that actually meant.

I checked my phone. Fifteen missed texts from Jenna. I grimaced. A lot had just happened.

"I need to get changed and go," I said, already thinking ahead. Then—hesitating—"Did you have my car brought here?" It was still registered under my parents. Another leash. Another way they could pull.

Something flickered across his face. Worry.

"What did you do?" The relief evaporated, anger snapping back into place.

"*Merda*," he muttered, dragging a hand through his perfectly styled hair and ruining it. "It was…sold." The way he said it—calm, explanatory, utterly unapologetic—made my blood boil.

"Lorenzo." My voice rose. "What the *fuck*? We literally just talked about control, and you went and sold my car?"

"*Calma, calma*." He lifted his hands. "*I* didn't actually sell your car."

That tone—light, almost amused—made it worse.

"It was registered to Blackwell Enterprises," he continued. "To cut the cord, it had to go. After your

apartment, it was the last thing they owned you with."
That landed harder than the anger. Owned you.

I opened my mouth, then closed it, my thoughts scrambling to catch up. He didn't give me time.

"Your new bank card will arrive in a few days," he said. "Your own account. The full balance from the old one has already been transferred."

I stared at him. "They can't touch it," he added. Then his gaze finally met mine. Steady. Intent. "They can't touch *you*."

The anger didn't disappear. But beneath it—unsettling, undeniable—was the same feeling as before. Relief.

And the terrifying realization that he'd taken control so completely, I wasn't sure where my freedom ended and his protection began. I didn't answer, but nodded.

"You'll have to take me." I lifted my chin like it was defiance. I hated the way I liked the curve of his mouth.

"I'll wait."

He leaned against the doorframe, his gaze following me down the hall to his—*our*—bedroom. For a moment, I considered keeping the blue sundress on. I'd make incredible tips, but at Last Call it wouldn't be the only thing I'd collect, and tonight I wasn't in the mood for overly flirtatious men.

I changed into opaque black tights, a black t-shirt dress, and my Docs. After fixing my makeup, I slipped on my usual jewelry, noticing how easily it complemented my newest piece. The ring caught the light when I moved—unapologetically beautiful.

I left my hair down. Despite the harshness of everything else, having my things here felt grounding. Like proof I existed beyond the contract. When I stepped back into the hall, he wasn't where I'd left him.

The door to the off-limits room stood ajar.

As if he sensed me, Lorenzo filled the doorway. Without a word, he stepped into the hall and closed the door behind him. The lock slid into place with a final, decisive click.

I exhaled and followed him toward the garage.

The drive to Last Call settled into a quiet lull—not tense, not uncomfortable. Just shared space. I pretended not to notice my phone connecting automatically to his Bluetooth. Pretended not to notice him noticing that I noticed.

Instead, I met the challenge.

The speakers filled with heavy, modern rock— slow-burning and relentless. A thick bass line crawled beneath the beat, the drums landing like measured blows.

It wasn't chaotic. It was deliberate. The kind of music that didn't rush the fight—it waited for it.

He glanced at me, one corner of his mouth lifting, and shifted the Maserati into gear. Then he took off.

******

"NO! For the last time, you can NOT stay here the entire time." I ran my hands across my face. We were standing in the lot outside Last Call.

"Then put your engagement ring back on." He was trying to keep his voice even but I could hear the edges of his control slipping. As we pulled in, I had taken my ring off, putting it in the glove compartment.

"Lorenzo, for fuck's sake," I seethed, my voice sharp with exasperation. "I haven't even told Jenna I'm engaged. I can't just show up after ghosting her for two days with a forty-thousand-dollar paperweight on my finger!" I searched his eyes, desperate for a flicker of something other than granite.

"Then I'm staying." He shrugged his shoulders, leaning back against his car.

"Jesus Christ, fine!" The words ripped out of me. I threw my hands up in surrender and spun on my heel, stalking toward the bar. I let the heavy back door swing shut behind me, a petty, childish part of me hoping it would slam into him. It was a useless gesture. He dodged it without even moving his feet, a fluid shift of weight.

His gaze lifted, slow and deliberate, and I knew he wasn't watching me walk away. He was watching his property enter the building.

I stormed into Gio's office, not bothering to see if Lorenzo followed. He would. The old man looked up from a stack of invoices, his brows arching in question as the door didn't close behind me. Lorenzo filled the frame, a silent, imposing shadow. I pinched the bridge of my nose, trying to summon the words to explain this nightmare, but Lorenzo stepped past me, cutting me off before I could even start.

He extended a hand, his movements smooth, practiced. "I don't believe we've met," he said, his normally dark, gravelly tone laced with a lightness, bordering on sociopathic. "I'm Lorenzo, Sierra's fiancé."

Oh my god. He was savoring every second of this.

"I didn't realize you were… so involved with someone," Gio stammered, his composure cracking. He scrambled to his feet, a forced smile plastered on his face. "Congrats!" He wrapped me in a clumsy side hug, the sheer insanity of the situation flying right over his graying head.

"Sierra is in the process of getting a new car, so I brought her tonight," Lorenzo continued, the lie rolling off his tongue like honey laced. It wasn't untrue, which made it all the more infuriating. "Instead of heading home then coming all the way back, would it be alright if I just… stayed?" He sounded so damn sincere, like he'd actually respect Gio's decision. The sly, predatory glance he shot me let me know this was just another move on the board. He was cornering me in plain sight.

"After her ex came in the other day," he added, his voice dropping with manufactured concern as he clapped Gio on the shoulder like old buddies, "I worry about her safety. I'll just sit in a corner and observe."

Giovanni rubbed the graying stubble on his chin, weighing the option as if he actually had one. "Well, I suppose that would be fine," he conceded, holding up a finger. "But you can't get in her way, you hear me? None of that jealous shit." He gave us both a pointed look that was utterly useless. I just rolled my eyes.

"Absolutely, signor," Lorenzo agreed with a deferential nod, shaking Gio's hand once before turning to follow me out. He paused at the door, turning back. "Oh, and Giovanni, is it? Call this number when you're ready to renew your liquor license." He slid a business card from his suit jacket, the motion fluid and effortless. "I know some people who owe my brother a favor. You won't get any pushback."

Gio's eyes widened slightly as he took the card. He just nodded, waving us out as the phone on his desk began to ring, a welcome distraction from the man who had just co-opted his life.

"You can't get rid of me, *amore*," he murmured, his hand a brand as it slid down my arm when I pushed past him to clock in.

"We'll talk about this at home," I said through my teeth. I needed Jenna. The air in the front bar was thick with the smell of stale beer and cheap perfume, the dance floor already a writhing, pulsing mass. I threaded my way through the bodies to the main bar. Jenna was a whirlwind of motion, shaking a cocktail mixer and laughing with a group of men who were all trying far too hard.

When she saw me, her eyes lit up like a firework. "SIERRA!" she yelled over the bass, pulling me into a hug that smelled like vanilla and everything stable in my life. I melted into it, just for a second.

"UM, so are you going to tell me WHY the building manager said you cut your lease?! I went to get you but you literally disappeared!" The words tumbled out of her in a rush. I opened my mouth to start the apology, the excuse, the story, but her gaze snagged on something over my shoulder and her eyes widened.

"I think you have a stalker."

I sighed, the weight of the last two days pressing down on me. "No, actually, he's my fiancé." I watched her face, a silent movie of shock, confusion, and dawning horror.

"You forgot your ring, amore." Lorenzo's voice was a low, wicked purr right behind me. He took my hand, his grip firm as he slid the cold, heavy band back onto my finger. Jenna's eyes whipped from him to me

and back so fast I was surprised they didn't just pop out
of her head and roll onto the sticky floor.

"Jenna, we need—"

"SHUT UP JAX—SIERRA IS ENGAGED!"
Jenna's squeal cut through the music, making Jax Vitelli,
who was polishing a glass, almost drop the damn thing.
He'd been working at Gio's for years, but Jenna's
enthusiasm was a force of nature that still caught him off
guard.

Jax recovered, his eyes narrowing as he looked
Lorenzo over, like he was sizing up a threat. "Do you
love her?" he asked, his voice cutting through Jenna's
giddiness.

Jenna squeezed my arm, her own attention fixed
on Lorenzo.

"I would burn the world down for her." Lorenzo's
voice wasn't a boast. It was a statement of fact. Steady,
firm, with the terrifying edge of something true in it. Heat
flooded my face, creeping up my neck. The way he said it
made me want to believe him.

"Wow, okay, tough guy, relax," Jenna said, fake-
punching his shoulder. She mimed calling me later and
let Jax drag her back to the thirsty customers.

"Ugh," I groaned, rubbing a hand over my face.
This was going to be a long night.

"Yeah, come on, tough guy." I grabbed his hand, pulling him through the crowd. We cut through the dark corridor separating the front and back bars, and I shoved him against the wall. "Rules for tonight," I said, holding up a finger. "Number one, you cannot sit at the bar. You'll scare all my customers away. Number two, you must be nice to Jenna and Jax. Number three—"

"Number three, you will keep your ring on, and I will stay out of your way." He shifted, using his weight to push off the wall, closing the distance between us until our faces were inches apart. One breath and we'd be kissing.

"Agreed," I whispered, letting my lips just barely brush against his. I felt the slightest hitch in his breath, a microscopic crack in his armor.

We walked into the back bar together. Marcus raised his brows but said nothing as I slid behind the bar. I was thankful for the group that walked in then—a bunch of young hot shots celebrating a promotion. I made their first round and took the drinks over to the pool tables. I could feel Lorenzo's eyes on me with every step. He'd found a quiet corner, a shadowed throne with a perfect vantage point of the door, the bar, and the hallway. A few patrons tried to flirt with me, but it was as if they all sensed him. He might not have been at the bar, but they felt his gaze the same way I did—a heavy, possessive weight.

Thankfully, the rest of my shift was a blur of easy orders and decent tips. When it was over, he was waiting for me by the door. He opened it, earning a shameless thumbs-up from Jenna, who was now shamelessly flirting with Jax. I slid into the passenger seat, the leather cool against my skin.

"Your friend seems to like me," his voice was amused as he got in.

"If anything happens to me, she will kill you." I wasn't sure why I said it, but it was the truest thing I'd said all night. Jenna might look like sunshine and bubblegum, but high society had sharpened her into a lethal social weapon.

"Nothing will happen to you." His words were heavy, like a vow carved in stone. "But, to humor you, I will file that away." He started the car, pulling us away from the noise and the chaos, and back toward his penthouse. Home.

******

***Lorenzo***

Even exhausted, she was beautiful. She leaned into the elevator wall on the ride up, like she needed it to stay upright. Her phone hadn't stopped buzzing since we left—Jenna, relentless, hungry for details. For proof.

The moment we stepped inside, I felt the shift. The apartment wasn't the same as it had been that morning when I'd walked out to meet her. Something had settled into the space.

Her presence was already altering my life, bending it around her in quiet, irreversible ways—and it had only been a day. But what a day it had been.

"I'm going to shower before bed," she said, her voice flat with exhaustion. She stood in the middle of the bedroom, a weary statue in the dim light.

"That's fine," I said, already turning toward the hall. "I have some work to do."

She didn't reply, just watched me go, her gaze unreadable. I didn't look back. The click of the bathroom door closing was the only sound that followed me down the hall. I entered my office, and the door slid shut behind me, sealing my sanctum. This wasn't a study. It was the command center. The nerve center of my world.

With a flick of a switch, the wall came alive. A dozen screens flickered to life, a mosaic of my domain. The kitchen, empty and sterile. The living room, a cavern of shadow. The elevator lobby. And there, the master bedroom. My bedroom. Our bedroom.

She was a blur of motion on the screen, peeling off the clothes she'd worn to the bar. Her movements were economical, tired. She tossed the dress onto a chair, her bra and panties following. She was a vision, all soft curves and pale skin under the sterile overhead light. My blood thickened, a slow, heavy pulse starting in my groin. I leaned forward in my chair, my hands resting on the cool leather of the armrests.

She turned toward the bathroom, but then she paused. Her head tilted. She walked back to the door, her expression thoughtful. And then, she flicked the lock.

A bolt of pure, unadulterated shock shot through me. She locked the door. Not against me, not really. She couldn't know I was watching. This was for her. A small, futile act of defiance in a world she thought she had no control over. A line drawn in the sand.

And then she did something that shattered my composure completely.

She didn't go to the shower. She walked to the bed and sprawled across my sheets, naked and unashamed. My bed. Her long limbs stretched out, a pagan goddess claiming her altar. Her hand drifted down her stomach, hesitated for a moment, and then slipped between her thighs.

My breath caught in my throat. *Merda.*

Her eyes were closed, her lips parted slightly as her fingers began to move, a slow, rhythmic circling that had my own cock straining against my trousers. This was a thousand times more potent than watching her undress. This wasn't vulnerability; it was ownership. She was touching herself in my bed, and the thought was so obscene, so perfect, it made my head spin.

Her hips began to lift, a subtle, desperate grind against her own hand. Soft, breathy sounds escaped her lips, little whimpers of pleasure that were amplified by the hidden microphone in the room. And then she said it. A whisper, a secret meant only for the darkness.

*"Lorenzo."*

My name. A prayer on her lips as her back arched, her body tensing as the orgasm washed over her. It was the most erotic thing I had ever seen. The shock was instantly incinerated by a wave of devilish, predatory excitement. She wasn't just in my bed; she was thinking of me when she came.

I was on my feet before I knew it, my hand fumbling with my belt. I leaned against the console, my eyes glued to the screen as she lay panting, a sheen of sweat on her skin. I wrapped my hand around my cock, the steel-hard length aching for release. I stroked myself in time with the memory of her gasps, picturing her face, the way she'd whispered my name. It didn't take long. A few rough, punishing pulls and I was coming, spilling myself into my own hand with a choked groan, my eyes locked on her image as she lay sated and oblivious in my bed.

On the screen, she finally stirred, rising with a languid grace and heading into the bathroom. The sound of the shower starting was my cue. I cleaned up quickly, straightening my clothes, my heart still hammering against my ribs. I left the office, the screens going dark behind me, and slipped into the bedroom just as the water shut off.

I was already changed and under the covers, propped up against the headboard, pretending to read something on my phone when she came out. She was wrapped in a towel, her skin pink from the heat, her hair damp.

"Enjoy your shower?" I asked, keeping my voice casual, letting gaze wash over every inch of her.

She shot me a look, a small, tired smirk playing on her lips. "Immensely. The water pressure is the only thing in this penthouse that doesn't have a stick up its ass."

I couldn't help but chuckle. She stepped into the closet, and I could hear the towel drop to the floor. She came back out in a pair of silk pajamas, before sliding into bed beside me without another word. The space between us was electric, a chasm of unspoken things. We both lay on our backs, staring at the ceiling, rigidly not touching. The air was thick with the scent of her clean skin and the ghost of her orgasm. I could still hear her moaning my name. And I knew, with absolute certainty, that neither of us would be getting any sleep.

******

I had never been woken by a scream before. The sound ripped through me—sharp, immediate—sparking a panic I didn't know I was capable of.

Sierra was upright beside me, chest rising too fast, skin damp with cold sweat. I reached for her on instinct.

She flinched, but didn't pull away—only drew her knees closer, folding in on herself.

"I'm fine. It's fine." The words sounded rehearsed, meant to convince herself more than me.

"It's not," I said quietly. I let the truth sit between us, unwilling to press. I already knew who her nightmare belonged to.

When I reached for her hand again, she let me take it. I leaned back against the headboard and drew her with me. She settled against my chest, the heat of her seeping through my thin t-shirt. I wrapped my arms around her and pressed a kiss into her hair, the clean scent of her shampoo grounding us both.

"Was it…?" I let the question fade. I wouldn't speak his name while she was in my bed.

She nodded, barely lifting her head.

"Nothing can touch you here," I murmured, low enough to feel like a vow. She answered with another small nod, her breathing slowly evening out.

She shifted, and I loosened my hold, letting my fingers trace her arm before slipping into her hair. I stroked it absently, guided by instinct. Every so often, she made a soft sound—unconscious approval. We stayed that way until her breathing caught once, then smoothed again. By the time I realized it, she was asleep.

Feeling the steady rise and fall of her against me, the quiet weight of her existence in my arms, I made two decisions.

I would keep her safe—regardless of cost.

And Matteo Rinaldi was already dead. He just didn't know it yet.

******

The sun sliced through the windows like a blade, too bright, too early. Sierra stirred beside me, a soft murmur escaping her lips. Yesterday's chaos was a film reel playing on the back of my eyelids. I leaned over and pressed a gentle kiss to her forehead before sliding out of bed. I pulled on a pair of grey sweats and swapped the white tee from last night for a black one, the fabric soft and familiar against my skin.

My phone buzzed while I was brushing my teeth. Emil. The message was simple: Bellandi was dead. I spat, wiping my mouth, and opened the screenshot. A news article, grainy and sensational. The Chief Acquisitions Manager for the Rinaldi Group, found near the east side docks, stabbed multiple times. His face was a mess of lacerations, matching cuts on both sides of his jaw. I froze, the toothbrush still in my hand. Sierra. The docks. Matteo. The pieces clicked into place with a sickening finality.

I fired off a text to our group chat. *Matteo. Has to be.* It was his calling card, his twisted signature. Rumors were swirling that he was holed up on his yacht, his father preparing to call an emergency board meeting. A public statement had been released, but it was a farce, a thin veneer over the rotting truth. Alessio sent his dog to start tying up loose ends.

My espresso was ready, the rich aroma filling the kitchen. I inhaled deeply, the scent grounding me, anchoring me to the present. I needed it. Our texts shifted from Rinaldi business to family matters. Emil and Dario were heading to California, scouting land for a stateside winery. Our parents had paved the way, but it was on us now to expand the Moretti brand, to cement our legacy.

The sound of water running in the bathroom, the soft click of doors opening and closing, told me Sierra was awake. I started making her a cappuccino, a peace offering after the whirlwind of yesterday. I needed her to know that despite the chaos, there were still constants. Like this. Like coffee.

She emerged from the bedroom, wearing a pair of shorts and my Moretti Vineyard crewneck. It was oversized on her, but it couldn't hide the curves beneath. Her dark hair cascaded over her shoulder, a waterfall of ink. She looked tired, but there was a spark in her eyes, a flicker of something I couldn't quite name. Seeing her in my clothes stirred something deep inside.

"Something smells good," she said, her voice soft, husky with sleep.

"For you," I said, handing her the cup. I watched as she took a sip, her eyes closing briefly, a small smile playing on her lips. "Can we write daily coffee into our contract?" she joked, and I nearly choked on my own breath. Her laugh was melodic, a sound I could get used to hearing.

"Um, thank you," she said, tucking a stray strand of hair behind her ear. "For last night - that usually happens 2 or 3 times a week, actually." Her voice trailed off, a hint of vulnerability in her words. "Just so you can be prepared, I don't always scream like that, but yeah."

I looked at her, really looked at her, taking in every line, every shadow, every secret she kept hidden behind those dark eyes. How could I tell her that I would burn the world down to erase the ghosts of her past? That Matteo would never draw breath in the same air as her again? That I would do anything, anything at all, to keep her safe, to keep her mine?

"Sierra -" My phone rang, shattering the moment. Marco. I tapped the green icon, already dreading whatever he had to say.

"Brother…you're sure?" I could feel her gaze on me, heavy and questioning. "That feels soon….if she agrees, yes, here, - Italy?" Her brows furrowed, confusion and something else - was it hope? - flashing across her face. "Whatever she decides, so it will be. *Sì, caio*" I ended the call, not waiting for her questions.

"Marco thinks it would be good for our image to host an engagement party and announce wedding details." I kept my voice even, my expression neutral. Her eyes widened, surprise and something else - was it excitement? - flashing in their depths.

"Lorenzo, this isn't a real engagement, getting married is not the end goal." Her words were automatic, but her tone was uncertain, like after just one night, she wasn't sure what the end goal was anymore. If the lines were blurring this easily, there was no telling how this engagement would end. Or if it would end at all.

******

### Sierra

I agreed to the engagement party—the kind that didn't just announce a future, but erased all doubt about it. No whispers, no speculation. An official declaration. In a month, at the historic Villa De Luca, candlelight and stone and legacy pressing in from every side. An evening designed to tell the world I belonged to Lorenzo Moretti.

He wanted me to plan it. That should have warned me.

"I can handle *all* of the details?" I asked, already imagining it—the guest list curated like a chessboard, every detail intentional.

Lorenzo studied me for a beat, the corner of his mouth lifting as if he'd anticipated the request. "Naturally," he said. "You're good at shaping impressions." Then, smoothly, "There's just one condition."

I tilted my head. "Of course there is."

"Security."

The word landed heavy, unmistakable. I exhaled through my nose. "Lorenzo—"

"You don't see the edges of my world yet," he cut in calmly. "But they're sharp." His gaze never wavered. "This isn't optional."

I weighed the argument, then discarded it. "Fine. Discreet. I don't want armed men ruining the illusion."

His smile deepened. "They won't be visible."

That should have unsettled me more than it did.

He reached into his jacket and placed his black Amex in my palm. The card was cool, weighty—an unmistakable symbol of access. Of permission.

"Whatever you need," he said quietly.

A thrill curled low in my stomach before I could stop it. As if that weren't enough, he disappeared into his office and returned with a slim laptop and a new phone, setting them in front of me like offerings.

"Your old phone was still linked to your parents' company," he said. "That's been handled. New number.

I've already transferred the contacts you actually need." I stared at the devices. I should have been furious. He hadn't asked. He hadn't even warned me.

Instead, warmth crept in, unwanted and unmistakable.

The contract was a cage, yes. But it was lined with silk. And Lorenzo didn't just protect what was his—he fortified it, wrapped it so completely you forgot what it felt like to stand unguarded.

"Plan everything," he said, his voice dropping, gaze locking onto mine. "Guest list. Menu. Music." I nodded, already slipping into the role.

"But," he added, stepping closer, close enough that I could feel the heat of him, "I'll choose your dress."

I opened my mouth to argue.

Then I saw the look in his eyes—not indulgent, not teasing. Possessive. Intent. This wasn't about fabric or fashion. It was about how the world would see me when I stood beside him. Marked. Claimed.

The words died on my tongue. In that moment, it became painfully clear: this engagement wasn't just a contract. It was choreography. A careful, dangerous dance of control and surrender.

And I wasn't just following his lead. I wanted to.

"Fine, but….not white." Giving him a condition made me feel like I was still in control. His smirk told me already had something in mind. "And I'm calling Jenna, she's going to come help me."

"I'll send Alexio to pick her up." He nodded, not even the tiniest bit surprised. "Will you be alright here while I'm gone?"

"Are you asking if I'll be here when you get back?" I teased, enjoying the glare I got in return. He crossed the room stopping just in front of me.

"I know you'll be here, *amore*." He held my chin in his hand, gently running his thumb down my cheek, tilting my face up to him. I couldn't help the way my breath stuttered. Real or not, I wanted to lean forward and sink into his lips.

Instead I leaned back against the island, crossing my arms over my chest and whispered, *"Stalker."*

His laugh was deep, dark. "You have no idea." I picked up my new phone, already responding to my biometrics and dialed Jenna as he disappeared towards the garage elevator.

******

Jenna walked into the penthouse and immediately stopped short.

She didn't scream.  She didn't swear. She just stared.

"...No," she said finally. "Absolutely not."

I shut the door behind her. "You said that last night too."

"That was *theoretical panic*," she snapped, gesturing wildly. "This is *architectural proof*."

She stepped farther inside, heels clicking sharply against the marble, her eyes jumping from the glass walls to the skyline stretched beneath them like it belonged to someone else.

"This is a lair," she decided. "Not a home. Villains live in places like this."

"It's a penthouse."

"It's a threat."

I leaned against the counter, watching her take it in—the clean lines, the restraint, the deliberate lack of warmth. Lorenzo's design choices were all control and precision. Nothing here was decorative unless it served a purpose.

Jenna frowned suddenly. "Wait." She crossed the room, pointing. "That candle is yours."

"Yes."

"And that throw blanket?" She touched it like it might bite. "That wasn't here before."

"I added it."

She turned slowly. "You *moved in*."

"I made it livable."

"You colonized it," she whispered. "Oh my God, you colonized the mob penthouse." I snorted before I could stop myself. Her eyes snapped to the bookshelf. "These are your books."

"They look better."

She spun on me. "You're nesting."

"Do *not* say that."

She dropped onto the couch with a dramatic huff. "I knew you were engaged. I knew that part." She waved a hand. "I was there. I heard the words. I processed them. This—" she gestured at everything "—is *different*."

"It's just where we live."

She laughed, sharp and disbelieving. "You said that like it's normal."

I didn't answer.

Her gaze sharpened. "Okay. Walk me through it again. Slowly. Because I still don't understand how a brunch confession turned into *this*."

I exhaled. "I told my mother we were exclusive."

"You lied."

"I improvised."

"And then Lorenzo *somehow* got your number." She made exaggerated air quotes.

"Yes."

"And invited *you* to brunch."

"Yes."

"And instead of being weirded out—"

"I told him the truth," I said. "What I'd said. Why I'd said it."

"And he didn't blink," Jenna muttered.

"He said if I'd already claimed exclusivity, then we should honor it."

Jenna stared at the ceiling. "That man does not do half-measures."

"No," I agreed. "He commits."

Her gaze dropped back to me. "And you're okay." It wasn't a question.

I thought about the driver who already knew her name. The new phone. The way this place no longer felt cold when I came home.

"I didn't plan it," I said. "But I'm not fighting it."

She was quiet for a moment. Then— "Okay," she said, pushing to her feet. "Rules."

"Rules?"

"If he turns out to be controlling in a scary way, we stage an intervention."

I raised a brow. "And if he's controlling in a... different way?"

She smirked. "Then I mind my business."

By the time we'd taken over the living room, Jenna had stopped spiraling and started organizing. The coffee table was buried beneath guest lists and timelines, half-scrawled notes layered over embossed stationery. Fabric swatches lay fanned across the marble like evidence—silk, velvet, chiffon—each one arguing for a different mood.

"This is not an engagement party," Jenna declared, crouched on the floor with a pen between her teeth. "It's a political summit."

"It needs to feel intentional," I said, sliding a seating chart toward her. "Nothing accidental."

She nodded, then held up a swatch of pale blush. "Okay, but hear me out."

I already shook my head. "No pink."

"*Sierra*," she pleaded. "Just a little. Soft. Romantic. You're getting engaged, not crowned."

I picked up two darker swatches instead—black velvet and a deep, wine-red silk that looked almost brown in low light. "Black and deep red."

She groaned. "You're allergic to joy."

"They're the Moretti colors," I said. "It makes sense. The villa, the family. It's legacy. Plus, you know I like black" I winked at her.

She paused, eyes flicking between the fabrics, recalibrating. "Fine," she said reluctantly. "Dark. Broody. Mafia chic."

"Thank you."

"But," she added quickly, reaching for a stack of floral mockups, "we add soft pink florals."

I blinked. "Jenna."

"Listen," she said, already flipping through images. "Not bubblegum. Not baby shower. Dusty rose. Blush. Same color family—warm undertones. It'll pop against the black and red without undermining the vibe."

I stared at the palette she'd laid out—dark linens, candlelight, then soft pink blooms cutting through it like something alive. "…You're annoying," I said slowly.

She beamed. "I'm right."

I laughed, actually laughed, the sound surprising both of us. "Fine. Pink florals. Minimal. Strategic."

She pumped a fist. "I saved romance."

The kitchen behind us smelled like garlic and sesame oil. Alexio had dropped off takeout earlier without asking—white containers stacked neatly on the island. Our favorites. Extra dumplings. Extra chili oil.

Jenna glanced over her shoulder. "How is this our new normal?" But she grinned, thoroughly enjoying it.

She shook her head, but there was a smile there now. "Okay. Color palette settled. Next: guest list triage." She sprawled onto her stomach, crossing out names with ruthless efficiency. I rearranged seating like it was a battlefield, grouping families by threat level rather than blood relation.

"You're good at this," she said after a moment.

"I've had practice managing people who think they own me."

She snorted. "Fair." She leaned back, surveying the room—papers everywhere, fabrics layered, chopsticks abandoned beside notebooks.

"You know," she said quietly, "this doesn't feel like you disappearing into his world."

I looked around the penthouse—no longer cold, no longer untouched. Marked by my handwriting. My choices.

"It's not," I said. "It's a merger."

She smirked. "Hostile or friendly?"

I picked up the deep red swatch, running it between my fingers. "That depends on who's watching."

She grinned. "God, I love you."

And for the first time since all of this had begun, planning didn't feel like surrender. It felt like control only… dressed better.

******

I didn't hear Lorenzo come in. Not at first.

Jenna and I were sprawled across the living room like we'd been there for days—papers everywhere, fabric swatches taped together, guest lists overlapping timelines. The coffee table was completely lost beneath it all.

"I'm telling you," Jenna said, waving a pen like a weapon, "if your mother sits anywhere near the Ashford's, someone will bleed."

"Figuratively," I said.

"Emotionally," she clarified. "Which is worse."

I snorted, reaching for a dumpling. "Okay, what if we stagger them? Buffer zones. Neutral parties in between."

"Like Switzerland," she said approvingly.

"And if Switzerland fails—"

"We drink," she finished.

Somewhere behind us, a door opened. Softly.

I felt it more than heard it—the subtle shift in the air, the awareness crawling up my spine. Jenna was mid-sentence, holding up a strip of deep red silk beside a mockup of black linens.

"—and I still think the pink florals are a *win*," she said. "They soften it without making it a bridal nightmare."

"They're a concession," I said. "A strategic one."

"That's all I'm asking—"

A quiet breath sounded from the hallway. Jenna froze. I turned.

Lorenzo stood just inside the penthouse, one hand resting loosely at his side like he'd paused there deliberately. He hadn't announced himself. Hadn't moved farther in. As if he were afraid that one wrong step would scatter us.

His gaze moved slowly—not sharp, not assessing the way it usually was—but curious.

The papers.
The swatches.

The takeout containers abandoned on the kitchen island.

Then his eyes lifted to me. For a moment, he didn't say anything.

Jenna recovered first. "Hi," she said, far too brightly. "Please don't murder me. I'm the emotional support human."

Lorenzo's mouth twitched.

"I wouldn't dream of it," he said calmly. "You seem… busy."

"We're planning," Jenna said. "Aggressively."

I pushed myself to my feet. "I wasn't sure when you'd be back."

"I heard voices," he said. "I didn't want to interrupt." That landed somewhere warm in my chest.

He stepped farther in now, careful where he placed his feet, navigating the chaos like it was something fragile rather than inconvenient. He stopped beside the coffee table, looking down at the layout.

"Black and red," he observed.

"The Moretti colors," I said.

His gaze flicked to me. Approval, quiet and unmistakable. "And the pink?" he asked, nodding toward the floral mockups.

Jenna held up her hands. "Accent florals. Same color family. It's a compromise."

Lorenzo considered this, then nodded once. "Balance," he said. "Good."

Jenna blinked. "That's it? No objections? No ominous warning?"

He glanced at her. "If I objected, you'd argue."

"Correct."

"And you'd win," he added mildly.

She beamed. "I like him."

He looked back at me, something unreadable passing through his eyes as he took in the scene again—not just the planning, but the way the penthouse felt different. Lived in. Loud.

"You've made yourself at home," he said softly.

I lifted my chin. "Is that a problem?"

"No," he said, stepping closer. "It's… impressive."

Jenna stood, stretching. "Okay, I'm going to pretend I'm not intruding on *something*. I'll be in the kitchen stealing dumplings." She vanished quickly.

Lorenzo's attention returned to me. "I didn't want to disturb you," he said again. "You looked… settled."

I smiled, unable to help it. "You snuck in, stalker."

"I didn't want to spook you."

The word shouldn't have felt intimate. But it did. And standing there, surrounded by plans and color palettes and the quiet proof that my life was no longer untouched by his, I realized something unsettling and true—

He wasn't afraid of losing control. He was afraid of breaking the moment.

"Anyway," Jenna said lightly, flipping a page on the guest list, "we're almost done. If you have any input?" Her eyes lingered on me instead of him. The question wasn't really for Lorenzo—it was a test. A probe.

He nodded once, but didn't answer her right away.

Jenna slid back onto the floor, propping her elbows on the coffee table like she was settling in for a long interrogation. Lorenzo sat on the edge of the couch, careful not to disturb the scattered papers. When he held out his hand, I took it without thinking, stepping over a fan of color swatches.

Jenna noticed.

I could tell by the way her mouth tightened—not disapproval, exactly. Surprise. Maybe concern? It felt natural, this small choreography between us, like we'd been doing it longer than we had.

We walked him through everything. The guest list. The colors. The seating strategy that read more like a ceasefire agreement than a celebration. Lorenzo listened, polite, attentive—but I caught it, the moment his focus drifted, eyes going distant as we debated floral heights.

Still, he waited until we were finished.

"You've done well," he said finally. "It's thoughtful. Controlled." His gaze flicked to me. "Intimate." The word landed heavier than it should have.

Jenna smiled, quick and sharp. I felt the tension coil anyway. Lorenzo wasn't pretending—he was pleased. Genuinely.

She tilted her head then, smile gone. "So," she said, voice casual but eyes hard, "are you going to let me have my best friend back tonight? Or are you planning to keep her locked up here like some kind of extremely well-dressed stalker?"

The room went still.

Even Lorenzo looked momentarily surprised—
just enough for a quiet breath of laughter to escape him
before his expression reset.

"Sierra goes where she wishes," he said, leaning
forward, forearms braced on his knees. His voice never
rose, but it sharpened. "She is not being kept here."

My heart stuttered.

"I understand this appears *sudden*," he continued,
gaze locked on Jenna now, unflinching. "But I care for
her safety more than my own." A pause. Intentional.
"And I would die before I harmed her."

There was no bravado in it. No performance. Just
truth, stated like a fact.

Jenna didn't look away. She studied him,
searching for cracks, for exaggeration, for the lie men like
him were supposed to tell.

Then she asked, quietly, "Do you love her?" The
air vanished from the room.

Lorenzo didn't answer immediately.

His thumb brushed once over the inside of my
wrist—grounding, possessive, barely there. When he
finally spoke, his voice was low, controlled.

"Love," he said, "is not a word I use lightly."

Jenna waited.

"So no?" she pressed.

His gaze shifted to me then. Not asking permission. Not seeking approval. Simply acknowledging the truth of my presence.

"I won't say a word until I can stand behind it," he said. "But nothing about this is casual." Silence stretched.

Jenna exhaled slowly, then stood. "Okay," she said. "That's… not reassuring. But it is honest." She looked at me. Really looked.

"Are you good?" I knew what she was really asking. Her family may not be Moretti-rich, but she would absolutely use every favor and resource available to get me out of here if I asked.

I gently pulled from Lorenzo's grip, leaning into her. "I am."

Jenna nodded, decision made. "Then I'll finish the guest list tomorrow." She wrapped me in a quick hug before grabbing her coat. "Text me when you're leaving! Or if you need an extraction." She sent a pointed look at Lorenzo.

Lorenzo's mouth curved faintly. "I assure you—"

"I wasn't talking to you," she said sweetly. The door closed behind her.

The penthouse felt quieter for it.

Lorenzo turned to me, expression unreadable. "Was that… acceptable?"

I swallowed.

"It was terrifying," I said honestly.

His eyes darkened. "Good." Somehow, that single word sent my pulse skittering. "So," he said, leaning back, suddenly infuriatingly casual, "where are you going tonight?"

"It's just our monthly girls' night," I said, stacking the guest list notes neatly, trying to pretend my heartbeat wasn't doing something strange. "Tonight it's one of those paint-and-sip things."

He blinked. Actually blinked.

For a moment he looked genuinely lost, and it struck me then—in everything Jenna and I had managed to dig up about him and his family, Lorenzo hadn't had a girlfriend in nearly two years. The few photos we'd found online were clearly old, probably survivors of a social media purge. Given his general disposition, I doubted he had much working knowledge of the things women did for fun.

"You know," I said, amused despite myself, "you go to a little studio and drink wine while you try to paint something."

His head tilted slightly. "You paint."

"I attempt to," I corrected, laughing when his confusion didn't clear. "The wine helps."

"Interesting."

I rolled my eyes. "Then we'll probably go back to Jenna's and hang out. It's a monthly thing. Sometimes it's a movie, sometimes a new restaurant. Depends on what everyone feels like."

He studied me for a moment, expression unreadable.
"You do this often."

"Yes," I said slowly. "Do you not… hang out with your friends?"

A low chuckle escaped him, dark and surprisingly warm. "Not like that."

"You need to live a little and relax, babe—"

The word slipped out before I could stop it.

His brows shot up.
Mine did too.

"I'm going to change," I blurted, already turning away. "I'll be quick." What the *fuck*, Sierra? I barely made it down the hall before my face felt warm.

When I came back out a few minutes later, dressed and ready, he was still on the couch, sleeves rolled, checking his phone, watching me with quiet focus.

"I'll drive you."

"No," I said immediately. "You absolutely will not."

A pause. Then, calm but immovable, "Then Alexio will."

"I can take—"

"Sierra." Not sharp. Just final.

I sighed. "Fine. Alexio."

"Text me when you arrive," he added. "And when you're leaving." It wasn't a request.

I headed for the door, then stopped. I don't know why. He was still sitting there, relaxed, familiar, like this was already routine.

Before I could overthink it, I crossed back to him. He looked up, surprised.

I leaned in and pressed a quick kiss to his cheek, soft, impulsive, barely there.

His skin was warm. His breath caught.

"See you later," I said, too fast.

His hand lifted like he might stop me, but he didn't. Just nodded once.

"Have fun."

The elevator ride down was quiet. Too quiet. By the time I slid into the backseat, my heart was racing like I'd done something reckless instead of ridiculous.

Why did I do that?

I stared out the window as Alexio pulled away from the curb, my reflection faint in the glass—silver jewelry catching the light, ring unmistakable on my hand.

It was just a kiss. On the cheek. Nothing major.

So why did it feel like I'd crossed a line I hadn't known was there?

And worse—why did I already want to do it again?

# Chapter 8

***Lorenzo***

Planning the engagement party, overseeing the acquisition of the California vineyard, keeping one ear trained for any whisper of Matteo—somehow, the month vanished.

Not quietly. Not gently. It burned.

Days collapsed into meetings and phone calls, into flights taken without noticing the takeoff, into decisions made on instinct because there was no time to deliberate. Contracts were signed. Staff reshuffled. Security expanded in ways Sierra would never see and never thank me for.

She shouldn't have to.

The party loomed now, close enough that I could feel it in my chest. Twenty-four hours, give or take. The final confirmations were already done. The guest list locked. The villa prepared to open its gates and announce to the world what had already become inevitable.

My fiancée.

Sierra had moved through the past few weeks with a careful steadiness, as if she were learning the weight of this new life by carrying it in measured steps. I watched her more than she realized—not because I distrusted her, but because I didn't trust the silence around us.

Matteo had gone quiet. Too quiet.

No rumors. No sightings. No reckless moves that would have announced his presence. That kind of restraint didn't come from fear—it came from planning. And I knew him well enough to recognize the shape of an ambush even when it hadn't yet revealed itself.

Marco thought I was overextended. The vineyard was legitimate work, the kind that demanded focus and precision. But even as Dario handled the details, my attention kept splitting—between contracts in California and the silence Matteo had left behind.

In truth, I was counting variables. Distance. Exposure. Timing. Sierra was the only constant I couldn't reduce to strategy.

At night, when the penthouse was quiet and she was asleep down the hall—or curled against me, warm and unaware—I allowed myself exactly one indulgence: the thought that after tomorrow, she would be untouchable.

Public. Claimed. Protected in ways even Matteo would hesitate to test.

I told myself that was enough.

But experience had taught me a brutal lesson long ago— the moments just before everything breaks are always the calmest.

And as the city glittered below us and the final hours slipped away, I couldn't shake the certainty that Matteo was still watching.

Waiting. Just like I was.

Sierra's voice drifted down the hall as she finished getting ready, bright and familiar. Of course she was on video with Jenna—those two were nearly inseparable.

I turned back to the window, studying my reflection in the darkened glass. The suit fit the way it always did—precise, unforgiving. Black jacket smooth across my shoulders, shirt crisp beneath it, collar open just enough to remind anyone watching that this was not a ceremony yet. Candlelight from the penthouse reflected faintly off the glass, catching the edge of my cuff, the watch at my wrist.

Appearances mattered tonight, but not in the way people assumed. This wasn't about looking impressive. It was about looking inevitable. The villa would be full. Eyes everywhere. Questions I would answer without speaking.

I checked my reflection once more—not for vanity, but for control. Calm face. Steady hands. No trace of the anticipation tightening in my chest.

I heard her before I saw her—the soft click of heels, the faint rustle of fabric. I turned as she stepped into the room, and for a moment, the city outside the windows ceased to exist.

The dress clung to her like it had been poured there. Champagne silk, warm and luminous, catching the light with every step she took. It wasn't white, not innocent or fragile—it was richer than that. Intentional. The kind of color that glowed against her skin and demanded attention without asking for it.

The cut was precise. Clean lines that skimmed her waist, a slit that revealed just enough of her leg to make the thought of her movement unbearable. The back dipped lower than propriety suggested, smooth and exposed, a quiet provocation I felt in my chest.

*Merda.*

I wanted her. Right there. Against the glass, against me, before anyone else could look at her, before the world had a chance to decide what she meant.

I didn't move.

That restraint cost me more than any tailored suit or calculated silence ever had. This wasn't the moment for hunger. This was the moment for control.

She was meant to be seen tonight. To stand beside me, unmistakable and radiant, proof of something irreversible. But as her eyes lifted to meet mine, soft and searching, I knew one thing with brutal clarity—

If I let myself touch her now, I wouldn't stop and the city below would learn just how little restraint I truly had.

"You did this on purpose," she said quietly, smoothing the silk at her hip, her voice light but her eyes anything but.

"I chose a dress," I replied, stepping closer. "You're the one wearing it."

Her lips curved, slow and knowing. "You look like you're reconsidering letting me leave the penthouse."

I met her gaze, lowered my voice. "I'm reconsidering letting anyone else see you."

Her breath caught, just for a moment. She brushed past me, close enough that the silk whispered against my jacket, and murmured, "Let's go, *stalker*."

"As you wish." I followed her—silent, attentive, exactly as she thought I was.

******

*Sierra*

The grounds of Villa De Luca were breathtaking. Blooming landscapes framed the old stone mansion in a way that felt almost unreal, like something lifted from a painting. Jenna had been right—this place was stunning.

Lorenzo opened my door and, without hesitation, pulled me up against him. The gesture was effortless, practiced, like he'd done it a hundred times before. A glittering crowd of guests was already making their way inside, voices low and expectant.

"Are you ready, *amore*?" he murmured.

His arm slid around my waist, his lips brushing my cheek just long enough to be felt. Despite the warmth of the late-summer evening, a shiver ran through me. I could feel his smirk without seeing it. These moments—quiet, charged, intimate—would be my undoing.

I nodded. It was all I trusted myself to do.

Cameras began flashing as we neared the entrance. I knew this was the point of tonight—to solidify us, to leave no room for speculation—but I still wasn't prepared for the attention. Marco had warned me. The second eldest Moretti brother, heir to one of the largest wine conglomerates in the world, announcing an engagement was always going to be news.

Add me to the equation—the eldest daughter of Blackwell Enterprises' CEO, freshly reappeared after the abrupt collapse of a very public engagement—and suddenly the story sharpened.

Lorenzo's hand settled at the small of my back, steady and warm, grounding me as we moved past journalists calling out questions I pretended not to hear.

Inside, the villa was just as stunning. Marble floors gleamed beneath our feet, architectural columns rising into shadow, a grand sweeping staircase softened by low candlelight. It was the vision I'd carried in my head for weeks, finally made real.

The floral arrangements Jenna and I had designed were perfect—lush without overwhelming, soft pinks layered against deeper wine tones. The Moretti colors threaded through the space effortlessly, creating an atmosphere that felt old-world and elegant… with just enough danger humming beneath it.

Love and power. Beauty and warning.

Lorenzo lifted his glass with an easy confidence that quieted the room without effort. He didn't tap it, didn't ask for attention. He simply waited, and somehow, everyone listened.

"Thank you for being here tonight," he said, his voice smooth, measured. "Villa De Luca has seen its share of celebrations, but tonight is a personal one for me." His hand found mine, his thumb brushing once across my knuckles—subtle, possessive. I felt it everywhere.

"I don't believe in grand speeches," he continued, a faint smile touching his mouth. "What matters is intention. And mine is very clear."

A few polite chuckles rippled through the crowd.

"Sierra has brought something rare into my life," he said, turning slightly toward me now. His gaze held mine, dark and unreadable. "Stability. Perspective. Purpose."

My chest tightened. None of that felt accidental.

"We're grateful you're here to celebrate with us," he finished, lifting his glass once more. "Enjoy the evening."

It was brief. Impeccably delivered.

The room erupted into applause, but I was too focused on the way his fingers curled more firmly around mine—like he'd said everything he needed to, and nothing at all. And for the first time that night, I felt a ripple of unease beneath the champagne glow.

Lorenzo and I moved through the room together, a practiced rhythm forming between us as we greeted guests, accepted congratulations, posed for photos. His hand never left me—steady at my back, guiding without pressure, while I smiled and nodded, playing my part with a grace I hadn't known I possessed.

Jenna found me almost immediately, glass of champagne already in hand, eyes bright as she swept me from head to toe.

"Oh my God," she breathed, grabbing my arm and leaning in close. "Okay, first of all, this dress? Criminal. Second of all—this place? Are you kidding me?"

I laughed, the tension in my chest easing just a fraction. "You helped design half of it. You can't act surprised."

She waved that off. "I knew it would be pretty. I didn't know it would be *this*. You look…" She trailed off, studying me, then smiled softer. "You look really good, Si. Like… steady." The word landed heavier than she probably intended.

"I am," I said, hoping it sounded true.

Her eyes flicked past me, toward where Lorenzo stood across the room, already deep in conversation, commanding attention without trying. "He's intense," she said quietly. "But if he ever forgets you're my best friend, I will end him."

I snorted. "Duly noted."

She squeezed my hand once before drifting off toward the bar, leaving behind the familiar comfort of someone who knew me before all of this.

I was refilling my wine when Marco approached.

He looked exactly like Lorenzo, same sharp lines, same dark eyes, but where Lorenzo was cold precision, Marco carried warmth. Or at least, the impression of it.

"Sierra," he said easily, offering a smile that felt practiced but not unkind. "I wanted to say—you've done something extraordinary here."

"Oh." I blinked. "Thank you. Jenna and I—"

He shook his head. "Still. You've honored the house beautifully. My parents would have loved this." Something in my chest shifted at the way he said it. Not polite. Not performative. Genuine.

"You'll have to come to the vineyard soon," he continued, as if it were already decided. "Italy, of course—but California as well. It'll be good for you to see everything you're becoming part of."

Part of. I forced a smile, my grip tightening slightly around my glass. "That's… kind of you."

Marco studied me for a moment, his expression thoughtful. "My brother isn't always an easy man. If you ever need anything," he said quietly, "you're family now."

Family.

As he moved away, a strange unease settled over me. It was easy to pretend Lorenzo was playing a role tonight. That this was all presentation, optics, illusion.

But Marco hadn't been acting. And that unsettled me far more than any champagne-fueled fantasy ever could. I watched as he moved through the ballroom to his brother and was surprised by what almost looked like a genuine smile on Lorenzo's face.

My parents found me near the edge of the room, smiles already fixed in place as if they'd been practicing them all evening. I groaned inwardly, I'd been dreading this more than the press coverage.

"Sierra," my mother said warmly, pulling me into a careful embrace that barely wrinkled my dress. "Darling, you look beautiful." As if our last interaction hadn't been laced with threats.

My father nodded his approval, eyes flicking briefly over my shoulder before returning to my face. "Very elegant. This place suits you." Relief loosened something in my chest. Maybe—just maybe—tonight wouldn't turn into a battlefield.

"Thank you," I said, meaning it. "I'm glad you came." I exhaled, the tension easing for just a moment.

"Of course we did," my mother replied, patting my arm. "We wouldn't miss something like this. An engagement party at a historic villa? It's all very… dramatic." She laughed lightly, as if it were a compliment.

My father lifted his glass. "You've always had a flair for spectacle." The word lingered too long between us. Dread pooled like a dark pit in my stomach.

My mother leaned in closer, lowering her voice with feigned concern. "We just worry about you, sweetheart. Things have moved so fast. Engagements should be… considered."

"I have considered it," I said evenly.

She smiled again, brighter this time. "Of course you have. It's just—well—you are already engaged. To Matteo."

There it was. My pulse thudded in my ears. "I am not—"

"I worked hard to secure that deal for our family," my father interrupted, his tone still pleasant, still reasonable. "Your responsibilities. This," he gestured vaguely around us, "is a detour."

"A mistake," my mother added through her teeth, squeezing my arm a little too tightly. "One you can still correct."

The room seemed to tilt. "I'm not correcting anything," I said, my voice low.

My mother's smile sharpened. "Sierra, don't be stubborn. This *arrangement*—whatever it is—it's not sustainable. Matteo will take you back. He's already asked."

My stomach dropped. "You don't get to decide that," I said.

My father's expression cooled, the warmth draining from his eyes. "We're only trying to protect the family. You've always needed guidance."

Something dangerous sparked in my chest—anger, humiliation, the old familiar weight of being managed. Before I could respond, a presence shifted beside me. Solid. Unyielding.

And suddenly, my parents' smiles faltered.

******

### *Lorenzo*

I noticed the shift before Sierra did.

Her smile faltered—not much, just enough. Her parents stood too close, voices low, faces arranged into something sweet and suffocating. I recognized it instantly. Concern weaponized. Authority disguised as love.

It only took a few strides to reach them. I slid my arm around her waist, my hand fitting there like it had always belonged. Her body softened against mine, the tension in her spine easing just enough for me to feel it.

Then I smiled.

"Mr. and Mrs. Blackwell," I said pleasantly. "I'm glad you could attend." Her mother's eyes flicked to my hand. I watched her notice. I wanted her to.

"We were just speaking with Sierra," she said lightly.

"I know," I replied. "That's why I joined you."

Her father gave a tight smile. "We're concerned parents."

"Of course you are." I inclined my head. "But concern should never sound like instruction." The space between us cooled, the polite hum of the party dimming at the edges.

"Sierra has already chosen," I continued, my thumb brushing once at her waist—subtle, deliberate. "There is nothing left to debate."

Her mother let out a small, practiced laugh. "You make it sound so final."

"It is," I said softly.

Her father's jaw tightened. "You're very confident."

I met his gaze fully now, smile unbroken. "I'm very prepared." The implication settled between us, heavy and inescapable.

"She will be my wife," I went on, my tone calm, conversational. "Which means any attempt to steer her elsewhere—toward old arrangements, old *mistakes*—will be interpreted as interference."

I felt Sierra's breath hitch against me. I didn't look at her. This wasn't for reassurance. It was for warning. "If Matteo has contacted you," I added mildly, "I would advise you to sever that connection immediately."

Her father opened his mouth. I leaned in just enough that only he could hear me. "I am not patient with people who mistake proximity for authority."

Then I straightened, smile returning to something perfectly social. "Enjoy the evening," I said.

They stepped back. Not offended. Corrected.

Sierra exhaled, her body pressing more firmly into mine now. My grip tightened reflexively, protective and possessive all at once.

I lowered my mouth to her ear. "You don't belong to them," I murmured. "Not anymore." I offered my arm, already turning us away.

The music was slow. Too slow. A low, velvet rhythm that pressed itself into the space between bodies and dared them to pretend it meant nothing.

"Dance with me?" I didn't wait for an answer as I drew her into me without ceremony.

There was no polite distance, no room for interpretation. Her front fit to mine like it had been waiting there, her breath stuttering when my hand slid from her waist to the small of her back, fingers spreading, anchoring her. I felt every inch of her through silk and heat and intention.

"You're not supposed to lead me in public, remember?" her voice was low, as she looked up at me through her long lashes. Was she flirting with me?

Her hand came up to my shoulder, then slid higher, fingers curling at the back of my neck like she'd forgotten where we were. Like she didn't care. Her thigh brushed mine with each sway, slow and deliberate, the slit in her dress doing nothing to hide the fact that she knew exactly what she was doing to me.

I lowered my head, my mouth close to her ear, not touching. Not yet. "They're watching," I murmured.

Her lips curved faintly. "Let them." That almost broke me.

My grip tightened. Possessive. Unapologetic. I guided her hips into the rhythm, subtle enough to pass as dancing, intimate enough that anyone close would have looked away out of instinct. She melted into it, her body responding like this was familiar, like it belonged here.

I felt it everywhere.

Her pulse. Her warmth. The quiet challenge in the way she moved against me, slow and unhurried, as if she knew exactly how thin my restraint had become.

"You're provoking me," I said softly.

Her breath ghosted my jaw. "You like it."

I did. God, I did.

I dipped my head, my lips brushing the shell of her ear—still nothing that could be called a kiss, nothing anyone could accuse. My hand slid just a fraction lower, firm enough to promise, restrained enough to deny.

"Careful," I warned. "I'm already past polite."

She tilted her head back slightly, exposing her throat to me in a way that felt reckless and deliberate all at once. "Then don't be polite," she whispered.

The room ceased to exist.

For a moment—one dangerous, razor-thin moment—I considered it. Considered taking her somewhere dark and quiet and proving to her exactly how much power she was playing with.

Instead, I exhaled slowly and pulled her closer, my mouth at her temple now, my voice low and lethal. "Later," I said. Not a promise. A certainty.

Her fingers tightened at my neck.

I ended the dance before either of us lost what little control we had left.

The rest of the evening unfolded the way these things always did—measured, elegant, inevitable. I spoke with Marco near the terrace doors, our voices low beneath the hum of conversation. He commented on the turnout, the optics, how smoothly everything had gone. He congratulated me again, quieter this time, his eyes flicking briefly to Sierra across the room.

"We'll talk tomorrow," he said, meaning Sicily without saying it. Business, family, obligations that never truly slept.

I nodded once. "Tomorrow."

He left me then, melting back into the crowd, and my attention returned to where it had been all evening. I found myself watching Sierra across the room as the music shifted and Jenna pulled her back onto the floor with the rest of their friends.

She laughed easily now, champagne-bright and unburdened, moving without thinking about who was watching.

Except she did think about it.

Every so often, her eyes lifted—searching, instinctive—and found mine across the crowd. Just a glance. A silent check-in. I didn't smile. I didn't wave. I only held her gaze until she looked away again, satisfied.

She was having fun. And she knew exactly where I was. That was enough.

The party wound down gradually, candles burning low, conversations softening as guests said their goodbyes. When Sierra finally returned to my side, she leaned into me without hesitation, her head resting briefly against my shoulder.

"Enzo, I'm ready to go home," her voice was soft, breath sweet with wine..

*Home*.

The word landed heavier than she realized. "Yes," I said, sliding my arm around her as we made our own goodbyes.

In the car, she leaned into me, tired now in the pleasant way that follows too much stimulation and too many eyes. Her head found my shoulder without asking. I didn't move. I never would have.

When we stepped back into the penthouse, the quiet wrapped around us immediately—familiar, grounding. She kicked off her heels near the door with a sigh and glanced around like she was orienting herself.

"I'm exhausted," she said. "It feels good to be home." Again. I noticed. I would always notice.

I followed her into the bedroom, unhurried. She turned to me then, close enough that her warmth seeped through the space between us. I cupped her face and kissed her—deep, steady, unclaimed by hunger. A kiss meant to settle, not take.

She melted into it, hands resting against my chest, trusting.

She stood still while I reached for the zipper at the back of her dress, my fingers careful, reverent. The silk slid away slowly, no rush, no urgency. Just the sound of fabric and breath and the quiet understanding that we had nowhere else to be.

We finished changing without speaking, sliding into bed with the ease of people who didn't need to prove anything. She curled against me, head tucked beneath my chin, already half-asleep.

I stayed awake a little longer, listening to her breathe, the echoes of the night settling into something heavier than celebration.

Tomorrow, the world would begin to press in again.

But tonight, she was here.

And that was enough.

# Chapter 9



**Sierra**

I woke to the sound of Lorenzo moving through the kitchen. Not quietly. Just… confidently. Like he had nowhere to be but everywhere to go.

I padded out barefoot, still wrapped in one of his shirts, hair a mess, and found him already dressed—dark slacks, crisp shirt, sleeves rolled. Coffee steamed between us like a peace offering.

"Morning," he said, eyes tracking me in that way that made me feel seen even when I hadn't said a word yet.

"Morning," I echoed, leaning against the counter.

We ate together in the easy quiet that had become familiar faster than I wanted to admit. He read something on his phone, occasionally glancing up to make sure I was still there. Like I might vanish if he didn't.

When it was time for him to leave, he stopped in front of me, adjusting his watch. I reached for his sleeve without thinking.

"Be careful," I said.

His mouth curved faintly. "Always." He kissed me then—soft, unhurried, deliberate. Not hungry. Not claiming. Just enough intent to remind me that last night hadn't been a dream.

"I'll see you tonight," he said.

I watched him go, feeling something settle behind my ribs. I thought back to my conversation with Marco last night. Like the both had forgotten about the contract for this engagement. Like there wasn't an expiration date for this little facade…there was, wasn't there?

***

That afternoon was work. Last Call. Loud, sticky floors, familiar faces. Normal in a way that felt almost defiant. I made drinks, laughed with coworkers, ignored the way my phone felt heavier in my pocket.

The next day blurred easily into the one after— sleeping in his bed, eating at his table, coming home to him like it was routine. Like this was just my life now.

It was starting to feel… claustrophobic.

Too quiet. Too watched. Too carefully contained. I needed to push something. Test a boundary. Prove to myself I still could.

Then Jenna texted.

**JENNA:** club tonight. no excuses.
**JENNA:** wear something that scares men!!!!

I smiled at my phone before I could stop myself. This was exactly what I needed.

"I'm going out tonight," I told Lorenzo over dinner, keeping my tone light, casual—like I wasn't already bracing for impact.

He didn't look up right away. That pause said everything.

"Where."

"A club. Jenna's idea."

He finally met my eyes. "No."

I laughed. "That wasn't a question."

His jaw tightened almost imperceptibly. "I don't like it."

"I know."

The phone rang then—something work-related, judging by the way his attention snapped away. He stood, already pulling on his jacket. "You shouldn't go," he said, voice low, dangerous in that quiet way. "If you do, I won't enjoy what happens next."

My pulse kicked. I waited until the door closed behind him before I went to change.

I dressed slowly. Deliberately. Something short. Something black. Something that made me feel sharp and untouchable. I caught my reflection and didn't look away. Before I left, I turned off my location.

I needed to remind us of the rules.

The club was all heat, noise, and bodies packed too close. Jenna screamed when she saw me, dragging me onto the dance floor before I could second-guess myself. I let the music take me, let the thrill of being seen without being *owned* wash over me. Just us and our friends chasing freedom.

But halfway through the night, it happened.

That prickle at the back of my neck. The sense of being watched. I didn't look at first. I didn't have to. I knew.

When I finally did, I spotted him at the edge of the room—dressed in black, half-hidden in shadow, still as a predator who didn't need to rush.

Lorenzo.

My breath caught. I didn't stop dancing. In fact, I did the opposite.

I let myself move closer to a stranger, let hands hover where they shouldn't, let my body speak a language I knew Lorenzo understood perfectly. I felt his gaze sharpen, darken, lock onto me like a promise.

A thrill ran through me—reckless and electric.

I met his eyes. Held them. And smiled.

That was all it took.

He moved.

One moment he was standing in shadow, the next he was cutting through the crowd with terrifying efficiency, bodies parting instinctively in his wake. He didn't rush, but he was fast—decisive, unstoppable. A predator who knew the kill was already his.

The stranger's hands fell away from me before I even registered why.

Lorenzo was there.

Too close. Crowding my space, his presence a physical force that stole the air from my lungs. His eyes dropped once—to the curve of my mouth, the line of my throat, the way my body was still moving with the music—then lifted again, dark and furious and unmistakably aroused.

"Enjoying yourself?" he asked quietly. Deadly calm. No accusation. No anger.

A promise.

My skin felt too tight, my heartbeat loud in my ears. I tipped my head slightly, defiant, breathless. "You told me to."

Something dangerous flickered across his face—approval twisted with restraint. His jaw flexed. His hand came up, not touching me, but close enough that I felt the heat of him, felt how badly he was holding himself back.

"Careful," he murmured, so low only I could hear it. "You're playing a game you don't intend to finish."

I swallowed, heat pooling low and traitorous. "You followed me."

His mouth curved, slow and sharp. "You turned off your location."

My breath hitched.

His eyes never left mine. "Did you think that would stop me?"

The music throbbed around us, the crowd oblivious, but in that small space between our bodies, everything went dangerously still. His gaze dragged over me once more, possessive and unashamed.

Lorenzo's fingers finally closed around my wrist then. Not rough. Not gentle. Certain. "Come," he said.

It wasn't a command. It was an expectation.

I let him pull me off the dance floor, my pulse roaring in my ears as we cut through the crowd. People stared. I didn't care. The heat between us was a live wire, snapping and sparking with every step.

Jenna spotted us near the bar, her eyes widening in instant understanding. She took in Lorenzo's grip on me, my flushed face, the look on his—and broke into a grin.

"Oh my God," she shouted over the music. "YES."

The rest of our friends caught on just as fast. Whistles. Laughter. Someone hooted as we passed.

"Get it, Sierra!"

"Finally!"

I laughed, breathless and reckless, letting Lorenzo tow me backward toward the exit. He didn't slow. Didn't look back. He trusted I'd keep up. I did.

Outside, the night air hit my skin like a shock. He stopped just long enough to look at me—really look at me—eyes dark, jaw tight, restraint stretched thin.

"You're coming home," he practically growled.

I didn't hesitate. "I know." That was all the permission he needed.

His hand slid from my wrist to my lower back as we moved toward the car, possessive and guiding, like this was where I belonged. Like this was inevitable.

I climbed in first and he shut the door.

Suddenly, there was nowhere else I wanted to be.

### *Lorenzo*

The silence in the elevator was a living thing, coiled and breathing between us. Sierra stood beside me, the scent of her perfume and the nightclub clinging to her like a second skin. She'd worn a black dress, a deliberate provocation, and I'd spent the entire drive picturing tearing it from her body.

The doors slid open, and I didn't give her a choice. My hand wrapped around her waist, my grip firm and I guided her into the penthouse. The door clicked shut behind us, the sound a final, definitive lock.

She turned to face me, her eyes dark, her chin tilted in that defiant way that made my blood sing. She didn't speak. She didn't have to. This was the reckoning she'd invited.

I closed the distance in a single stride, my hand cupping the back of her neck, my fingers tangling in the soft hair at her nape. I crushed my mouth to hers, not a kiss but an invasion. It was all teeth and tongue, a hungry, desperate clash. I tasted the wine she'd drunk, the mint on her breath, and the unique, intoxicating flavor of her surrender. She kissed me back with equal fury, her hands fisting in the collar of my shirt, pulling me closer, demanding more.

My hands were everywhere, tracing the line of her spine, the curve of her hips, the smooth, exposed skin of her back. The dress was a flimsy barrier, an offense. With a low growl, I found the zipper and yanked it down. The whisper of metal teeth was the only sound for a moment before the fabric pooled at her feet, leaving her in nothing but a scrap of black lace and her heels. She was a fucking goddess, all soft curves and sharp angles, bathed in the cold light of the city.

I shed my own clothes with impatient efficiency, my shirt discarded, my trousers kicked away. I stood before her, naked and hard, my cock aching with a need that bordered on pain. I saw her gaze flick down, her breath hitching, a flicker of triumph in her eyes. She'd wanted this. She'd wanted to see how much she affected me.

"On the bed," I commanded, my voice a low rumble.

She didn't hesitate. She moved with a liquid grace, lying back against the dark sheets, a creature of shadow and light. I followed her down, not to cover her, but to worship her. I knelt at the foot of the bed, my hands wrapping around her ankles, spreading her thighs wide. Her breath hitched, her eyes locking onto mine, a silent question in their depths.

I didn't answer with words. I lowered my head, my mouth finding the inside of her knee, placing a soft, deliberate kiss. I worked my way up, my lips and tongue tracing a path of fire along her sensitive skin. I could feel the tremor that ran through her, the way her muscles tensed in anticipation. I took my time, savoring every gasp, every shiver, every soft sigh.

When I finally reached the apex of her thighs, I paused, my breath ghosting over her. She was already so wet, so ready for me. The scent of her arousal was intoxicating, a drug I knew I would never get enough of.

"*Lorenzo*," she whimpered, her hands fisting in the sheets, her hips lifting in a silent plea.

I gave her what she wanted. I flattened my tongue and licked her from her entrance to her clit, a long, slow, deliberate stroke. She cried out, her back arching off the bed. I did it again, and again, my movements a slow, torturous rhythm. I explored her, my tongue delving inside her, tasting her, memorizing her. I circled her clit, teasing her, building the tension until she was writhing beneath me, her body a taut, trembling bow.

Then I focused on her, my lips closing around the sensitive bundle of nerves. I sucked, hard, my tongue flicking against her in a relentless, demanding rhythm. I could feel her getting closer, her breaths coming in ragged, desperate pants, her thighs trembling against my ears.

"Come for me, *amore*," I commanded against her flesh, my voice a low, guttural growl. "Let me feel you fall apart."

My words were her undoing. With a sharp cry, her body convulsed, her orgasm tearing through her with the force of a tidal wave. I held her down, my hands on her hips, my mouth never leaving her, drinking in every drop of her pleasure. I didn't stop until she was a boneless mess beneath me.

Only then did I rise, my body humming with a primal satisfaction. I positioned myself at her entrance, the head of my cock teasing her, a slow, deliberate pressure. She was still pulsing from her orgasm, her body welcoming. I sank into her in one slow, deep thrust, burying myself to the hilt. We both groaned, a shared, guttural sound of pure, unadulterated pleasure.

Then I began to move.

I set a punishing rhythm, a hard, deep, relentless pace that was designed to claim, to conquer. Each thrust was a statement, a reminder of who she belonged to. I watched her face, the way her eyes fluttered closed, the way her lips parted, the way her brows furrowed in a mixture of pleasure and pain. She was beautiful, so fucking beautiful, and she was mine.

"You are mine," I growled, my voice harsh, unyielding. "Every inch of you."

Her body responded, her inner muscles clenching around me, her hips rising to meet my every thrust. I could feel her building again, the tension coiling tighter and tighter, a spring ready to snap. I reached between us, my thumb finding her clit, rubbing it in tight, fast circles.

"*Lorenzo*" she moaned my name again, her body arching off the bed, her second orgasm tearing through her. Her name was a prayer on my lips. I followed her over the edge, my own release a brutal, all-consuming wave, pulsing deep inside her.

But we weren't done. Not by a long shot.

Before I could catch my breath, she rolled us over, her strength surprising me. She straddled my hips, her eyes blazing with a fury and a need that matched my own. She was in control now, and the sight of her, wild and untamed, was the most erotic thing I had ever seen.

She rode me, her movements slow, deliberate, a sensual dance that was both a tease and a demand. She leaned forward, her breasts brushing against my chest, her lips finding mine in a searing kiss. Her hands roamed, exploring my body, her touch setting me on fire.

Then she did something that surprised me again. She took my hand, guiding it to her throat. It was a silent, dangerous request, a test of my control. I complied, my touch gentle but firm, a promise and a threat all at once. I didn't squeeze, just held her, my thumb stroking the delicate skin over her pulse point. She gasped, her body responding to the restriction, to the edge of danger.

"Is this what you want?" I asked, my voice a low, dangerous purr. "To dance with the devil? To play with fire?"

"Yes," she hissed, her hips rolling, her body demanding more. "I want it all. I want you. I want the storm."

And so I gave it to her. I flipped us again, pinning her beneath me, my hand still on her throat. I fucked her with a wild, abandon, a raw, primal need that I had never felt before. I gave her everything, every dark, twisted, obsessive piece of me. I gave her the man who would stalk her, who would claim her, who would never, ever let her go.

When it was over, when we were both spent and sated, I collapsed beside her, my body trembling, my heart hammering against my ribs. I pulled her into my arms, her head resting on my chest, her breathing soft and even.

After a moment, I rose quietly, leaving her curled in the sheets, eyes heavy with sleep and trust. I disappeared into the bathroom and returned with a warm cloth, steam curling faintly in the low light.

I moved slowly, deliberately, as if haste might fracture something sacred.

My touch was gentle as I cleaned her, careful and thorough, every movement considered. Not claiming. Not taking. Tending. Worshipful. She stirred once, a soft sound leaving her throat, then relaxed again, yielding without question.

Reverence settled over me, heavy and unexpected.

I had done terrible things in my life. Violence had never cost me sleep. Killing had never cost me peace. But with her, my brutality found a different purpose. Not destruction—control. Not restraint—devotion.

I pressed a kiss to her shoulder when I finished, lingering there for a breath before settling back beside her. She turned instinctively, fitting against me like she had always known where she belonged.

She was mine. And not in the way men bragged about or abused. Not in the way ownership corrupted. She was mine because I chose to protect her. To watch. To guard. To carry the weight so she wouldn't have to.

I wrapped my arm around her and held her there, anchoring us both to the quiet certainty of the moment, knowing with absolute clarity—Whatever darkness waited for me in the world, it would never touch her without going through me first.

******

Morning light spilled across the penthouse like it owned the place. Gold and unapologetic. I watched her pad barefoot across the marble, my shirt hanging off one shoulder, sleeves swallowing her hands. It shouldn't have undone me the way it did.

She caught me looking. Her cheeks flushed—soft, pink, unmistakable—and she dropped her gaze to her coffee like it had personally offended her.

I smiled into my espresso. "You're staring at me like I've done something wrong." Her eyes flicked up again. Color bloomed instantly in her face.

"I'm not staring," she said too quickly.

"Mm," I murmured. "Liar."

She huffed, grabbed her plate, and moved to pass behind my chair. I caught her wrist as she went by and tugged. She gasped, balance gone, and a second later she was in my lap, knees bracketing my hips.

Her hands came up automatically, curling around my neck. One slid into my hair, fingers tightening like she'd done it a hundred times already. I stilled. So did she.

Her voice was quieter when she spoke. "Lorenzo... what is this?"

The question landed heavier than it should have.

"This," she continued, eyes searching mine, "this isn't in the contract."

I opened my mouth to answer—and my phone rang.

I ignored it. Her brow furrowed.

My phone rang again. Still ignored.

A third time, sharper now. Insistent.

I cursed under my breath and reached for it, keeping one arm locked around her waist so she didn't move away. Marco's name lit the screen. The moment I answered, dread and exhilaration slammed into me at once.

"They spotted him," Marco said without preamble. "Matteo. Back in Sicily."

The room narrowed. My pulse thundered.

"Where?" I asked.

"Palermo. Your engagement party pulled him out of hiding. He wanted to be seen—new girlfriend, some model. Idiot thinks visibility makes him untouchable."

It took everything in me not to smile. This was it. Answers. Revenge. For my parents. For *her*. "I'll handle it," I said. "I'm coming."

I ended the call and looked down at her. She was still in my lap, still holding my neck, but her expression had changed—sharper, more aware.

"I have to go to Sicily," I said smoothly. "Land acquisition."

Her lips parted like she wanted to argue. She didn't. But I could see it—she knew I wasn't telling her everything. After a beat, she nodded. "Okay."

I brushed my thumb along her jaw. "Promise me something."

"What?"

"Don't go anywhere without Alexio while I'm gone."

Her mouth twitched. "Are you… banning me?"

"I'm watching," I said lightly. "Always."

She smiled then—soft, amused. "*Stalker.*"

"Only yours."

I kissed her before she could reply. Deep. Possessive. A promise and a warning wrapped into one. An hour later, my bag was packed. I didn't look back when I left. I didn't need to. Everything I was going to destroy was waiting for me in Sicily.

# Chapter 10

*Sierra*

The door clicked shut with a finality I hadn't expected. The penthouse went quiet instantly—too quiet.

I checked my phone out of habit. Jenna was out of town, some big weekend trip with her family. She'd tried to convince me to go, had practically begged. If I left now, I could still have my ass in the sand by dinner.

I laughed out loud at the thought of Lorenzo finding out I'd disappeared right after he did.

Still, there was something about being here that settled me. The space felt… protected. I crossed to the windows and leaned against the cool glass, watching the city move far below. Cars, people, lives intersecting and diverging in neat little patterns.

Up here, none of it could touch me. None of it could hurt me.

I pulled one of my favorite books from the shelf and curled into the chair by the window, legs tucked beneath me. I had a few shifts at Last Call over the next couple of days, but otherwise—nothing. No obligations. No expectations.

It struck me how rare that was.

If I was being honest with myself, it had been a long time since I'd truly been alone. Lorenzo had stormed into my life and never really left. Not that I wanted him to—but still. He filled space effortlessly. Took up oxygen. Made everything feel sharper, louder.

He'd even been pushing me to come work for him after something Marco had said. It wasn't the first time I'd felt that pull—this quiet awareness that Last Call wasn't meant to be forever. I loved the bar, loved the chaos and the regulars and the way a good night felt like a small victory, but I couldn't shake the truth.

I didn't want to still be pouring drinks ten years from now.

Jenna and I had planned a beautiful engagement party—truly beautiful. I'd felt something click while we worked, the way details stacked into something seamless and alive. Lorenzo had noticed it too. He'd mentioned Marco was interested in hiring me to plan events for the vineyard. Tastings. New releases. Experiences. The kind of work that looked effortless only because someone obsessed over every detail behind the scenes.

Marco had told me he'd love to have me. Said I had an eye for it. That I brought order without killing the magic. I'd told him I was flattered. That I'd think about it.

The truth was, I didn't just want a job. I wanted a direction. A reason to wake up and know where I was headed. And for the first time, I wasn't sure Last Call could give me that.

The hours drifted by slowly, lazily, the way they only do when you're not waiting for anything to happen. But nothing did, the rest of the day passed without much ceremony.

I showered, dressed for my shift, pulled my hair back the way muscle memory demanded. Normal things. Familiar things. The kind that grounded me when everything else felt too big.

Alexio was waiting downstairs when I finished. He straightened when he saw me, all seriousness until I smiled.

"Relax," I said, grabbing my bag. "I'm not trying to escape."

He snorted. "Boss wouldn't believe that."

"Your boss is a broody nightmare," I shot back as we climbed into the car. "You're not allowed to sit in silence all night in the corner like he does. It's unsettling."

Alexio laughed as he pulled into traffic. "Fair enough. I'll try to be charming."

"You'd fail," I said sweetly.

He shook his head, amused, then hesitated—just a second too long. "You know… Lorenzo's not like this with anyone else."

I glanced at him. "Like what?"

"Protective," he said. "Overprotective, really. But—" He shrugged. "He loves hard. Always has." The word settled somewhere in my chest.

*Love.*

I didn't say anything after that.

Last Call was busy in the predictable way—music loud, glasses clinking, regulars arguing over nothing. I moved through it all on autopilot, smiling, pouring, listening. But the word followed me from customer to customer, echoing in the back of my mind.

*Love.*

I tried not to think about what it meant. About whether it was real. About whether it was dangerous. After my shift, Alexio was there again, exactly where he'd said he'd be. He drove me back in companionable silence this time.

Alexio said goodnight at the elevator, and I was left alone with my thoughts again.

Lorenzo had texted when his flight landed, then off and on throughout my shift. I wasn't sure what time it was for him, but I sent a quick goodnight anyway. My thumb hovered over the screen, Alexio's words replaying in my head.

Love.

Before I could talk myself out of it, I hit send.

*Goodnight*

I practically threw my phone onto the bed, refusing to look at it.

What was I doing?

This was business. Contractual. A carefully constructed arrangement meant to buy me time—time away from my parents, from Matteo's control, from expectations that had always felt like a trap. I was helping Lorenzo keep the tabloids quiet. Helping him with whatever he and Marco refused to discuss in front of me.

They acted like I was clueless. I let them.

Being engaged to me, being seen with me—it was a means to an end. I just didn't know what that end was.

I flopped back onto the bed dramatically, still refusing to reach for my phone. My life had flipped so completely it still felt unreal. It had been months since we'd entered into this arrangement, and despite Lorenzo's constant attempts to micromanage my life— the new phone, the new car, the contract itself—I wasn't unhappy.

It felt… claustrophobic sometimes. But I was calm.

*Peace.*

The realization hit me hard enough that I sat up.

For the first time in my adult life, I wasn't bracing myself. I wasn't worried about stepping into my place at Blackwell Enterprises—whether I wanted it or not. I wasn't worried about society gossip or saying the wrong thing at the wrong time. I wasn't worried about the man I was supposed to marry. About whether he'd be drunk. Or high. Or whether his grip would tighten when no one was watching.

I wasn't afraid of him coming home. I wasn't living in the *what ifs*. I wasn't scanning the shadows.

Lorenzo *was* the shadow.

I didn't need to look for him—I knew he'd be there. I didn't worry about embarrassing him or misstepping because he gave me the confidence I'd never had. He put me in the driver's seat. Even with the contract in place, he'd engineered it so I held the power.

He gave me peace. Maybe that was what love was.

My phone buzzed. I hesitated, then picked it up and brought the screen to life.

*I hope you think of me before you fall asleep.*

Such a simple text, but it destroyed me. I lay back against the pillows, phone still warm in my hand, his words echoing louder than the quiet room ever could. I tried to distract myself—counting breaths, staring at the ceiling—but my body wasn't interested in restraint.

A slow smile spread across my face. He was pushing, testing the limits even from thousands of miles away. And God help me, I wanted to be pushed. My mind drifted, unbidden, to the night before. The way he'd looked at me, the raw, possessive hunger in his eyes. The way he'd touched me, his hands and mouth claiming every inch of my body. The memory was a fire, and I was the kindling.

I closed my eyes, my breath hitching as I replayed the moment he'd knelt before me, his mouth on me, his voice a low, guttural command.

*Come for me, amore.*

The memory was so vivid, so intense, it was almost as if he were here. I could feel the phantom weight of his hands on my hips, the ghost of his breath on my skin.

My own hands began to wander, tracing the same paths his had taken the night before. And I let myself think of him.

******

The sun was just beginning to rise over the Sicilian coastline, casting a soft, golden glow over the vineyards. I was in my office at the villa, a glass of dark, rich espresso in my hand. But my attention wasn't on the breathtaking view or the reports spread across my desk. It was on the screen of my laptop.

The screen was divided into a dozen smaller feeds, all showing different views of the penthouse. The living room, the kitchen, the hallway. And the master bedroom. I had wanted to watch her sleep, to see her peaceful, unguarded face before I had to face the day, before I had to face Matteo. But then her text had come through, a simple heart, and a dark, possessive impulse had taken hold. I had to push her. I had to know.

*I hope you think about me before you fall asleep.*

I watched as she read my message, a slow smile spreading across her face. My own lips curved in response. She was playing along. Good.

I leaned forward, my elbows resting on the desk, my gaze fixed on the screen. I watched as she closed her eyes, her hands beginning to roam over her body. My blood thickened, a slow, heavy pulse starting in my groin. I knew what she was doing. I knew she was thinking of me.

I watched as her fingers found her clit, her movements a slow, deliberate rhythm. I could see the flush on her cheeks, the way her chest rose and fell with each ragged breath. I was hard, straining against the fabric of my trousers, aching with a need that was almost painful. I wanted to be there, to replace her fingers with my own, to hear her cries, to feel her shatter in my arms.

I watched as her movements became more frantic, more desperate. I could see the tension building, the way her body arched off the bed, the way her brows furrowed in concentration. She was close. So close.

I unbuckled my belt, my hand fumbling with the zipper of my trousers. I wrapped my hand around my cock, aching for release. I began to stroke myself, my movements in time with hers, a shared, intimate rhythm across continents. I pictured her face, the way she'd looked when she came for me, the sound of her cries.

On the screen, she came, her body convulsing, her lips forming my name. That was it. That was my undoing. I came with a low groan, my release a brutal, all-consuming wave. I leaned back in my chair, my body trembling, my heart hammering against my ribs.

I watched as she lay there, a sated heap on the bed. I wanted to be there, to hold her, to clean her up, to take care of her. But I was here. And I had a job to do. A promise to keep. I would kill Matteo. And then I would go home to her.

The screen went dark, and with it, whatever softness I'd allowed myself to feel.

I had indulged the illusion long enough. The warmth. The ache. The dangerous fantasy that I could stay in that penthouse and pretend this was life instead of a battlefield. Sicily had a way of stripping things down to essentials—of reminding you who you were born to be.

I had killed before. Not recklessly. Not for pleasure. But to protect what was mine—my family, our business, the fragile order that kept predators at bay. Violence had never been foreign to me. It was a language I spoke fluently when diplomacy failed.

The Moretti's and the Rinaldis had shared this soil for generations, but we had never been the same kind of men. My family were stewards—vineyards rooted deep in history, patience measured in decades instead of quarters. The Rinaldis built empires meant to dazzle: luxury resorts, curated excess, experiences polished until no one thought to ask what lay beneath. Alessio Rinaldi was the mind behind it all, clever enough to stay clean, distant enough to seem respectable. Matteo was his blunt instrument, sent to intimidate when money failed. And Bellandi—always Bellandi—made sure the blood never showed on paper.

My parents saw the pattern before it became legend. They understood Matteo wasn't reckless; he was deadly. Alessio decided who broke and Bellandi ensured the world never noticed. By the time I was old enough to be useful, the lines were already drawn. I was sent to watch, to learn, to trace the machinery quietly instead of confronting it loudly. We believed knowledge would be enough—that proof would protect us.

It didn't.

When I came back with answers instead of doubts, the response was immediate and absolute. My parents weren't killed for ambition or territory. They were erased because they'd seen too clearly how the Rinaldi machine worked—and because they'd started collecting the evidence to dismantle it. Their deaths weren't strategy. They were panic.

That was why this was happening now. Why Matteo had to be drawn out into the light. Why Sierra—bright, visible, inconvenient—became the perfect lure once my brothers and I connected the dots between her and him. The engagement, the spectacle, the contract—it was never about appearances alone. It was a summons.

Whatever peace she gave me, whatever softness I allowed myself when I watched her sleep—or move, or breathe—that was mine to carry. What came next was business.

And I had never failed to finish business before.

I left the villa without a backward glance, the taste of Sierra's phantom pleasure still lingering like a sin I didn't have time to atone for. The drive blurred into asphalt and olive groves, each mile pulling me farther from softness and closer to the stench of the sea—and the man I intended to erase.

Marco's intel looped in my head with ruthless clarity. Matteo, spotted publicly in Sicily. His yacht docked at a private marina, a floating monument to excess and ego. He'd been showing off after Sierra's engagement went public—parading a new woman like proof he hadn't lost. The tabloids ate it up. According to them, Sierra had been seen with him last. Now she'd "upgraded."

He hadn't just been replaced. He'd been humiliated.

The gravel crunched beneath my tires as I pulled into the docks. And there it was. White and gold. Obscene. Gaudy. Screaming money without taste or restraint. His yacht.

I sat there for a moment, engine idling, letting the city inside my head go silent. This wasn't business. This was blood.

I checked my weapons with mechanical calm. Two suppressed SIGs in the double holster beneath my jacket. A stiletto blade strapped to my left side. A heavier serrated knife on my right. I adjusted my signet ring— cold, familiar, a reminder of who I was and what I owed—then stepped out of the car.

I moved down the gravel path without hurry. Tailored Italian wool. Polished shoes. A civilized exterior wrapped around something far less polite. The sea air was thick with diesel and salt. The warehouse door stood slightly ajar—steel, scarred, waiting.

I pushed it open. The scream of metal echoed through the cavernous space.

Inside, a single chair sat beneath a bare bulb, its light swaying gently. A redhead slumped forward in it, her back to me. A model. His latest accessory.

"So, Matteo," I said, my voice low, conversational, deadly. "Tired of the view already? Or did she finally realize you're nothing but—"

I stopped.

Blood. Too dark. Too still.

The body wasn't a woman.

It was a man.

I closed the distance in two strides and tipped his head back with the butt of my gun. A familiar face. One of Matteo's associates. His eyes were glassy, a single precise bullet hole centered in his forehead.

Pinned to his chest with a throwing knife was a folded piece of paper. My hand shook—not from fear, but from the kind of rage that narrows the world to a point— as I tore it free.

*She's next.*

The air vanished. Sound dropped out entirely, like the world had cut power. This wasn't a kill site. It was a message. A decoy. A declaration.

I turned and ran.

My boots thundered across concrete as I tore back to the car, slammed it into gear, and spun out of the lot. I was already dialing Sierra. Once. Twice. Again.

No answer.

Alexio. Nothing.

"Marco," I roared when he finally picked up, my voice ripping itself apart. "THE PENTHOUSE. IT'S A SETUP. SIERRA."

I was flying now—toward the private airstrip, toward anything that would get me back faster. I called her again.

Ring.
Ring.

A man answered.

"You won't get here in time."

The line went dead.

Everything narrowed.

There was no road. No sky. No consequence. Only purpose. I had spent my life learning how to destroy men like Matteo Rinaldi. Slowly. Precisely. Completely.

And now?

Now I would burn the world down to get to her.

# Chapter 11



**_Sierra_**

I was asleep when the sound pulled me out of it. Not loud. Not sudden. Just… wrong.

I shifted beneath the sheets, half-conscious, my body reaching for familiarity before my mind caught up. "Lorenzo," I mumbled, rolling onto my side, chasing sleep.

Then I sat bolt upright. The room was dark. Too dark. And Lorenzo was in Sicily.

My heart kicked hard against my ribs. "Alexio?" I called softly, then louder. "Alexio?" Nothing answered me but silence.

I reached for my phone on the nightstand. The screen lit up my face, blinding in the dark. One missed call.

Lorenzo.

Relief and panic tangled in my chest as my thumb hovered over his name. That was when someone laughed. Low. Amused. Close.

"I told you," a voice said from the shadows, thick with satisfaction, "you're mine, little dove."

The world tilted.

I screamed and lunged off the bed, instinct screaming *run*, my mind flashing to the nightstand—Lorenzo's gun, always there, always—

Hands closed around my throat.

Matteo slammed me back against the wall hard enough to knock the air from my lungs. Pain burst behind my eyes. I clawed at him, choking, terror ripping through me as he laughed, breath hot against my face.

"You should've listened," he said, almost fondly.

My phone rang.

The sound cut through everything. He glanced down, then back at me, eyes bright with something vicious. He plucked it from the floor and answered it without breaking eye contact.

"You won't get her in time," he said calmly. He ended the call and tossed the phone aside. I shook my head, trying to scream again, but he was already reaching into his pocket. A cloth.

"No—" I gasped. He clamped it over my mouth and nose.

The room spun. My limbs went heavy. His face blurred, the edges of the world dissolving as darkness rushed in.

The last thing I heard was his breath in my ear. And then nothing at all.

******

Pain pulsed behind my eyes as I blinked, fighting to clear the fog in my head. My body ached everywhere at once. When I tried to move, rope bit into my wrists and ankles—rough, unforgiving. The reality of it crashed down on me, sharp enough to steal my breath.

Tears burned, threatening to spill. I forced myself to slow my breathing, to ground myself, to wake up fully. This wasn't a dream. The cold chair pressed against my bare skin, the chill seeping deep. I was still wearing Lorenzo's shirt. That somehow made it worse.

Water dripped somewhere behind me. Steady. Relentless. I heard men speaking in low voices off to my left, words indistinct but close enough to make my pulse race. The light was dim—not darkness, but not safety either.

A ship's horn sounded outside. Understanding settled in with sick clarity.

The Rinaldi warehouse. East side docks.

Everything rushed back at once. Matteo in the penthouse. The cloth over my face. The way he'd smiled. The keycard in his hand—Alexio's.

*Alexio.*

My chest tightened painfully. I prayed he wasn't dead. Matteo answering my phone. His voice, calm and cruel. *You won't get her in time.*
It had to have been Lorenzo.

I clung to that thought even as terror curled tighter around my ribs. I wasn't sure I could survive Matteo a second time.

Time slipped strangely, distorted and unreliable, but I knew enough to be afraid of it. It would have taken nearly two hours to get here from the penthouse. Even if Lorenzo caught a charter the moment he realized—Sicily was still almost ten hours away.

Eight hours. Matteo could do a lot of damage in eight hours.

And I was tied to a chair, counting every second.

"Well, well, little dove." His voice sliced clean through my thoughts.

I didn't look at him. I stared at the floor instead, at the cracks in the concrete, at anything that wasn't his face. His footsteps echoed as he moved closer—unhurried, deliberate.

Then his fingers tangled in my hair.

He yanked my head back hard enough to make my vision spark, forcing my eyes up to his. "Look at me when I'm speaking to you." It wasn't a request. It was a promise—*look, or I'll make you.*

His pupils were blown wide, his eyes rimmed red and frantic.

Cocaine.

Cold clarity cut through my fear. I couldn't stall him. Not for eight hours. Not like this. If I pushed too hard, he'd snap—I'd seen him do it before. But if I did nothing, I wouldn't survive either.

I swallowed and made my choice.

"I thought I'd gotten rid of you," I said, wrenching my head out of his grip despite the sting.

His mouth curved, slow and delighted. "Oh," he breathed. "How bold."

It was almost admiration. Like I'd entertained him.

"What do you want?" I asked, forcing my voice steady even as my heart battered my ribs. He leaned closer, invading every inch of space I had left.

"You belong to me," he said softly.

"My fiancé is coming," I said, lifting my chin despite the way my body shook. "And when he gets here, you'll regret this. I'm not yours to push around anymore."

Matteo laughed, sharp and ugly. He straightened, wiping his hands on his jeans like I was already beneath him. "Your fiancé?" he echoed. "That's adorable."

He circled me slowly, boots scraping against concrete. "Tell me, little dove—how much do you really know about Lorenzo Moretti?"

I held his gaze. "Enough."

His smile widened, all teeth and menace. "You think so," he said softly. "You think he's the hero in this story." He leaned down until his mouth was close to my ear. "Men like him don't come running because they're good. They come because they already belong to the darkness."

He straightened and stepped back, already bored. "Rest," he said lightly. "We've got time." Then he turned and walked away, the sound of his footsteps fading, the warehouse swallowing him whole.

And I was alone again—with his words, and the echo of his laughter ringing in the dark. My vision blurred, the world going sideways again.

******

The wheels hit the tarmac hard enough to rattle my teeth.

I didn't wait for the plane to taxi. The door wasn't even fully open before I was moving, phone already in my hand, Marco's voice still echoing in my skull from the flight. Sicily was predictable if you understood its rhythms. Matteo didn't hide—he displayed. And when he wanted to be seen, when he wanted to make a point, there was only one place he would take her.

Two hours to the docks.

A warehouse he thought was untouchable. Rinaldi-owned land. Familiar. Isolated. Close to the sea, where screams dissolved into wind and machinery.

I should have known sooner. I *had* known sooner. Grief had taught me to think like this—cold, brutal math that never lied. I counted the hours whether I wanted to or not.

Two to transport her from the penthouse. Hours restrained. Drugged. Alone.

By the time I hit the private terminal, the numbers had already finished carving themselves into my skull. Nearly 10 hours. That's how long he'd had her.

I replayed it until the time stopped being abstract and became physical. Two in the morning—her call unanswered. The sedative window. The drive from the penthouse to the docks. The gaps where Matteo would leave her alone just long enough to convince himself she couldn't escape.

Eight hours of fear. Of restraint. Of waiting.

My hands clenched until my knuckles burned. I'd killed before. For family. For the business. For men who thought leverage made them untouchable. I'd slept after every one of them. This was different.

This wasn't strategy or necessity. This was survival.

I saw her every time I closed my eyes—sleeping, wearing my shirt like it belonged to her. The thought of Matteo's hands on her made something feral claw its way up my spine.

The car was waiting, engine already running. I slid into the back seat and barked the address, the tires screaming as we tore onto the road.

He hadn't forced his way in. That much was clear now. The entry logs Marco pulled mid-flight confirmed it—no breach, no alarms. Just one clean scan.

Alexio's keycard. My chest went hollow.

Matteo hadn't just taken her—he'd wanted me to know that he could reach her without breaking a door. That no perimeter I built mattered if he could rot it from the inside.

The airport faded into the city. I pictured the warehouse—east side docks, Rinaldi property. A place Matteo liked because it made him feel untouchable. A stage for men who mistook patience for control. He'd learned that from his father, Alessio.

I'd killed men for less. For threats made in half the time. I'd done it without hesitation, without guilt, because that was the cost of protecting my family and the business. But Sierra—

Eight hours with him was not time. It was torture.

My phone vibrated in my hand. I didn't need to look to know it wasn't her.

"I'm close," I said when Marco answered. "Get eyes on the docks. If anyone moves—*anyone*—I want to know."

I leaned back as the car devoured the road, forcing my breathing steady, my mind narrowing to a single point of inevitability.

Matteo thought he was playing a long game. He was wrong. He'd already lost the moment he touched what was mine.

******

**Sierra**

I wasn't sure how long I had been out, but the gray light of morning was starting to cut through the dirty windows. Matteo hadn't bothered me in several hours, at least. My body still ached, my shoulders felt numb from the strain of being tied to the chair. The ropes had turned my wrists into a raw, bloody mess.

The heavy metal door screeched open, and he was back, a silhouette against the dim light of the outer room. In his hands, he carried a plate with a sandwich and a bottle of water. He set it down on the floor in front of me, the gesture mocking.

"Eat," he said, his voice flat.

I turned my head away, the very thought of food turning my stomach.

He sighed, a long-suffering sound. "It's not drugged, Sierra. Not yet, anyway." The joke was sick, a thin veil over the threat beneath. My throat was parched, a desert of need. I managed a small, jerky nod. He twisted the cap off the water bottle and held it to my lips. I sipped, just enough to wet my tongue, the water tasting metallic and cold.

He sank onto a crate across from me, pulling a switchblade from his pocket. He flicked it open, the *snick* of the blade unnaturally loud in the silence. He began to clean his nails with the tip, his movements casual, but my heart hammered against my ribs, a frantic bird in a cage. The glint of steel in the low light was a predator's eye.

"You know," he began, his voice conversational, as if we were old friends catching up, "your new fiancé…

Lorenzo. He's quite the man. Confirmed kills. Not just business, you understand. Brutal things. Things he's done to protect that precious family of his." He looked up at me, his eyes glittering. "Things that would make you sick."

"I don't care." I stared back, forcing myself not to flinch. "That's what you do to protect the people you love."

He laughed, a sharp, unpleasant sound. He latched onto the word, his smile widening, turning predatory. "Love? You think he loves you?! You stupid girl."

He rose and crossed the small space in a single step. I flinched as he trailed the cold, flat side of the blade over my cheek, down my jawline, the touch a terrifying caress. My breath hitched, my body rigid with fear.

"He's using you," he whispered, his voice a venomous hiss. The tip of the knife pricked my skin, not enough to break it, just enough to promise.

"He found out you were connected to me. That little scar on your face? It's a brand, isn't it? He knew. The second he saw it, he knew. And he used you. You are nothing but bait, Sierra. A pretty, desperate way to draw me out. He played you to get to me."

My mind recoiled, the words striking me like physical blows. It couldn't be true. But the sick feeling in my stomach said it felt true. The way he had just appeared in my life, the way he'd agreed without a second thought to becoming exclusive, the way he'd claimed me so publicly. The contract.

"But unlike you, I refuse to be played," Matteo continued, his voice rising with fevered intensity. He was high, his eyes wide and unfocused, lost in his own obsession. "So I played him instead. He thinks I'm on a yacht in Sicily with some cheap redhead. He's probably on his way to an empty dock right now."

He laughed again, a triumphant, unhinged sound. "And while he's chasing shadows, I have you."

He leaned in closer, his face inches from mine, the scent of his sweat and cologne suffocating. "You know, his plan worked. In a way. Your father was ready to give you to me. You were promised. And I will have you. You're mine, Sierra. You were always meant to be mine." The knife pressed a little harder, and I felt a sting as it broke the skin. "And if I can't have you, no one can. Especially not him."

The blade skimmed my skin again, light but deliberate, and I focused on my breathing instead of the cold terror curling in my chest. Matteo was talking too much. Repeating himself. Circling the same thoughts like they were wounds he couldn't stop picking at.

That's when I heard it.

The distant grind of an engine outside. Low. Industrial. A truck, maybe. Or a boat shifting in the marina.

Matteo froze.

Not just paused—*froze*. His head snapped toward the sound, pupils blown wide, breath hitching like he'd forgotten how to inhale. The switchblade stilled against my collarbone.

I felt it then. Not just fear—*certainty*. He wasn't in control anymore.

"You hear that?" I asked softly, barely moving my lips.

His gaze flicked back to me, wild and sharp. "Shut up."

The sharp *crack* as his open palm connected with my face. A stinging sensation radiated from my eye. Something warm was running down my face. Blood.

Another sound—metal clanging, far away but real. Normal. Harmless. But Matteo stepped back like he'd been struck.

"They're early," he muttered, more to himself than to me. His hand dragged through his hair, leaving sweat-slicked strands sticking up. "I told them not yet. I told—"

He laughed suddenly, too loud, too fast. "Doesn't matter. Doesn't matter at all." The knife snapped closed, then open again. His fingers fumbled with it.

I watched him unravel, piece by piece, my pulse steadying as a strange calm settled over me. This was it.

Men like Matteo didn't plan their endings—they *panicked* into them. "I'll be back, little dove." He left without waiting for a response. The door slammed, and the warehouse swallowed the sound.

I didn't waste the silence on panic. My body screamed as I shifted—hours bound had turned my muscles into stone—but I ignored it, focusing instead on the ropes biting into my wrists. Blood had soaked the fibers, dark and slick.

I twisted carefully, testing—not pulling yet. Learning. The chair rocked under me, unsteady. Too light. Too old. Hope flared, thin and dangerous.

I rocked again, slower this time, measuring the scrape of wood against concrete, memorizing the sound. If he came back, I needed to look helpless.

But if he didn't—I leaned into the pain and kept working.

The screech of the door announced his return. My heart seized, I froze. He wasn't alone. Two men flanked him, broad and brutish, their faces blank, devoid of emotion. They didn't even look at me, as if I were just another piece of furniture in this sick tableau. They were men who followed orders, no questions asked.

"Cut her loose," Matteo commanded, his voice flat, cold.

One of them stepped forward, a heavy-duty knife in his hand. He sawed through the ropes in two brutal, efficient slashes. The tension vanished, and with it, all my strength. I fell out of the chair, my limbs useless pins and needles, my body crumpling to the dirty concrete floor.

Adrenaline, sharp and electric, surged through me. Get up. Run. I scrambled, my hands scrabbling for purchase on the gritty floor, trying to push myself up. I made it to my knees, my gaze fixed on the open door, a sliver of gray light, a promise of freedom.

A laugh, dark and mocking, cut through my hope. A sharp, brutal kick connected with my ribs, sending me sprawling again. The air whooshed from my lungs in a pained gasp.

"You have to do better than that," Matteo sneered, standing over me. "There is no escaping me."

He reached down, his hand tangling viciously in my hair, and hauled me to my feet. He pulled me flush against him, his body a hard, unwelcome cage. The scent of his cologne was gagging, his grip like iron.

"We will get married," he whispered, his voice a grotesque parody of intimacy. "Today. We will say the vows, and you will be mine forever."

Blood from my split lip filled my mouth. I gathered it, spat it directly into his face.

The world exploded. For a second, there was only shock in his eyes. Then, pure, unadulterated rage. He roared, a sound of pure animal fury, and threw me. I flew through the air and crashed hard onto the concrete, the impact stealing my breath and bringing stars to my vision.

Pain, blinding and absolute, was my only companion as I lay there, broken, on the floor of my own personal hell. The tears I'd been holding broke, flowing freely down my face mixing with blood on the cold concrete.

I lay there, cheek pressed to the cold concrete, tears blurring everything into streaks of light and shadow. The world pulsed in and out, pain eclipsing thought.

Footsteps approached.

I squeezed my eyes shut, bracing.

Then— a sound I didn't recognize. Not laughter. Not Matteo's voice.

A sharp crack split the air.

Matteo jerked, a startled sound tearing from him as his body dropped out of my line of sight. Something heavy hit the floor. The vibrations shuddered through me.

Another figure moved into view—tall, dark, indistinct. My ears rang, the warehouse muffled like I was underwater. I couldn't hear words, only impacts. Motion.

Another man stepped forward—too fast, too close—

The dark figure raised his arm.

Another crack. The man folded, collapsing bonelessly to the concrete.

There was no pause.

The figure was already moving again. A flash of steel. A swift, brutal motion I felt more than saw. The second man made a choking sound before he went down, blood blooming dark against the floor.

Silence rushed in, thick and suffocating.

I blinked hard, trying to make sense of the shapes around me. Three bodies. One standing. The figure turned toward me. I tried to focus. Tried to breathe.

And then—through the ringing, through the haze—I knew.

Even before he reached me. Even before he dropped to his knees at my side.

Even before his hands—warm, steady, shaking—touched my face.

*"Amore,"* he said, voice breaking through the fog like a lifeline.

# Chapter 12

**Lorenzo**

I didn't see the blood at first. I only saw her.

Curled on the concrete like she'd been discarded. Shirt torn. Skin bruised, mottled, marked. Too still. Too small in the middle of all that empty space.

Something inside my chest caved in.

"*Amore*." My voice didn't sound like mine as I dropped to my knees beside her. My hands shook when I touched her face—gentle, reverent, terrified I'd hurt her more. "Baby. Look at me."

Her eyes fluttered, unfocused. She was breathing. Shallow. Ragged. Alive.

Thank God.

I slid an arm beneath her shoulders, lifting her slowly, carefully, drawing her against me. She was light—too light. Every bruise felt like an accusation carved into my skin.

"It's over," I murmured, pressing my forehead to her temple. "I've got you. I'm here."

Footsteps thundered behind me. My men. Familiar voices. Emil's among them—tight, alert, already assessing threats that no longer mattered. I got her to her feet, one arm locked around her waist, turning us toward the door.

That's when she screamed. Not loud—raw.

"Wait."

The word tore out of her like it hurt to exist. She twisted in my arms with sudden strength, panic and fury flooding her face. Before I could stop her, she wrenched free and dropped to the floor beside Matteo's body.

"Sierra—" Too late.

She was already reaching into his jacket, fingers wet with blood. She pulled out the switchblade like she'd been born knowing where it was.

"No," I said, rising, horror slamming into me. "Sierra, stop—"

The blade snapped open. And then she was on him.

She stabbed him again and again, screaming words that weren't words—just sound, just pain made audible. Blood splashed up her arms, soaking into my shirt like it belonged there. Like this was inevitable.

Emil froze beside me. Even he—who had killed more men than most could count—looked away. "Take it from her," I snapped, moving forward. "Now."

"She's gone," Emil said under his breath, but he moved.

I grabbed her wrists from behind, trying to ground her, trying to anchor her back into the world. "Sierra. Look at me. It's over. He can't hurt you anymore."

She thrashed, wild, feral.

"Let me go!" she screamed. "Let me finish it!"

Emil lunged for the knife. She jerked.

Pain flared sharp and hot across my side—a line of fire as the blade caught me. I barely felt it. I knew it wasn't deep, I'd be fine.

Emil wrestled the knife from her grasp, tossed it away, pinned her arms as she collapsed in on herself, sobbing so hard it sounded like she was breaking apart from the inside.

I dropped to my knees with her, pulling her against my chest, uncaring of the blood soaking through my clothes. "You're safe," I said fiercely, over and over. "I've got you. I won't let anything else happen to you. Ever."

Her breathing slowed. Her body sagged. Then she went still. She pulled back just enough to look at me. Her eyes were clear now. Too clear.

"You used me too," she whispered.

The words hit harder than any blade.

"You're just as bad," she went on, voice hollow, devastated. "At least Matteo admitted his sins."

I didn't deny it. I couldn't.

She saw it then—everything I hadn't said. The guilt. The recognition. The truth.

"I hate you," she whispered. And then her eyes rolled back.

I caught her as she collapsed, gathered her into my arms like she weighed nothing at all. Like she was everything.

I carried her out of the warehouse without looking back. Behind us, my men moved. Orders were given. Gasoline spilled. Flames climbed.

I laid her gently into the back seat, brushing blood-matted hair from her face, my hands steady even as my soul fractured. The fire roared to life behind us.

The warehouse went up in flames—bright, violent, final. Just like my parents' plane. A warning. A promise. A reminder.

And as we drove away, Sierra unconscious in my arms, I knew one thing with brutal certainty—Saving her had cost me everything.

And I would gladly pay for it again.

******

I drove straight through the gates of the private facility without slowing.

No signage. No press. No questions. Money and favors ensured that much.

They took her from my arms gently—too gently, like they were afraid she'd shatter—but I didn't let go until the doors forced the choice from me. I followed anyway, boots silent against polished floors, my presence unquestioned. Everyone here knew who I was. And more importantly, what I would do if anyone failed her.

They sedated her.

I watched it happen, my jaw clenched as her body finally relaxed, tension bleeding out of her inch by inch. IV lines followed. Monitoring leads. Careful hands cleaning blood that never should have been there.

Bruises bloomed even as they worked—deep purples and angry reds surfacing like truths that couldn't be hidden. Cuts along her wrists. A split lip. Marks I catalogued without blinking, each one filed away somewhere dark and permanent.

I didn't leave her room.

A nurse knelt beside me at one point, quietly tending the shallow slice along my ribs. She cleaned it, stitched it with efficient hands. I didn't look down. My eyes never left Sierra's face.

"She's stable," the doctor said softly. "Physically." I nodded once.

That word—*physically*—hung in the air between us.

Marco arrived an hour later, his presence a shift in gravity. He didn't speak at first, just took in the room, the machines, Sierra's still form. His expression tightened in a way that mirrored my own.

"Alexio's alive," he said finally. "Drugged. Stab wound to the abdomen. Missed anything vital. He's in surgery now, but he'll make it."

My chest loosened just enough to breathe. "Good."

Marco continued. "The fire's being handled. Electrical fault. Accelerant traces explained away as industrial runoff. One of our friends at the outlet pushed the story through early—no speculation, no names. Warehouse fire. Tragic. Contained."

I nodded again.

Optics mattered. Not because I cared what they thought—but because chaos invited questions. And questions invited enemies.

"Rinaldi assets tied to the property are already being frozen," Marco added. "The rest of Bellandi's people are panicking. Alessio hasn't surfaced yet."

He didn't need to say more. This wasn't over.

Marco glanced at Sierra. "She said—"

"I know," I cut in quietly. He stopped.

I reached out, brushing my thumb over the back of her hand, careful of the IV. Her skin was warm. Alive.

"I know what she said," I repeated.

Marco held my gaze for a moment, then inclined his head and stepped back. He left without another word. The room settled into silence again, broken only by the soft, steady rhythm of the monitors.

I sat there for hours.

Watching her breathe. Counting the rise and fall of her chest like a prayer I didn't deserve to make. I had saved her.

And somehow, I had broken her too.

I didn't know yet which of those truths would cost me more—but as I sat beside her hospital bed, blood drying on my hands, one thing was certain:

I would not leave her again. Not now. Not ever.

******

### Sierra

Consciousness came back in pieces.

Beeping. Too steady. Too loud. My mouth tasted like metal and cotton, my limbs heavy, distant. I tried to move and felt resistance—IV lines, sensors, the quiet insistence of a hospital bed.

I opened my eyes. White ceiling. Soft light. No windows.

My gaze shifted slowly, deliberately, taking inventory the way you do when you're not sure if you're safe yet.

That's when I saw him.

Lorenzo sat slumped in a chair beside the bed, head tipped back, eyes closed. His shirt was gone, discarded over the armrest. Fresh stitches ran along his side, angry and red against olive skin. One arm hung loosely at his side, fingers slack with exhaustion.

He looked…wrecked.

I swallowed, my throat tight, and the memories came rushing back all at once—concrete, blood, fire, his hands shaking as he held me, the look in his eyes when I said it.

*I hate you.*

The door opened quietly. Marco stepped in with two coffees in his hands, moving like he belonged here. Like this was routine.

He froze when he saw my eyes open.

"Well," he said softly. "You're awake."

I stared at him, my pulse ticking up with every breath. "Get away from me."

Marco set the coffees down slowly on the counter. "Sierra—"

"No," I snapped, my voice hoarse but sharp. "Don't say my name like you didn't know exactly what was happening."

Lorenzo stirred in the chair, brow furrowing, but didn't wake. Good.

Marco's jaw tightened. "You should rest."

I laughed—a brittle, broken sound. "You knew. All of you knew."

He didn't deny it. That was the worst part.

"You used me," I said, each word deliberate. "You paraded me in front of him. You let him see me. You let him think—"

"That you were leverage?" Marco finished calmly. "Yes." The word landed like a slap.

My hands curled into the sheets. "You're monsters."

Marco met my gaze evenly. "We're realists."

"Don't," I hissed. "Don't justify it."

"I'm not," he said. "I'm confirming it."

Something in my chest cracked open. "You knew he'd come for me."

"Yes."

"You knew he'd hurt me."

Marco hesitated. Just for a fraction of a second. "We calculated risk," he said finally.

I turned my head away, blinking hard. "You're all the same."

"No," Marco said quietly. "We're worse. Because we knew exactly who Matteo was—and we still chose to bait him."

That finally woke Lorenzo. He sucked in a sharp breath, sitting forward, eyes immediately finding me. "Sierra—"

I didn't look at him.

Marco straightened. "He's dead," he added, not unkindly. "And Alessio Rinaldi will follow. That part is inevitable."

I turned back to him, fury burning through the exhaustion. "And what happens to me?" Marco didn't answer right away.

"That," he said carefully, "depends on whether you believe Lorenzo when he tells you he never meant for this to happen."

Lorenzo stood, slow and deliberate, pain written into every movement. "Marco," he warned. But Marco didn't back down.

"You deserved the truth," he said to me. "Even if it costs us."

I looked at Lorenzo then. Really looked. The stitches. The blood still under his nails. The devastation he hadn't bothered to hide.

"I meant what I said," I whispered. "About hating you."

His face tightened—but he nodded. "I know."

"And if you lie to me again," I continued, my voice deadly calm, "I won't scream. I won't run."

I held his gaze. "I'll disappear."

Silence fell heavy between us.

Marco picked up one of the coffees, glanced between us once, and stepped back toward the door. "I'll give you time," he said.

The door closed behind him. Lorenzo stayed where he was.

And for the first time since this began, neither of us knew how to move forward without destroying what was left.

******

The days blurred together under antiseptic lights and hushed voices. Recovery came in fragments— measured breaths, monitored pain, the slow return of feeling to places that had gone frighteningly numb. Everything was quiet by design. Conversations stayed clipped and careful, as if speaking too loudly might crack something open. Nurses rotated. Doctors spoke in soft absolutes. And Lorenzo never left for long.

When he slept, it was in the chair beside my bed. Always close. Always watching, even in rest.

Jenna had been blowing up my phone since the first story broke. Missed calls stacked on top of one another, texts veering wildly between fury and fear. When she finally showed up, she took one look at me—at the bruises blooming beneath hospital gowns, at the way Lorenzo hovered without touching—and I saw the shift in her immediately. She stayed less than an hour. Long enough to hold my hand. Long enough to tell me, quietly but with steel beneath it, *You can leave. Come stay with me. No contracts. No men like him.*

I didn't answer her. I just nodded, filed the offer away, and watched her walk out knowing the door was still open if I decided to take it.

Lorenzo came back not long after she left. That's when everything finally broke open.

"I'm leaving."

The words left my mouth cleanly. No tremor. No room for interpretation.

He stilled, watching me. Not shock—never shock. Calculation. The kind that came from knowing I meant it. "You're not well enough to—"

"Don't." My voice was rough, scraped raw, but it held. "The contract was insurance. Matteo was the threat. He's dead. So it's over."

Silence stretched between us. Heavy. Telling. He didn't deny it.

"Matteo was a symptom," he said quietly.

I let out a short, humorless laugh. "He was the nightmare."

"Yes," Lorenzo agreed. "And nightmares leave echoes."

I swung my legs over the side of the bed, ignoring the way my body protested, the way pain flared like it wanted attention. "You promised it would protect me from him. You got what you wanted. You killed him. So don't pretend this is anything else."

He stepped closer, careful—like I might bolt, like I might shatter. "If you leave," he said, "every family watching Sicily will see it as an opening."

I turned on him sharply. "I'm not bait anymore."

"No," he said without hesitation. "You're leverage." The word hit harder than any slap.

"So you admit it."

"I admit the truth." His voice stayed even, steady. "Matteo made you visible. His death made you valuable."

I shook my head, fury sharpening my movements. "That's not my problem."

"It becomes your problem the moment someone decides you know too much," he countered. "Or that hurting you is the fastest way to test me."

I opened my mouth to argue—then stopped. Because I knew he was right.

He pressed on, relentless, not loud. "If you walk away, you're a woman who survived Matteo Rinaldi. A story. A liability. A question mark."

"And if I stay?" I snapped.

His jaw tightened. "You're untouchable."

I scoffed. "Because I belong to you?"

"No," he said. "Because anyone who touches you declares war on me. On paper. Publicly. Permanently. And they know how it ends"

I searched his face for the lie. There wasn't one. Somehow, that made it worse.

"So the contract isn't protection anymore," I said slowly. "It's a warning label."

"Yes."

"And the leverage?"

A beat. "It cuts both ways."

My pulse spiked. "Explain."

"You stay," he said, "and you become part of the structure. Not hidden. Not erased. Seen." He paused. "Which means if anything happens to you, there are consequences I can't quietly bury."

My throat tightened. "You're saying I hold *you* hostage."

"I'm saying," he replied softly, "that for the first time, I can't afford to lie to you." The room hummed with it—truth, ugly and exposed.

"You used me."

"Yes." No excuses. No hesitation.

"And you're still asking me to stay."

"I'm asking you to decide," he said. "Leave, and I'll protect you as long as I can." His mouth hardened. "Stay, and no one will dare test whether I fail."

I looked away, jaw trembling—not weak. Furious. "If I stay," I said, "it's not because of the contract."

"I know."

"It's because I refuse to be hunted."

His voice dropped to a whisper. "That's all I ever wanted you to understand."

I met his gaze again. Sharp. Wounded. Still alive. "Don't confuse this for forgiveness."

"I won't."

"And don't mistake it for trust."

"I wouldn't dare."

A long beat. I lay back against the pillows, staring at the ceiling, letting the choice settle into my bones.

"I'll stay."

He closed his eyes for half a second—relief, guilt, something dangerously close to reverence.

"But," I added, turning my head just enough to pin him with my gaze, "we renegotiate everything."

His lips curved—not a smile. Respect. "Of course we do."

He was already on the phone by the time I pressed the call button for the nurse. Whether I was ready or not, I had to get out of this hospital room. I needed to feel the sun on my skin. I needed to find a way out of this.

# Chapter 13

**Lorenzo**

We'd been home for a few days. Sierra sat across from me like this was a hostage negotiation. I supposed, to her, it was. The softness I'd come to recognize in her eyes was gone—replaced by distance, calculation. Her skin was too pale, the split on her lip still a violent, unforgiving red. She had barely spoken to me since she woke up in the hospital, but she didn't need to. Her eyes said everything. The fire I'd come to crave was gone. In its place was something colder. Clearer.

I leaned back, stretching my arms. The stitches pulled, sharp but distant. It didn't hurt. Not compared to this.

The door opened quietly and Marco stepped inside, the same leather briefcase in his hand. Only now, we both knew why he was here.

I'd found a way to keep Sierra with me—but only for a while. She would find an exit eventually. She always did. I'd had Marco revise the contract, strip it of loopholes, seal every weakness I could find. I'd convinced her that leaving me wouldn't erase the danger I'd brought into her life. It would only change its shape.

Alessio would be searching for leverage. Against my family. Against me.

The warehouse fire had buried his son and erased evidence—but it was also a message. A reminder. My parents' plane had fallen from the sky in flames; this was simply business in return. But Alessio wasn't stupid. He knew we'd connect the dots. Matteo had been violent, reckless—but he'd never been the architect of the Rinaldi Group's power. That had always been his father.

And now, in Alessio's eyes, I'd stolen what belonged to him. Sierra—his future daughter-in-law. And then his son.

The blinders I'd so carefully put in place were gone. Sierra could see the fractures now, the danger beneath the surface no matter how carefully I'd hidden it. She felt the scrutiny, the constant attention. She knew I was always watching.

Marco glanced between us, then set the briefcase on the table and opened it with soft, deliberate clicks. He removed the folder and spread it open before us.

"This isn't necessary," Sierra said. "I haven't broken the contract."

Marco nodded. "Correct. This is an amendment to the engagement agreement."

Her shoulders loosened a fraction. Not relief—curiosity.

"Given recent developments," Marco continued, sliding the folder closer, "certain provisions require clarification."

"Section Four," Marco said. "Mutual Risk Acknowledgment."

Sierra sighed. "If this is about how leaving Lorenzo doesn't make me safe, you've already made that point."

"Verbally," Marco replied. "This makes it enforceable."

He read. She stared at the table, jaw tightening with each line. "So," she said when he finished, "separation doesn't reduce risk. I understand that."

Marco turned the page. "Section Seven. Extended Protection Mandate."

Her eyes flicked up. "Define extended."

"Thirty-six months minimum," Marco said. "Post-separation."

She looked at me. "Three years."

"At least," I said.

"And who decides when it ends?"

"Threat reassessment remains under Lorenzo's authority," Marco answered.

She exhaled sharply. "Of course it does."

"Section Nine. Non-disclosure."

She didn't bother looking down. "I don't speak. I don't write. I don't hint. If I do, protection is revoked."

"Yes."

"And if protection is revoked—"

"You're exposed," Marco said.

Her fingers curled into her palm.

"Section Eleven," Marco continued. "Proximity Clause."

She scanned the page now. "One hundred miles," she said flatly. "You're joking."

"No," Marco replied. "Rapid response necessity."

"So I can leave you," she said to me, "but I can't leave your reach."

"That's the idea."

She laughed quietly. Brittle. "You really know how to dress up a cage."

"We'll refine it," I said, cutting in. Marco paused, then wrote in the margins.

"You will continue to live here with me, " I continued. "No extended absences without my approval."

Her head snapped up. "This isn't about response time. This is about watching me."

"It's about access," I said evenly. "If Alessio looks for leverage, he won't find distance."

Her smile was thin. "So I don't get to disappear."

"No," I said. "You don't."

Marco cleared his throat. "The clause also stipulates shared security routes and unrestricted monitoring within common living spaces."

Her mouth parted slightly—not in surprise. In understanding.

"Third-Party Contact Restrictions," Marco added. "All communication outside a pre-approved list will be monitored." He didn't hesitate.

"This includes Jenna." She flinched.

Marco aligned the papers carefully. "Those conclude the engagement amendments."

Sierra exhaled slowly. "Fine. I don't like them, but none of that is new."

She lifted her gaze to Marco. "There's something else."

Marco closed the folder then pulled out a new document.

"To address remaining exposure," he said, "the engagement agreement will include a conversion provision."

Her brow furrowed. "Conversion to what?"

Marco met her eyes. "Marriage." The word hit the table like a dropped plate.

"I'm sorry," she said. "What?"

"Legal marriage," Marco clarified. "By contract."

She laughed—sharp, disbelieving. "You can't just add a husband to an engagement."

"You can," Marco said, "when the contract allows structural modification in the event of escalated threat."

Her gaze snapped to me. "You knew."

"Yes."

"This wasn't an engagement," she said slowly. "You were just buying time."

"It was protection," I said.

Marco slid the page toward her. "The provision establishes immediate legal marriage upon execution. No public filing is required at this stage."

Her voice dropped. "At this stage."

"Public disclosure increases risk," Marco said. "However, legal status ensures continuity."

She shoved the paper away. "You don't get to marry me on paper without my consent."

"Your signature *is* the consent," Marco said quietly.

She stood so fast her chair tipped back, clattering across the tile. "This is insane," she said. "You're telling me I sign this and I belong to him."

"No," I said. "You survive with me."

Her eyes burned. "You think Alessio will look at me and see a liability."

I didn't answer fast enough.

"Something he can use," she went on, voice tightening. "Something disposable. Something that proves even *you* have a weakness."

"You aren't a weakness."

"That's what *he* would think," she snapped. "That if I'm not legally tied to you, I'm fair game."

"He'll think you're unprotected," I said.

She laughed softly, broken. "Unprotected or expendable?"

The word hung between us.

"Like the difference," she said quietly, "is supposed to matter to me."

Marco spoke again. "There is a final additional recommendation."

She stared at him. "Of course there is."

"A formal ceremony," he said. "Public. Timed. Controlled."

I felt her recoil without touching her.

"A wedding," she whispered.

"Yes," Marco said. "Within sixty days."

She turned to me then, like she was seeing me clearly for the first time. "So this is it," she said. "I don't just wear your ring. I wear your name."

I didn't deny it.

"You don't need to love me," I said. "You just need to stay alive."

Her hands trembled as she pressed them to the table.

She swallowed hard. "I thought the ring meant maybe," she said. "That there was still time."

Her voice cracked. "You were already deciding what I was worth to him."

The room felt smaller. Denser.

Marco's voice cut through it, polite and final. "The engagement agreement will convert into a legal marriage within sixty days of signing."

Marriage.

Not protection. Not proximity.

Permanence.

She looked at me again, and there was nothing left to misunderstand. The cage didn't pretend to be beautiful anymore.

And I knew—too late—that whatever I told myself this was, I had just finished sealing her inside it.

Marco slid the pen across the table. "When you're ready," he said.

Sierra looked at the contract. Then at me. She pressed the pen down hard enough to crease the paper. When she finished, she stared at the signature like it didn't belong to her.

"I don't love you," she said.

Then, softer—but worse:

"And I hate you for letting me think I might.

****** 

***Sierra***

I threw the pen onto the table. It clattered once, too loud, and I hated that sound because it meant it was done. I didn't look at either of them. If I did, I wouldn't leave. Or worse—I would beg.

I turned and went down the hall toward the bedroom, my heart slamming so hard it felt like it might crack my ribs from the inside. I needed air. I needed noise. I needed to scream until something in me broke open.

All I could think about was Jenna. The way she would pull me into her without questions, without contracts, without conditions. I wanted to crawl into that safety and tell her everything I'd been too stupid to see.

*How could I have been so blind?*

Even when I signed the original agreement, there had been something—heat, tension, attraction I'd mistaken for choice. For agency. Now I could see it for what it was. Manufactured proximity. Engineered emotion. A role written for me before I ever knew the script existed.

I hadn't fallen for him. I'd been placed.

Even now—*even now*—with the man who hurt me most dead and buried, I still wasn't free of his reach.

Marco was right. Alessio would come looking. He always did. I didn't need the details to know the shape of it.

I'd known Alessio the moment I met him. At my engagement to Matteo, his eyes had lingered too long, too sharp—not desire, not interest. Inventory. Like I was something he could pick up and turn over in his hands.

A tool.

Matteo was dead, and I was glad. But Alessio wouldn't see justice—he would see opportunity.. He'd find a way to use me anyway. To hurt me. Or worse—to hurt Lorenzo *through* me. And that was the sickest part.

Because beneath the anger, beneath the humiliation, something in me still ached. I still wanted to protect him.

I still wanted to believe there had been something real between us—something that hadn't been written into a clause or decided in advance. That the way he looked at me sometimes hadn't been calculation. That the way I'd felt in his arms hadn't been another carefully closed trap.

Even knowing he'd used me. Even knowing I'd signed my name into his hands,

I still wanted to love him. And that was the part of me I hated the most.

I braced my palms against the floor-to-ceiling glass and let my forehead fall forward. The window was cool. Unmoved. The city stretched beneath me, indifferent and alive.

My bruises were fading, yellowed at the edges, but they were still visible. Proof. Not of weakness—of survival. I closed my eyes and breathed until the shaking stopped.

He didn't get to cage me here. Not completely.

I pulled my phone from my purse and typed without hesitation.

*911 please come get me*

Sent.
Delivered.
Read.

*Five minutes.*

That was all I needed. I slipped my phone away, lifted my purse, and walked back toward the kitchen at an unhurried pace. Deliberate. Controlled. Like I hadn't just declared war in twelve characters.

They were both still sitting at the table. Lorenzo and Marco, too still, voices low. They stopped the moment I entered. Their attention snapped to me like I'd yanked a wire.

I didn't slow. "I'm going out with Jenna," I said.

I wasn't asking. I walked past them. Lorenzo moved—instinctive, possessive. His hand reached for my arm. I stopped and turned just enough to look at him.

"Don't fucking touch me." The words were flat. Cold. Razor-sharp.

"Sierra—" His voice dropped, warning threaded through it. Control trying to reassert itself.

I laughed softly. Not amused. Not nervous. Just cruel. "We'll stay within a hundred miles," I said. "I'll grab one of your guards downstairs."

I met his eyes fully now, letting the hatred show. Letting it *burn*.

"Relax," I added, venom dripping from every syllable. "I wouldn't want to break your contract."

Then I turned and walked out before he could decide whether stopping me was worth proving I'd been right all along.

I stepped into the warm sunlight as I saw Jenna's car approaching.

"Don't follow too closely and please, leave us alone." I addressed one of the security team assigned to me. Alexio was still recovering. He nodded silently.

Her gaze cut to the mountain of a man behind me as I opened the door, sliding into her passenger seat. "Just drive," I breathed.

Jenna's apartment still smelled like vanilla and laundry detergent, like a life that didn't require permission.

The door had barely shut before my composure gave out. I didn't sob. I just sagged, knees soft, breath coming wrong. Jenna caught me and pulled me in, arms tight around my shoulders.

"Hey," she murmured. "You're safe. You're here."

I nodded against her collarbone, even though the word *safe* felt provisional now.

She sat me on the couch and crouched in front of me, her eyes scanning my face. The split lip. The fading bruises. The way my hands wouldn't stay still. Her mouth tightened.

"I saw the news," she said quietly. "The warehouse fire. Matteo."

I didn't flinch.

"I figured," she went on. "You don't disappear for days and come back looking like this unless something went very wrong."

"He's dead," I said. The relief in my voice surprised even me. Jenna studied me. Not judgment. Not shock.

Understanding.

"Okay," she said slowly. "And somehow that didn't fix anything."

I shook my head. I told her *just* enough.

Not how it happened. Not who pulled the trigger. Just the aftermath. The contracts. The security. The way leaving didn't mean leaving. How the engagement had quietly turned into something else entirely.

Jenna leaned back against the arm of the couch, folding her arms. "So the fire wasn't an ending," she said. "It was a warning."

"Yes."

"And now they're afraid someone will come looking for leverage." I didn't answer. I didn't have to.

Her gaze sharpened. "You." I nodded.

"That's why they won't let you go," she said. "Not because you're in love. Because you're exposed."

The word landed heavy.

"Does he care about you?" Jenna asked.

I looked away.

She exhaled, long and controlled, like she was filing something away for later. Jenna watched me for a long moment, head tilted, eyes narrowed in that way she got when she was thinking three steps ahead.

"So there *was* something," she said quietly. Not a question. "Before all of this."

I didn't answer, but my silence did.

She nodded once, like she'd just confirmed a theory she didn't want to be right about. "And then Matteo happened," she went on. "And whatever rules they live by snapped shut."

Her jaw tightened. "I don't need the details. I just need to know this isn't what you chose."

"It isn't," I said. That was enough.

She straightened, resolve settling into her bones. "Okay. Then we treat this like what it is."

"And what's that?" I asked.

"A battlefield," she said calmly. I huffed out a breath that might have been a laugh. "You've got a wedding coming," she added. "Which means we'll plan it, but plan it smart."

I looked at her. Really looked. The steadiness. The refusal to panic. The way she'd already moved from shock to strategy.

Then, lighter—but no less serious—"First step: we get your nails done."

For the first time all day, my mouth almost curved into a smile. Not because things were okay. But because whatever this had turned into—love, leverage, war—I wasn't walking into it alone.

We left Jenna's apartment ten minutes later.

I noticed the security immediately—too polished to be coincidence, too far back to pretend subtlety. A black sedan idled half a block away, rolling forward when we did. Jenna followed my line of sight.

"Do I need to alert your handler?" she asked lightly, like she was asking whether I wanted oat milk.

"No," I said. "I'm done playing fair."

She smiled at that. Sharp. Pleased.

As we crossed the street, she lifted her hand and gave the car an exaggerated little wave. Even blew a kiss for good measure. The window stayed up. The car slowed.

"He looks confused," she murmured.

"Good," I said.

******

The nail salon smelled like acetone and sugar scrub, the air humming with dryers and quiet conversation. Ordinary. Crowded. Safe in the way only public places could be. We sat side by side, hands soaking, our shoulders almost touching.

Jenna's eyes drifted—just once—over my knuckles, the faint discoloration near my wrist. I felt it the moment her gaze lingered. I didn't pull away.

"I know," I said quietly. She looked at me.

"I can't talk about it," I added. "Not yet."

That was enough. She nodded, immediate and absolute, and didn't look again. "What color?" she asked instead, like she was giving me an out.

I scanned the samples until my fingers closed around one without thinking.

"This," I said.

The technician smiled. "Oxblood?"

"Yes." Dark. Almost black. Red only if the light caught it just right.

Jenna hummed approvingly. "Bold."

"Appropriate," I said.

As the polish went on, layer by careful layer, we talked logistics. Not feelings. Not fear.

Sixty days.

Venue options that wouldn't draw attention. Invitations that were understated, clean, impossible to misinterpret. Who needed to be there. Who absolutely could not. Black and sage-green, we decided. Controlled. Elegant. No softness to mistake for weakness.

My phone buzzed.

Once.
Twice.
Again.

I turned it face-down on the counter.

Jenna didn't comment. She just leaned back in her chair and crossed her arms, watching the reflection in the mirror instead. That's when I saw him.

His car was parked across the street, angled just enough to be deliberate. Lorenzo sat inside, motionless, his gaze fixed on the salon window like he could see straight through the glass.

The oxblood polish gleamed under the dryer, dark and deliberate. I held my hand up and watched it like proof that I still belonged to myself.

It wasn't romantic. It wasn't gentle. It felt honest.

I imagined it against black silk and muted green and felt something settle in my chest. If there was going to be a wedding, it wouldn't be bloodless. I glanced out the window again.

He didn't call.
He didn't come inside.

He just watched.

Fine, if he wanted to see me, he could watch me choosing myself—one small, defiant decision at a time. Jenna's technician finished a moment later. Her blush-pink stiletto nails were flawless—soft, precise, unmistakably *her*. We paid and stepped out into the late afternoon sun.

She pulled me into a tight hug, squeezing like she was trying to remind me I was still solid. Still real.

Then she stepped back, turned, and pointed one long nail directly at Lorenzo. Without breaking eye contact, she dragged it across her throat.

Quick. Clean. Intentional.

Not a threat—*a promise*.

She winked at me, then blew exaggerated kisses toward the security SUV before spinning on her heel and heading for her car. I choked on the laugh rising in my throat. It felt dangerous. Necessary.

Lorenzo had already stepped out of his car, moving automatically to the passenger side, hand reaching for the door.

I stopped. There it was—the choice.

If I got into his car, it would be another quiet surrender. Another step away from myself. From the small, stubborn part of me that still believed I got to decide things. I glanced instead at the SUV I'd arrived in with Jenna.

The guard hesitated, thrown by Jenna's theatrics, but not stupid. He read my face. Threw a careful look toward Lorenzo. Then he jogged around, opened the back door of the SUV, and waited. I slid inside without looking at Lorenzo.

The door shut. Final.

A second later, the engine turned over, and we pulled out of the parking lot—leaving him standing there, watching, as control shifted just enough for me to feel it. Just enough.

We made it back to the penthouse before Lorenzo. I let out a breath I hadn't realized I'd been holding. The guard slowed at the curb, clearly unsure, clearly running through the consequences in his head.

"I'll make sure you don't get in trouble," I said, softer than I'd been all day.

He hesitated—just a flicker of doubt—then nodded and pulled away.

The elevator doors slid shut behind me, sealing off the lobby and the city and the watching eyes. As the car rose, I leaned back against the mirrored wall, grateful for the brief, fragile mercy of being alone.

Just a few minutes.

Enough time to breathe.

Enough time to remember who I was before everything hardened.

Because I could already feel it—the pressure building, the storm gathering. And I knew when Lorenzo arrived, there would be no more quiet.

# *Chapter 14*



**_Lorenzo_**

I stood silently next to my car, the door hanging open in my hand. I watched as my hired security, a man I paid to follow my orders, made a split-second decision of his own. He saw her hesitation, the raw, fractured look in her eyes, and he acted. I watched as Sierra slid into his backseat, her gaze never leaving mine until the car door shut, severing the connection. They pulled away from the curb, leaving me alone on the street. I wasn't sure if I was impressed by his initiative or pissed that he'd just enabled her escape. I settled on a cold, simmering fury.

I got back into the driver's seat, the engine a low, predatory growl as I navigated the city streets. The silence in the car was a physical weight, pressing down on me. My mind replayed the last few hours, the sterile office, the contract amendments, the look on her face when Marco said the word "married."

Then, the word she'd thrown at me like a rock. *Love.*

*You don't love me.*

*I hate you.*

I had told her she didn't need to love me. It was the truth. Love was a liability, a weakness to be exploited.

I'd seen it destroy my father, seen it used as a weapon against my family. It was a fairytale for people who didn't live in the dark. But my chest tightened anyway, a phantom ache from a memory that was still too fresh. Seeing her on that warehouse floor, broken and bleeding… for a moment, the world had ceased to exist.

There was only her, and the terrifying, all-consuming need to get to her. That feeling, that visceral, gut-wrenching terror—that wasn't tactical. It was something else. Something I refused to name.

Love was supposed to be unconditional. Our contract was nothing but conditional. A list of clauses and contingencies. A business arrangement with a body count.

I made a pit stop, pulling up to a small, unassuming Chinese takeout place. I went inside and ordered her favorites—spicy kung pao chicken, steamed dumplings, an extra order of crab rangoon. A peace offering. I knew it would do no good, not yet. It was a pathetic gesture, a bone thrown to a wolf that had already tasted my blood. But I did it anyway.

Back on the road, heading toward the penthouse, the thought solidified in my mind. I would do everything in my physical power to ensure nothing else happened to her. I would burn cities, drain fortunes, and erase men from the earth to keep her safe. I would follow her to the ends of the earth, a silent, lethal shadow. Even if it meant that she never looked at me with anything but hatred and contempt.

I had decided that this was what love was. Not the soft, gentle thing from stories. Not the unconditional sacrifice. Love was a vow. It was a promise of protection, of ownership, of absolute, unwavering devotion, no matter the cost. It was the iron will to keep someone safe, even if you had to become their monster to do it. It was ruthless.

She didn't need to love me back. She just needed to be mine. And she was. I had signed the papers. I had drawn the blood. She was mine, and I would protect what was mine. Always.

******

"Sir, I—" I lifted a hand, cutting him off.

"Your job is to follow her instructions while maintaining proximity," I said calmly. I nodded once. "You made the right call."

I stepped closer, lowered my voice. "But if she changes plans again and I'm not informed, you won't work another day." I didn't wait for a response. He already understood.

Once I reached our floor, I heard it before I ever opened the door. Hard rock. Heavy bass. The kind she never played unless she wanted the world to know she was angry.

I stepped inside.

She was on the living room floor, legs crossed, laptop open in front of her. A notebook lay to one side, pages torn free and scattered like she'd been pacing, thinking, ripping ideas out of herself. Wedding sites glowed on the screen. Dates. Color palettes. Lists.

So that was how she was fighting. I set the bags of food down on the coffee table without a word. She glanced up at me—just a flick of her eyes—but there was nothing soft there. No curiosity. Just heat. Anger sharpened into purpose.

I didn't speak.

I turned and went to my office. The door closed quietly behind me.

I sat, logged in, and pulled up the camera feeds. Every angle. Every room. She moved across the screen, focused, efficient, furious. Leaning back, I watched her plan the war I'd dragged her into.

******

I learned quickly that having her was not the same as keeping her.

The first morning, she told me she needed to meet with a florist. She didn't ask if I was coming. She didn't look at me when she said it. Just stood at the kitchen island, scrolling through her phone, hair twisted up like she didn't expect anyone to touch it.

"I'll have the car ready," I said.

278

She paused. A fraction of a second. Then, "I already called one."

I smiled anyway. "Cancel it."

She did not argue. That was new. She simply tapped the screen, set her phone down, and walked past me toward the bedroom to change. No thank you. No glance back.

I followed her to the florist on Fifth. I stayed a step behind, silent, my presence an invisible weight at her back. The woman arranging samples looked between us with bright, hopeful eyes.

"Wedding?" she asked.

"Yes," Sierra said flatly.

I watched her hands while she spoke—how they moved with purpose, how she touched the flowers like they were enemies she intended to defeat. She chose dark blooms. Burgundy. Nearly black. Roses stripped of softness. The florist hesitated.

"They're a bit… intense," she offered.

"That's fine," Sierra said. "So is the marriage." I felt it then, sharp and unwelcome: pride.

In the car afterward, she stared out the window. I stared at her reflection in the glass. When I reached over to adjust the air, she flinched. Just barely. Enough that it lodged under my ribs.

That night, she worked at the dining table. Guest lists. Seating charts. She crossed out names with vicious strokes. I sat across from her, pretending to read reports, watching the set of her jaw.

"You don't have to hover," she said without looking up.

"I'm not."

She finally lifted her eyes. They were cold. Assessing. "You always are."

I didn't correct her.

The next day it was a tailor. She disappeared into the fitting room while I waited outside, arms crossed, jaw tight. When she stepped out in a half-finished dress, white fabric clinging to her like a lie, the air left my lungs.

She didn't look at me. She looked at the mirror. Turned. Adjusted the strap herself.

"Do you like it?" the seamstress asked.

"Yes," Sierra said. "It'll do."

I didn't speak. If I opened my mouth, something unmanageable would come out. On the drive home, my phone buzzed. Marco. I ignored it. Then again. And again.

Back at home, she closed herself in the bedroom. No doubt to talk to Jenna, as if the walls between us could stop me from listening. She stayed in there nearly all night. She didn't even come out when Marco's sharp knock sounded throughout the quiet space.

"You're unraveling," Marco said, standing in my office, arms crossed. "You've doubled security, tripled surveillance, and you're following her like—"

"Watch your mouth."

"She's not a package," he snapped. "She's a person. And you're losing sight of Alessio."

I said nothing.

"You should end the contract," he continued. "Let her go."

The idea hit me like a physical blow. Let her go. As if she hadn't already slipped through my fingers while standing three feet away.

"She's mine," I said quietly.

Marco stared at me for a long moment. "That's the problem." He pinched the bridge of his nose, I sighed heavily.

"Fine, I'll…" I hesitated, barely. "I'll refocus. I'll pull back." That lie seemed to smooth the lines on his face. It was enough to get him out the door.

Despite her body only laying inches from me, the nights were cold and restless. Marco was right. I was losing everything that wasn't her.

By the fifth day, I had managed not to follow so closely. She needed to go back to the florist and refused being in the same car as me. She walked the city, earbuds in, sunglasses on. I followed at a distance, driving when she moved, blending into traffic when she didn't. On her way back, she stopped at the café I had taken her to for brunch.

I watched a man smile at her as she left, holding the door open for her. Watched him step closer as she walked away. Watched him reach for her as she shook her head.

I was out of the car before I thought about it.

The sound of bone breaking was loud. Satisfying. Final.

Sierra didn't scream. She didn't cry. She just stared at me like I'd confirmed something she already knew.

"Get back in the car," she said. We drove home in silence.

The penthouse was a cage of glass and steel, and I could feel her fury from across the room. She stood by the floor-to-ceiling windows, a silhouette against the glittering city, her posture radiating a cold, barely contained rage. She'd been quiet since she came home, the silence a weapon she was sharpening. I knew what was coming. I'd been waiting for it.

It wasn't forgiveness. It wasn't forgiveness. It wasn't peace. It was violence with a pulse.

She turned, her eyes finding mine in the dim light. "You broke his nose." It wasn't a question. It was an accusation, a verdict.

I didn't move from my position on the couch. "He touched you."

"He flirted," she shot back, her voice tight. "He was an idiot. You didn't have to… you didn't have to do that."

"He put his hands on what's mine." My voice was flat, a statement of fact. I wasn't going to apologize for it. I'd do it again in a heartbeat.

Her chest rose and fell with a sharp, angry breath. "You're always watching me. Following me. I can't even walk down the street without you lurking in the shadows."

I still didn't deny it. I let the truth hang between us, thick and suffocating. "And you haven't stopped me."

That was it. The spark that lit the fuse. Her face crumpled, the anger giving way to a raw, wounded fury. "I hate you," she whispered, the words trembling with a violence that promised more. "I hate you so much."

I stood then, my body responding to the challenge in her voice. I crossed the room, closing the distance until I was standing in front of her, close enough to feel the heat radiating from her skin.

"Show me," I said, my voice a low, dangerous rumble. "Show me how much you hate me."

Her eyes widened, a flash of shock in their depths before they hardened again. And then she moved. She didn't slap me. She didn't scream. She launched herself at me, her hands fisting in my shirt, her body crashing against mine. Her mouth found mine, and it wasn't a kiss. It was an attack. All teeth and fury, a desperate, angry clash that was meant to wound.

I let her. I stood there and took it, my hands hanging loosely at my sides as she poured all of her rage, her fear, her frustration into me. She tore at my shirt, sending buttons flying, her nails raking down my chest. The sting was sharp, a welcome pain. She was trying to mark me, to hurt me, to make me feel even a fraction of what she was feeling.

She shoved me back, and I let myself stumble, my legs hitting the back of the couch. I fell into a sitting position, and she was on me in an instant, straddling my lap. Her hands were everywhere, tearing at my belt, at the zipper of my trousers. She was a storm, a beautiful, destructive force, and I was the ground she was determined to break apart.

She freed me, her hand wrapping around my cock, her grip almost punishing. I groaned, my head falling back against the couch as she began to stroke me, her movements hard, fast, and completely devoid of any gentleness. This wasn't about pleasure. This was about punishment. Hers and mine.

She rose up on her knees, positioning herself over me, and then she slammed down, taking me in one hard, brutal thrust. We both cried out, a shared, guttural sound of pure, unadulterated aggression. She set a punishing rhythm, her movements wild and unrestrained. She rode me like she was trying to erase herself, to fuck the memory of me, of the florist, of the entire world, out of her system.

I watched her, my hands gripping her hips, not to guide her, but to hold on, to anchor myself in the hurricane of her fury. Her head was thrown back, her hair a wild tangle around her face, her breasts bouncing with each powerful movement. She was magnificent, terrifying, and more alive than I had ever seen her.

"Is this what you wanted?" she panted, her eyes burning into mine. "Is this what you get off on? My hate?"

I didn't answer. I just watched her, my gaze unwavering, letting her see the truth in my eyes. Yes. Yes, it was. I wanted all of her. Her fire, her passion, her pain, her hate. I wanted it all.

She leaned forward, her mouth finding my neck, her teeth sinking into my skin, hard enough to leave a mark. I hissed, my hips bucking up to meet her, my control finally starting to fray. I could feel myself getting closer, the tension coiling tighter and tighter, a spring ready to snap.

With a final, desperate cry, she came, her body convulsing, her inner muscles clenching around me in a way that pulled my own orgasm from me, a brutal, all-consuming wave that left me shaking and breathless.

She collapsed against me, her body trembling, her face buried in my neck. For a long moment, we just sat there, the only sound in the room was our ragged breaths. Then, she pushed herself up, her movements slow, heavy. She climbed off me, her expression unreadable, and walked away toward the bathroom without a backward glance.

I sat there, my shirt ripped, my body aching, her bite mark throbbing on my neck. I could still taste her fury on my lips. And I knew, with a chilling certainty, that I had never wanted anything more.

I lay awake long after she fell asleep, staring at the ceiling, my own words closing in around me.

She didn't need to love me.

But loving her, I was beginning to understand, would be catastrophic

# Chapter 16

**_Sierra_**

Nothing fit.

That was the problem the attendant kept trying to solve, adjusting straps, pinning fabric, stepping back with hopeful eyes like the right angle might suddenly make this feel like a choice instead of a sentence.

I stood on the small pedestal in my underwear while mirrors fractured me into versions I didn't recognize. White silk. White lace. White crepe. All of it looked like someone else's life draped over my body.

Jenna sat on the couch, legs crossed, coffee balanced on her knee. She was quiet in the way that meant she was watching me, not the dresses.

"Do you hate it," she asked gently, "or do you hate… everything?"

I huffed a breath that wasn't quite a laugh. "Is there a third option?"

The attendant smiled too brightly. "We can try something with sleeves? Or a higher neckline?"

"Sure," I said, because it didn't matter. I stepped back into the dressing room. The curtain swished closed, cutting off the mirrors. I leaned my forehead against the wall for a second longer than necessary.

My phone buzzed.

Unknown number.

I stared at it. Let it ring out. It buzzed again, immediately.

Still unknown.

I silenced it and dropped it into my bag like it might bite me. When I stepped back out, the attendant was waiting, a different dress draped over her arm.

Jenna cleared her throat. "So," she said carefully, eyes still on me in the mirror. "You look like someone who hadn't slept well."

I met her gaze. Held it. "We didn't," I said.

Her eyebrow lifted a fraction. "Fighting or…?"

"Yes."

That got a huff of a laugh out of her. "That bad?"

"He watched me like I was already gone," I said. "And I let him touch me like I hated him for it."

Jenna exhaled slowly. "Jesus, Si."

"I know," I murmured. "It didn't fix anything."

"No," she agreed. "It never does."

The attendant reappeared then, smiling, hands full of another white dress—perfect timing, as always. "Someone called for you," she said. "They asked for you by name."

"I'm not taking calls," I said automatically.

She hesitated. "They called the shop phone." My stomach tightened.

Jenna's head snapped up. "Who?"

The attendant glanced down at the receiver in her hand, lowering her voice as if the dresses might overhear. "She said she was your mother."

The room tilted—not violently, just enough to make everything feel slightly off-center. Like a picture knocked crooked on the wall.

"I didn't tell her where I was," I said.

"She just said that it was important," the attendant replied. Of course she did.

I took the phone. It was heavier than my own, tethered by a cord I suddenly resented. "Hello," I said.

"Sierra." My mother's voice was warm. Careful. Tuned to the exact frequency of concern. "Thank God. I was starting to worry."

I closed my eyes. "I'm fine."

"We heard about Matteo," she said, and there it was—the name slipping into the room like smoke. "What happened was… horrific. We wanted to make sure you were safe."

Jenna was watching me now, her expression unreadable.

"I am," I repeated. "How did you know I would be here?"

A pause. Calculated. "Your father and I were hoping we could have dinner. Just us. We'd like to see you. Talk. Make sure you're being taken care of."

I pictured my parents' dining room. The long table. The way conversations there always felt like negotiations dressed up as concern. "You didn't answer my question," I said. "Besides, I was busy."

"Of course," my mother replied quickly. Too quickly. "We understand. But maybe tomorrow? Or the next day? We're family, Sierra."

Family. The word landed wrong. Heavy.

"We've been so worried," she continued softly. "Everything has happened so fast. An engagement, a tragedy… We just want to check on you."

I opened my eyes and caught my reflection in the mirror across the room—half-dressed, half-undone, wrapped in white that didn't belong to me. "I'll think about it," I said.

"That's all we're asking," she said, relief threading through her voice. "We love you." The line went dead. Of course, when all else failed, my mother relied on emotional blackmail.

I handed the phone back to the attendant without a word. She smiled politely and retreated.

Jenna stood. "That was… unexpected."

"Was it?" I asked.

She studied me. "Do you want to go?"

I looked down at the dress still pinned to my body. I looked at the mirror. At the version of myself that looked like a decision someone else had already made.

"I don't know."

Outside the dressing room, the shop hummed with soft music and hushed excitement. Somewhere, someone laughed about cake flavors. About flowers. My phone vibrated in my bag again. This time, I didn't check it.

I had the distinct, unsettling feeling that whatever my parents wanted to say to me over dinner had nothing to do with my safety—but everything to do with who they thought I belonged to.

******

Lorenzo watched me the entire time I got dressed, sharp and unblinking. His expression stayed cold, distant, as if proximity were a concession he hadn't agreed to. He asked questions the way men asked them when they already assumed guilt.

Where were we going.
Why was I going.
Who would be there.
What was the purpose.

We both knew the concerned-parent routine was a façade. The difference was that I still had to see mine through. I needed to understand. Matteo was dead, and with him the excuse that everything had been done for my protection. Now I had to know why they had put me in that position in the first place—and how.

I didn't explain that to Lorenzo. I didn't explain anything. But the thought followed me as I fastened earrings and smoothed fabric into place: if I had never been pushed toward Matteo, would Lorenzo and I have ever crossed paths at all?

It was time for answers. Whether he believed it or not, there were still choices I needed to make. And they were mine. Naturally, he insisted on going with me. I refused. He tried to be the one to drop me off. I refused again.

Alexio was back, and I trusted him. I felt safe with him.

Something flickered in Lorenzo's eyes at that—brief, sharp, gone almost before I could catch it. Then he relented, at least on the surface.

Our joke about him being my stalker was starting to feel less like humor and more like prophecy. He was everywhere. And even with my explicit instructions to stay away, I knew he wouldn't be far tonight.

The car pulled to a stop in front of an older brick-and-stone building. We had settled on a private restaurant, somewhere neutral. It was only dinner with my parents, so why did it feel like stepping onto the front lines?

There was no sign. No awning. Just a single iron-framed door set back from the street, its glass dark enough to reflect my own silhouette back at me. Controlled. Composed. Armored.

Alexio opened my door and I stepped out, taking a deep breath. Inside, the air changed—cooler, quieter, perfumed with citrus and something sharp beneath it. A host stood waiting as if he'd been positioned there for me alone.

"Sierra," he said, already smiling. Not a question.

I nodded once. No correction. No hesitation.

"Your table is ready."

He didn't take my coat. He didn't ask if I preferred the bar. He turned and led me through the dining room as though I already belonged to it.

La Verrière unfolded in glass and iron, candlelight fracturing across pane after pane until it was impossible to tell where one reflection ended and another began. Every table was discreetly spaced, every conversation muted, every diner carefully pretending not to notice anyone else. Privacy, curated.

I spotted my parents before I reached them. Of course I did. My mother sat perfectly straight, hands folded atop the table, pearls catching the light. My father leaned back in his chair, composed, surveying the room like a man who liked to know where the exits were.

They saw me at the same time.

My mother's smile bloomed first—relief, affection, calculation braided together so tightly it was hard to separate them. My father stood, just slightly, enough to signal courtesy without surrender.

There it was. The opening move.

I crossed the remaining distance, heels striking stone in steady, measured beats. Each step felt deliberate.

Not a daughter arriving late. A negotiator entering the room.

"We're so glad you could make time for us, darling," my mother said, her voice sugared to the point of nausea. She reached across the table, her hand cool and insubstantial as it settled over mine. "We've missed you."

I resisted the urge to pull away. "It's good to see you both."

My father, who had never wasted words where leverage would do, leaned back in his chair. "This situation with Lorenzo Moretti," he said, "has become complicated."

I let the silence stretch. Complicated was one word for it. Blood-soaked was another.

"We're worried about you, Sierra," my mother continued, eyes wide with a concern polished to perfection. "Your association with the Morettis has placed you in a very precarious position. There are people who are… displeased. People who remember old obligations."

The phrase landed like a blade between my ribs.

"Old obligations," I repeated quietly.

My father nodded once. "Debts," he said. "The kind that don't disappear just because time passes." The room seemed to tilt. Not violently—just enough for everything to slide into alignment.

An old friend of the family, they had said once. A powerful ally. A union that would secure our future. Matteo hadn't been chosen for love, or even strategy. He had been chosen because he was convenient. Because he was owed. The engagement hadn't been an alliance.

It had been payment.

"An old friend has reached out," my father continued. "Alessio Rinaldi is willing to be… generous, given recent events. He understands that loyalties can become confused. He is prepared to offer you protection. Permanently."

I stared at them as the truth finished assembling itself, piece by horrifying piece. Matteo had been the first offering. A son to settle a balance sheet written in blood. And now that son was dead. So they were sending the debt to the father.

This wasn't a dinner. It was a negotiation. My parents weren't worried—they were brokers, acting on behalf of Alessio Rinaldi. The man who had ordered the hit that killed Lorenzo's parents.

The man they had already paid once with my body and my future. They were trying to pay him again.

"I'm not discussing my relationship with Lorenzo," I said, my voice going flat. Hard.

My father's smile vanished. "You will show respect. This is a generous offer. Alessio Rinaldi is not a man who extends mercy lightly." They said his name without flinching. As if he were a banker. A benefactor. Not the architect of half the violence that had shaped my life.

I thought of Lorenzo—watchful, obsessive, relentless. He had bound me to him with force and fire, but never with lies. He didn't pretend I was free while tightening the leash. He didn't dress ownership up as protection. My parents did. With them, it was always velvet gloves and knives in the seams. I wasn't a daughter. I was currency. A ledger entry passed from one powerful man to another. Lorenzo wanted to possess me. They wanted to dispose of me.

The difference mattered.

"No," I said. The word felt solid. Final.

My mother's face tightened. "Sierra, don't be foolish. This is for your own good."

"Is it?" I asked, my eyes locking on my father. "Was it for my own good when you gave me to Matteo to settle a debt you owed Alessio Rinaldi? When you dressed it up as a prestigious match and told me it was my duty?"

My father's face darkened. "Watch your tone."

"No," I said again. "You don't get to correct me now."

His voice dropped, dangerous. "You will tell us what you know about the Morettis. Their operations. Their weaknesses. It's the only way to prove where your loyalty lies."

"I won't," I said, pushing my chair back. The scrape echoed too loudly in the sudden quiet. "Not a single word."

His hand came down on the table, silverware rattling. "You ungrateful little bitch. You are our daughter."

"I was," I said, my voice shaking with a cold, furious clarity. "Until you decided I was easier to trade than to protect. First to Matteo. Now to his father. You don't get to use that word anymore."

I stood, turning to leave. My father's voice, sharp as glass, stopped me at the edge of the table. "Be careful, Sierra. The Moretti name is a target. You might just get caught in the crossfire. It would be a shame for something to happen to that pretty face of yours. Again. Alessio is not a man who appreciates being denied what he's been offered."

The words hung in the air, a venomous promise. My hand froze on the back of my chair. My mother's face was a mask of sickly satisfaction, my father's a rigid mask of authority. They thought they had me cornered, that the threat of Alessio Rinaldi was a chain I couldn't break. That's when the restaurant's heavy door swung open, and the ambient chatter seemed to die. Lorenzo walked in.

He wasn't just dressed; he was armed in Italian wool and bespoke fury. His suit was a charcoal gray that seemed to absorb the light, his shirt a stark, severe white. Every line of him was a threat, from the cold glint of his signet ring to the dangerous stillness in his posture. He moved with an unnerving grace, his eyes finding me instantly, a flicker of something unreadable in their depths before they slid to my parents.

He stopped beside my chair, his presence immediate and oppressive, like the air had learned to fear him. He didn't look at me, but slid one arm around my waist—steady, possessive. A claim made without ceremony.

His gaze fixed on my father. Blank. Assessing. His voice was low enough that it barely carried past the table, yet it cut through the silence with surgical precision.

"You threaten her like you've forgotten how easy it would be for me to kill you."

The room seemed to lose its breath. My parents stared at him as if he had stepped out of thin air, their composure cracking just enough to reveal confusion beneath the polish. Lorenzo shifted, releasing me. He took one measured step forward and extended his hand to my father.

The handshake was firm. Civil. To anyone watching, it would have looked like nothing more than a courteous greeting between two men. Up close, it was something else entirely.

"You talk about crossfire," Lorenzo said quietly, his mouth near my father's ear, "as if you're not standing in the kill zone. She is the only reason you're still breathing. Don't give me a reason to reconsider."

My father's jaw tightened. He didn't pull away. Lorenzo released him first.

He turned back to me then, finally meeting my eyes. Whatever fury lived beneath his skin was locked down, controlled, reserved for later. He slid his hand back to my waist, grounding, unmistakable.

"We're leaving," he said. Not a question.

I didn't look at my parents as we stepped away from the table. I didn't need to. I could feel their silence behind us, thick with humiliation and something darker—fear, finally catching up.

The restaurant parted around us as we moved toward the door. Conversations resumed too loudly, chairs scraped, glasses clinked. Everyone oblivious as if something irrevocable hadn't just happened.

At the threshold, Lorenzo paused just long enough to glance back—not at my mother, not at the room, but at my father alone. The look promised an ending.

Then we were outside, the heavy door closing behind us, sealing the threat inside and letting the night rush in like relief.

<h1 style="text-align:center">Chapter 17</h1>

Lorenzo

The penthouse was dark when we stepped inside, the city spread beneath the windows like a field of quiet embers. I locked the door behind us out of habit, not necessity. Anyone who wanted to come for her wouldn't knock.

She slipped out of her heels first, careful, unhurried. No shaking hands. No tears. That mattered. It told me she was still mentally where I needed her—present, aware.

I watched her from across the room as she crossed to the bar and poured herself a drink she didn't offer to me. She leaned back against the counter, glass cradled in both hands, and finally looked at me.

Not guarded. Not afraid. Listening.

"I meant what I said," I told her.

She didn't pretend not to understand. "I know." I moved closer, slow enough not to crowd her. I needed her to hear this, not feel cornered by it.

"If your father threatens you again," I continued, "if he puts a hand on you, if he tries to move you toward

Alessio—if I even believe he's considering it—I will kill him."

No heat. No emphasis. Just fact.

She inhaled once, steady. Her eyes didn't drop. "And my mother?" she asked.

I didn't hesitate. "She won't survive him." That earned a flicker of something in her expression—not shock. Recognition. The moment where people realized the edge they were standing on was real.

"I'm not saying this to frighten you," I said. "I'm saying it because you deserve to know where the lines have been drawn."

She turned then, really looked at me. Not measuring distance—measuring truth.

"You weren't trying to scare them," she said.

"No."

"You were setting a boundary."

"Yes."

She nodded once. Like something clicked into place.

"I think," she said slowly, "I'm starting to understand the difference."

I waited.

"They use fear to move people," she continued. "You use certainty."

I didn't correct her. She set her glass down and crossed the space between us herself. Stopped close, but not touching. Choice, not gravity.

"You don't want to decide for me," she said. "You want to make sure no one else does." That was close enough to the truth that I let it stand.

I reached out then—not to pull her in, just to rest my hand at her waist. Steady. Present.

"You should know," I said quietly, "that I don't bluff."

She met my eyes. Held them. "I know," she said again. This time it meant something different. She rested her hand on my chest, not asking, not yielding.

The silence after that wasn't empty. It was aligned. And for the first time in days, neither of us was circling. We were standing on the same ground. I let my lips brush against her forehead before watching her walk away to get ready for bed.

******

The next morning I worked with the door closed. Not for secrecy. For focus.

My desk was littered with fragments of Alessio Rinaldi—flight manifests, stills pulled from security feeds, grainy photos taken from angles meant to stay unnoticed. Marco's notes were blunt. Emil's were precise. Together, they told the same story. Alessio wasn't in the States anymore.

One screen showed him moving through a private terminal, coat draped over his arm, face turned slightly away from the camera. The timestamp blinked in the corner. Thirty minutes ago. Destination codes scrolled beneath the image.

Sicily. Running wasn't the right word. Alessio didn't run. He repositioned.

The plan to kill him had existed since the year my parents were put in the ground. Last night hadn't created it, but it had removed any remaining patience.

I leaned back, eyes lifting to the wall of monitors. Most tracked Alessio's network—cars, couriers, men who mistook anonymity for safety.

One screen was different.

Jenna's car idled at the curb. The boutique windows glowed softly against the early evening dark. Ivory & Silk. Third appointment. Sierra would be inside, pretending this was about lace and silhouettes instead of armor.

Her location pulsed steadily on the map.

Another feed refreshed. Same street. Opposite side.

A man stepped into frame, pausing just long enough to check his phone before looking up—too casually, too deliberately. I recognized him immediately. Alessio's courier. Not important enough to know, valuable enough to send.

My jaw tightened as I stood. My phone vibrated against the desk. Marco.

"He's airborne," Marco said. "Private charter. Heading for Sicily."

"I know," I replied.

A beat. "You seeing what I'm seeing?"

"Yes."

"Family office," Marco said. No hesitation. "Now."

"I'm leaving," I said, already moving.

I shut down the monitors one by one—Alessio's routes, his men, the flight path arcing east over black water.

I left hers on. Her dot remained steady, unaware of how close the line had been drawn. This wasn't a message. It was a mistake.

And mistakes were fatal.

******

The restaurant was too bright for the conversation we were having. Sunlight spilled across the table, catching on the rim of Jenna's glass, the edge of her fork. The place felt exposed, all white surfaces and open windows, like nothing ugly was supposed to be said here.

"So," Jenna said, breaking into her eggs. "How did it actually go last night?"

I let out a breath through my nose. "They didn't pretend this time."

Her gaze sharpened. "And?"

"And they framed it as concern." I shrugged. "They said they were worried about the kind of danger I was inviting into my life. About who I'd aligned myself with."

Jenna snorted quietly. "That's rich."

"They asked if I felt protected," I continued. "If I was sure I knew what kind of man I was getting married to."

Jenna leaned back. "Did Lorenzo go with you?"

"No." I shook my head. "I had Alexio drive me."

Her brows knit together. "But let me guess, he still showed up."

"Yes." The word landed heavier than it should have.

"He didn't ask what they'd said to me," I said. "He already knew. He always knows."

Jenna was quiet for a moment. "That should scare you."

"I know."

"But it didn't," she pinched the bridge of her nose, sighing loudly.

I looked down at my plate. Pushed a piece of toast I hadn't touched. "No."

She waited.

"The last thing my father said was about me being in the crossfire," I said slowly, "That's when he appeared. He didn't raise his voice." I swallowed.

"He told them that my safety was the only thing keeping him alive."

Jenna's hand stilled. "Jesus, Sierra." Her eyes were wide with shock.

"It wasn't a threat," I said. "But it wasn't a promise." I met her eyes.

"It was a vow." The silence stretched.

"And how did that make you feel?" Jenna asked carefully.

I hesitated. Not because I didn't know — because saying it felt like crossing something. "It didn't scare me like it should have," I said.

Jenna didn't flinch. That almost made it worse.

"I liked that he didn't ask me what I wanted," I continued. "Not because he was taking control — but because he already knew. Because my safety wasn't negotiable to him."

"That's obsession," Jenna said quietly.

"I know."

"And that didn't bother you?"

"It did," I said. "After. Later."

"But in the moment," she pressed.

"In the moment, it felt like someone finally drew a line and meant it."

Jenna studied me. "Do you love him?"

The question settled low in my chest. "I don't know," I said honestly. "But I know this isn't just about being protected anymore."

She nodded once. "Are you afraid of him?"

"No."

"Then what are you afraid of?"

I thought about the way he'd stood beside me. The certainty. The calm.

That I'm starting to understand him," I said. "And I can feel myself meeting him halfway."

Jenna reached across the table, covering my hand. Her grip was steady. "Just promise me one thing," she said.

"What?"

"That you don't lie to yourself about what this is."

I squeezed her fingers once. "I won't." Outside, the city moved on. Inside, something had already shifted — and there was no undoing it.

******

We walked to Ivory & Silk after brunch. Jenna joked with the bridal attendant that the third time was the charm. They'd called earlier, saying they'd found something in storage—something that might finally be what we were looking for.

Soft, but dangerous. Sharp. Confident.

She led us to a private dressing room with velvet couches and a three-panel mirror that showed every angle. No flattering tricks. No hiding.

I stepped behind the curtain and pulled it shut. Slipped out of my clothes, laid them carefully across the chair, and unzipped the black garment bag.

A small gasp escaped before I could stop it.

Ivory first—clean, structured. The skirt fell in a smooth, uninterrupted line, heavy enough that it barely moved when I shifted the hanger. Restrained. Almost obedient. The kind of well-behaved dress that didn't reveal its teeth right away.

Then the black lace came into focus. It wasn't soft. It wasn't romantic. The pattern was bold and deliberate, laid over the ivory like something claimed rather than adorned. Flowers, yes—but sharp-edged ones. Intentional. Meant to be seen, not admired.

The bodice held its shape without a body inside it. Boning. Control. It didn't sag or apologize. It looked like it expected a spine strong enough to meet it.

I stepped into it slowly, gathering the skirt as I slid my feet through. The lining was cool against my skin, smooth and substantial. When I pulled it up, it didn't flutter or whisper—it fell into place, decisive, like it already knew where it belonged.

The bodice required intention. I fastened the inner clasps, feeling the structure guide me upright. My shoulders rolled back without permission. My spine straightened.

The attendant slipped in behind me, quiet and focused. I lifted my hair automatically, exposing my neck. Vulnerable. Unprotected. The zipper slid upward in one smooth pull. Final.

When I stepped out from behind the curtain, the room went still.

I walked to the center of the room, the skirt moving around my legs with controlled restraint—nothing playful, nothing forgiving. The mirror caught me from every angle.

The mirror didn't soften me.

No romantic haze. No illusion of becoming someone gentler. The woman staring back at me was sharp. Awake. Unsheltered. The dress didn't disguise it—it frames it.

Ivory beneath. Structured. Almost severe. A body built to carry weight.

And the black lace—

It climbed over me like a confession. Thorns and shadow, unapologetic. Not an accent. A declaration. It darkened the white without asking permission, turning something ceremonial into something edged.

For the first time all day, my chest loosened.

This dress didn't feel like a lie.

Behind me, Jenna made a sound—soft, startled. "Oh."

I don't look at her right away. I was afraid if I did, the spell would break. That she'd say something practical or cautious or kind in the wrong way.

Instead, I lifted my chin. Studying the way the lace cut across my ribs. The neckline that refused sweetness. The reflection that didn't ask me to pretend I'm untouched.

"This is…" Jenna trailed off, then laughed quietly, almost in disbelief. "This is the one."

"You did say the third time's the charm," I murmured.

"I know." She stepped closer, eyes flicking between my reflection and my face. "But you look like yourself. This isn't the version everyone expects. This is the real one."

The attendant had gone very still. Her professional smile faltered slightly as she circled me, hands hovering just off the fabric.

"It's beautiful," she was choosing her words carefully. Then, after a pause—soft, certain—

"And dangerous."

The word settled low in my stomach.

Not wrong.
Not ruined.
Not too much.

I curled my fingers into the fabric at my waist. "That's okay," I said quietly. "I don't need it to be safe."

Jenna met my eyes in the mirror. There was worry there—but threaded with recognition.

"Yeah," she said softly. "I didn't think you did."

I turned back to the reflection. To the woman who knew what she was choosing. Who understands the cost and was ready to step forward anyway.

This dress didn't promise forever. It promised truth. And for me, that was enough.

***

A quick swipe of my card and a few hugs with Jenna, and it was done. Alexio picked me up and brought me back to the penthouse.

Lorenzo and I had started taking steps in a better direction. Baby steps—but still steps. Careful ones. Measured. Toward something that almost felt like peace if I didn't look at it too closely.

He'd been working in his office when I left, so I didn't bother him when I got back. I showered, letting the heat rinse away mirrors and lace and too many truths, then pulled on black leggings and an oversized tee. Something comfortable, neutral.

The penthouse was quiet.

Not the usual quiet—the kind that existed because Lorenzo was somewhere nearby, aware, listening. This was hollow. Empty. As if the space itself was holding its breath. I padded down the hall and called his name softly.

Not because I was worried about startling him—Lorenzo Moretti didn't startle—but because the silence had begun to itch. No answer.

The office door was slightly ajar. That stopped me cold. He never left it open.

I knocked once, gently. "Lorenzo?" Nothing.

Concern slid into my stomach, heavy and unwelcome. I pushed the door open and stepped inside. The click of it closing behind me sounded louder than it should have.

His office was cold. Not just in temperature, but in intention. Dark wood. Steel accents. Everything was precise. Aligned. Disciplined. There was no clutter, no softness. No evidence of anything human lingering too long. It felt like stepping into a vault.

I exhaled a quiet laugh, trying to shake the creeping unease. This was it? This was the mystery? Men and their sanctuaries.

Still, I moved farther in.

The bookshelves were lined with binders—black, gray, navy—each one labeled in his sharp, angular handwriting. Dates. Locations. Names. Everything was categorized like an archive.

His desk was immaculate. Laptop closed. Pens aligned. A neat stack of folders rested at one corner, except the top one was slightly crooked. Barely. Enough to notice.

That's when I felt it.

The sensation of being watched. I turned slowly. The far wall was black—too black. Matte and seamless except for a faint glow in the corner.

I stepped closer. My breath left me all at once.

Monitors. Dozens of them. A wall of screens stacked and tiled, some dark, some dim, one still fully lit. The front entrance of Ivory & Silk. Jenna and me, earlier that afternoon. Laughing. Unaware.

My stomach dropped. "What the fuck," I whispered.

I backed up instinctively, my hip slamming into his desk. The impact sent the folders tumbling to the floor, paper scattering like startled birds.

"Fuck."

My heart was pounding so hard it hurt. I crouched quickly, hands shaking as I gathered the papers. I just needed to put them back. Leave. Forget.

Then I saw the names.

*Cole, Jenna*
*Marcello, Giovanni*
*Blackwell, Charles*
*Rinaldi, Matteo*
*Blackwell, Sierra*

My name stared back at me in Lorenzo's handwriting. This wasn't work. These were dossiers. The room tilted. I stood slowly, pulse roaring in my ears. I dropped the stack onto the desk—except one.

Mine. My fingers felt numb as I opened it.

Photographs slid free. Grainy stills pulled from security footage. Polaroids. Screenshots from social media. Me walking down the street. Me sitting at a café. Me laughing with Jenna.

Moments I didn't remember consenting to.

Some of the dates made my vision blur. They were before we met. Before the accidental collision in the dress shop. Before the contract. Before *everything*.

The edges of the desk dug into my palms as I leaned forward, fighting the sudden urge to vomit. Taped to the back of the folder was a flash drive.

Just numbers written in marker. I stared at them until my brain caught up. The yacht party. The night Matteo almost killed me.

"No," I breathed. I opened Lorenzo's laptop. No password.

That hurt worse than anything else. The monitors flickered to life, flooding the room with cold light as I plugged in the drive. Every screen reflected me back at myself—small, pale, trapped in a room that suddenly felt too tight.

One file appeared. A video.

I double-clicked.

The screen filled abruptly.

A high-angle view of the warehouse. The dock lights flickering. The metal door shrieking as it rolled open, the sound sharp enough to make my teeth ache. Matteo's shoes on concrete—slow, unhurried. Like he had all the time in the world.

The camera followed as he dragged me into frame. My body went limp the way it does when panic outruns strength. I watched myself shoved into the chair, watched my wrists disappear into restraints. Too tight. Too final.

Then my head snapped sideways. The crack of skin on skin was loud in the quiet office.

I gasped, fingers flying to my cheek, breath stuttering as my body reacted before my mind could catch up. My pulse hammered in my ears, drowning out everything but the echo of that sound.

Matteo laughed. The noise crawled up my spine—wrong, delighted, intimate.

That stupid switchblade appeared in his hand, flashing once under the lights as he toyed with it. Close enough to see the edge. Close enough to remember the cold.

My scream tore out of the speakers, raw and breaking, filling the room until it felt like the walls were vibrating with it.

"SIERRA."

My name cut through the sound like a gunshot.

I spun. Lorenzo stood in the doorway.

His face was stripped bare—rage, fear, something violent and unguarded colliding in his eyes—as the footage continued to play behind me, my screams echoing between us.

And suddenly, there was no air left in the room.

***

***Lorenzo***

I knew the second I heard her scream.

Not the one coming from the monitors—the one ripped out of her in my office, sharp and real and close enough to split me open.

I was in the hallway before I thought. In the doorway before I decided.

The room was flooded with light and sound. Her past alive on the walls. Her pain echoing between us. She stood there shaking, hand pressed to her face like she could hold herself together if she just didn't move.

I had done this. I took a step forward and felt something in me fracture.

"I was supposed to be watching him," I said, and my voice betrayed me, rougher than I'd ever allowed it to be. "That was the job. Matteo Rinaldi. His movements. His temper. His patterns. I was hunting the man who ordered my parents' deaths."

Her shoulders tensed.

"I needed proof," I continued, words spilling now, too fast, too honest. "I needed to know who he answered to. Who protected him. Who gave the order. He was the thread. You were never supposed to be part of it."

I swallowed hard.

"But then there was you."

My chest ached. I pressed a hand to it without realizing it, like it might cave in if I didn't.

"I saw you before the dress shop," I admitted. "I saw you laughing with Jenna. Walking. Living. And something in me shifted. I told myself it was strategic. Proximity. Access. A way in."

It was a lie.

"I kept the cameras on Matteo," I said hoarsely. "I did. I watched him. But every time you were on a screen, my eyes went to you. Every time I had to choose, I chose you."

The word cracked.

"I wasn't watching you to control you," I said, desperation edging in now. "I was watching because I was afraid. Because if I looked away, something would happen. Because the one time I wasn't watching—"

My gaze flicked to the screens behind her. To the frozen image of her tied to that chair.

"—he got to you."

The room felt too small. I dropped to my knees before her, the motion sudden, instinctive, unguarded. The sound of it hit the floor hard.

"I failed you," I said simply.

I pulled my gun from my jacket and placed it on the floor. Then my knife. Then my phone. Everything that made me dangerous. Everything that made me me.

"My life," I said, looking up at her now, my vision blurring for the first time in years. "Or my death. I don't get to choose anymore. You do."

I bowed my head.

"If you tell me to leave, I will. If you tell me to stay, I will spend the rest of my life making this right. If you tell me to kill myself—" My voice broke. "I won't fight you."

Silence.

Then she laughed. Not cruel. Not hysterical. Empty. She stepped closer. I felt her shadow fall over me. I looked up.

Her eyes were dry. Distant. Exhausted. "I don't care," she said quietly. "Do you know why?"

I shook my head once.

"Because there are always more men," she said. "Men who watch. Men who use me. Men who decide what I'm for before I ever get to choose."

Each word flayed.

"You offering me your life or your death doesn't make you different," she finished. "It just makes you honest."

The truth landed like a blade. I stayed on my knees.

Because even broken open like this, even stripped of every weapon, I knew one thing with terrifying clarity:

I would still choose her.

Every time.

I didn't hear Marco enter. I felt him. The shift in the air. The weight of another presence. A line drawn where there hadn't been one before.

Footsteps stopped behind me.

"My brother," Marco said. His voice was steady. Too steady. The kind of calm that only came when something had already gone wrong. He looked past me— to her.

"Sierra," he began.

One look silenced him. She didn't raise her voice. Didn't move toward him. She simply turned her head, eyes sharp and unreadable, and Marco stopped mid-step like he'd run into glass.

The room held its breath.

"No," she said evenly. "Not yet."

Marco inclined his head once. A concession. Not an argument.

She gestured vaguely toward the screens still glowing on the wall. "The contract," she said. "The one you all keep pretending is about protection and alliances and leverage."

Her gaze cut back to me. "It doesn't say anything about surveillance," she continued. "It doesn't say anything about being watched before I ever agreed to belong to any of you."

The word landed heavy.

"You broke it," she said. "Whether you meant to or not."

I opened my mouth. She didn't let me speak.

"And before you start justifying it," she added coolly, "don't. I've heard enough vows for one lifetime." She stepped back, reclaiming space. Reclaiming air.

"Get out."

The words were final. Not shouted. Not shaken.

A command.

Marco moved immediately. He crossed the room and reached for me, hauling me up off the floor. My legs nearly gave out beneath me. I caught myself against him without meaning to, weight sagging into my brother like I'd taken a bullet I hadn't noticed yet.

He steadied me without comment. To her, he said, "We will."

Then, quieter—just for me—"Family office." I nodded once, jaw tight, vision still blurred. Marco turned me gently, guiding me toward the door. I leaned harder than I should have. I felt it—the weakness, the exposure—and hated myself for it.

At the threshold, Marco paused. He looked back at her.

"I'll stay," he said calmly. "We'll talk, next steps."

Then, softer, meant only for me:

"You go before you say something you can't survive."

His hand tightened briefly at my shoulder. I let him lead me away. Behind us, the door closed.

And for the first time since I could remember, I walked down the hall knowing I'd left something irreplaceable behind me.

***

I got into my car and slammed it into gear. Marco had given clear directions. Family office. Sit. Wait. Let him handle it. I didn't follow them.

The city blurred past the windshield as I turned the wheel hard and aimed south, toward the airstrip. Toward the one place Marco would never authorize and every instinct in me demanded.

My phone buzzed once on the console. I ignored it.

The engine growled beneath me, a living thing responding to pressure, to speed, to intent. I drove faster than I should have, every red light an insult, every second stretching too thin.

This wasn't panic. It was clarity.

Sierra's face replayed in my mind—not screaming, not breaking—but standing there, unmovable, looking at me like I was something she'd finally seen clearly.

I needed to fix it. No—end it.

The Rinaldi's had taken too much. Not just blood. Not just fear. They'd carved themselves into her, my life,

life in ways that still echoed, and I had let that echo live longer than it should have.

I told myself it had been strategy. Intelligence. Patience.

It was a lie. The truth was uglier.

Watching Matteo had started as a necessity. A name I needed to understand. A man whose shadow touched my parents' deaths in ways no one had been able to prove. But somewhere along the way, my attention had shifted.

I stopped watching him.

I watched her.

I memorized the way she moved through rooms, the people she trusted, the moments she didn't know anyone was looking. I told myself it was protection. I told myself it was preparation.

It was obsession.

The road opened up, dark and empty, the airstrip lights faint in the distance like a promise. I thought if Matteo was dead, the past would close its mouth. But the threat hadn't disappeared, it had gotten worse in the face of his father. Maybe if the threat was gone entirely, she'd understand.

She'd have to.

I tightened my grip on the wheel, knuckles white, pulse steady in a way that should have scared me more than it did.

This was how I proved it.

Not with my words scripted into vows she no longer believed in.

But with a vow written in blood.

Maybe then—just maybe—she would see the truth:

That my obsession was love. And that I was willing to burn everything else to prove it.

# Chapter 18

**Sierra**

I stood in Lorenzo's office, staring at the remnants he'd left behind.

His phone lay on its side near the desk, screen dark. His knife sat where it had fallen, familiar, intimate in a way that made my stomach twist. The gun rested farther away, heavy and final.

A line of discarded truths.

He had placed his life in my hands and walked away from it like it was nothing. Or like it was everything.

I forced myself to breathe. Forced my gaze up as Marco returned to the room. He didn't look at me at first. Instead, he crossed to the far wall with the same calm efficiency he used for everything that mattered.

The monitors went black one by one.
The footage vanished.
The dock. The chair. My scream.

Gone.

He removed the thumb drive from the laptop with two fingers, like it might burn him, and slipped it into his pocket before closing the computer. The click of it echoed too loudly in the sudden quiet.

Then he exhaled. Long. Heavy. Like he'd been holding that breath for years. "Sierra," he began. He stopped.

The silence between us stretched—not empty, but crowded with everything he wasn't saying.

"You could have told me," I said. The words fell flat, not angry. Worse. Certain.

Marco's jaw tightened. He didn't argue. That told me more than any excuse could have.

I let my eyes drift back to the floor, to the evidence of Lorenzo's confession scattered like an offering. "You saw it," I continued quietly. "The footage. You knew I disappeared. You knew I ran from my fiancé in the middle of the night."

My throat tightened. "You knew something was wrong."

Marco opened his mouth, then closed it again.

"I hated Matteo," I said, the admission heavy but honest. "I would have given him up. Hell—" I exhaled, rubbing at my chest. "I might have helped."

The words hung there, unfinished.

Helped how?

Helped who?

Helped kill the man I was supposed to marry?

The thought made my stomach churn.

Marco held my gaze longer than he needed to. When he finally spoke, his voice was steady—but there was strain beneath it, like something pulled too tight.

"He was supposed to be watching Matteo," he said. "That was it. Containment. Information. We knew Matteo was reckless, violent. We didn't know when he'd move, only that he would."

I said nothing. I didn't trust myself to.

Marco exhaled again, slower this time. "Lorenzo doesn't half-watch anything. When he locks onto a target, he studies every angle. Patterns. Weaknesses. Escape routes." His mouth tightened. "At first, you were just… proximity. Collateral."

My stomach twisted, but I didn't interrupt.

"Then you stopped being that," he continued. "Somewhere along the way, the focus shifted. I noticed it—but I told myself it was strategy. That he was keeping you close to draw Matteo out faster."

"And you believed that?" I asked quietly.

Marco's expression flickered. Not denial. Recognition.

"I wanted to," he admitted. "Because the alternative meant admitting my brother was losing control." The words landed hard. Losing control.

"He stopped reporting the way he should have," Marco went on. "Stopped sleeping. Started making decisions that weren't… efficient." A humorless huff escaped him. "That's how I should have known."

I glanced at the knife on the floor. The gun. The phone.

Obsession didn't look like chaos in Lorenzo. It looked like precision taken too far.

"I thought he was managing it," Marco said. "That he understood the line."

I laughed softly, the sound sharp and wrong. "He erased the line."

Marco didn't disagree. "He convinced himself it was protection," Marco said quietly. "That watching you meant keeping you safe. That if he saw everything, nothing could happen to you without him stopping it."

My chest tightened. "And then it did."

"When it did," Marco said, his voice dropping, "Matteo knew exactly what he was doing."

"He fed Lorenzo a trail," he continued. "False movement. Offshore chatter. A sighting that couldn't be ignored." His jaw tightened. "He made it look urgent. Personal."

My hands curled at my sides. The sudden "work trip" to Sicily.

"Lorenzo took the bait," Marco said quietly. "Left the country. He thought he was intercepting Matteo before he could make a move."

"And instead," I said, already knowing.

"Matteo never left the city," Marco finished. "He used his resources to make sure Lorenzo was gone. And the moment you were alone—"

"He came for me," I whispered.

Marco nodded once. No excuses. No softening. "He took you from his own bed," he said. "From a place Lorenzo believed was untouchable."

The word rang in my ears. Untouchable.

"I was on the phone with Lorenzo when we realized," Marco added. "When the feeds went dark. When your phone stopped responding." His voice went tight at the edges. "I've never seen him like that. Not before. Not ever."

I thought back to waking up tied to a chair, again, with Matteo smiling at me. I thought about the way Lorenzo appeared at the last moment. Watching Matteo's body slump to the ground. How I'd taken his precious switchblade and plunge into him over and over.

"So this—" I gestured weakly at the screens, the office, the wreckage of obsession. "This was him trying to make sure it never happened again."

"Yes," Marco said. Then, after a beat, "And punishing himself for letting it happen at all." The silence pressed in around us.

"I should have shut it down," Marco said. "Taken the surveillance from him. Told you the truth. Destroyed the contract, but I didn't." His eyes met mine, unflinching. "That's my fault."

I swallowed. "He watched me," I said. "Before Matteo. Before the contract."

Marco didn't deny it.

"He told himself it was intel," Marco said. "That knowing you meant knowing the threat." A pause. "By the time he realized it wasn't that anymore, it was too late."

Too late.

I stared at the darkened monitors, at the blank wall where my life had been reduced to angles and timestamps. "And now?" I asked.

Marco exhaled shakily. "And now…" His voice broke despite the effort to hold it steady.

"Now he's unraveling. And I'm not sure I know how to stop him."

***

Marco left me standing in the wreckage of Lorenzo's office. He paused at the door, one hand braced against the frame like he needed it to stay upright. "I'll release you from the contract," he said quietly. "But I need time."

I laughed once, sharp and humorless. "You're negotiating?"

"I'm prioritizing," he corrected. "My brother comes first." Of course he did.

"Fine," I said, because fighting him would change nothing. "Go."

He didn't look relieved. He looked tired. Older than he had an hour ago. And when he left, the quiet rushed back in, thick and suffocating.

I didn't let it settle. I called Jenna.

She answered on the second ring. "Sierra?"

"I need you to listen," I said, already pacing. "And you can't interrupt me."

Silence. Then, softly, "Okay."

So I told her.

Not every word. Not every detail. But enough. The contract. Matteo. Alessio. Lorenzo watching me from the shadows long before I ever noticed him. The office. The cameras. The video from the yacht party gone wrong. His confession. The way he'd knelt. The way he'd offered himself up like something already dead.

I talked until my throat burned and my hands stopped shaking.

"And the worst part," I said finally, staring at the dark window, my reflection warped in the glass, "is that I'm worried about him."

Jenna didn't say anything right away.

"I should hate him," I went on. "I should feel relieved that Marco's ending it. That this is over. But all I can think about is whether he's alone. Whether he has backup. That his gun is still here, sitting on our coffee table."

"That doesn't sound like relief," Jenna said carefully.

Before I could answer, my phone buzzed.

Marco. *Do you know where he went?*

My stomach dropped.

*No,* I typed back. *He didn't tell me.*

The reply came almost immediately.

*He's missing. His last known target was Alessio Rinaldi. Sicily. Family estate.*

The room tilted. I told Jenna. All of it. The name. The place. The implication hanging between every word.

"You can't be serious," she said. "Sierra, this is—this is obsession. You're crossing a line."

"I know," I said, already grabbing my keys.

"You're not responsible for him."

"I know."

"He made his choices."

"I know," I repeated, sharper now. "And he made them unprepared. He didn't take a gun. He didn't take a knife. He didn't take anyone with him."

"Sierra—"

"What if he gets hurt?" The question tore out of me before I could stop it.

The line went quiet.

Finally, Jenna exhaled. "You're already gone," she said softly.

"I have to be."

"Then promise me one thing."

"What."

"Come back."

I didn't answer. I hung up and yelled for Alexio.

He argued. Of course he did. Until I took Lorenzo's gun off the coffee table. His knife. Until I slid them into my bag with hands that didn't shake at all.

"Airstrip," I said. "Now."

He didn't look happy about it. But he drove.

At the terminal, I used Lorenzo's name like it belonged to me.

*Moretti.*

It opened doors. It greased palms. It erased questions.

The flight attendant smiled too brightly when she handed me the boarding pass. "You just missed him," she said. "About two hours ago."

Two hours.

I nodded like that didn't feel like a countdown.

The flight was long. Too long. Nine hours trapped in a narrow seat with nothing but my thoughts and the steady hum of engines dragging me farther from anything safe.

*What was I doing?*

Flying across the world to what—stop him? Save him? Kill someone for him? Kill him myself for making me feel like this?

I pressed my forehead against the window, watching the black stretch endlessly beneath us. This wasn't loyalty. It wasn't an obligation.

It wasn't even love, not the kind people talked about when they wanted it to sound clean. This was something else. Something sharp and coiled and deliberate.

***

A few hours into the flight, my phone buzzed. Thank God for in-flight Wi-Fi.

An unknown number. No preamble. No warning.

The image loaded slowly, each detail cutting deeper than the last.

Lorenzo sat slumped in a chair, his head tipped back against something hard. Blood traced a thin, lazy line from his temple, slipping down his cheek, soaking into the collar of his shirt. His eyes were closed. Not unconscious—*contained*. Displayed.

Beneath the image, a single sentence waited.

*I have something of yours.*

The last soft part of me went quiet.

Lorenzo had crossed oceans for vengeance.

I was crossing one because someone had mistaken possession for ownership.

The thought didn't frighten me. It settled. Locked into place.

Alessio Rinaldi didn't know it yet. But I wasn't coming to negotiate.

I was coming to collect.

***

Lorenzo

I came back to myself in pieces.

The chair first. Hard wood digging into my spine. My wrists bound behind me, the burn of circulation returning too slowly. The copper taste in my mouth. Blood drying as it ran down my face, sticky where it reached my collar.

I didn't lift my head. I already knew where I was.

The Rinaldi villa smelled like arrogance—polished stone, expensive silence, the kind of place that believed itself untouchable because no one had ever made the mistake of testing it properly.

What had I thought I was going to do? March through the front door and crack Alessio Rinaldi's skull open with my bare hands?

The thought almost made me laugh. I had left everything behind.

My gun.
My knife.
My phone—abandoned on the floor of my office for her.

As if I hadn't needed them.
As if this had ever been about survival.

Alessio's arrogance had done the rest.

Minimal security. Familiar faces. Men who believed reputation was enough. The first one I'd killed at the gate with force alone—his throat crushed under my forearm before he could finish reaching for his weapon. The second had been sloppier. I'd taken his gun when he hesitated, used it before he understood his mistake.

Two bodies before the house even realized I was there.

After that, the tone had changed. Alessio hadn't wanted me dead.

He'd wanted me contained. Neutralized. Displayed.

Personal security. Professionals. Too many angles. Too much patience. I'd fought longer than I should have. Harder. Like a man who didn't care if he made it out.

Maybe I hadn't.

The memory of Sierra rose unbidden.

Her face as Marco hauled me out of the office. The way she'd looked at me—no softness left, no illusions. Just clarity sharp enough to cut. I thought about her before she knew.

Before the cameras.
Before the truth.

When I'd believed—stupidly, dangerously—that maybe we could love each other anyway. I had used her. Just like Matteo. Just like her parents.

I had simply dressed it up better. Told myself it was protection. Strategy. A necessary evil. Now I was the one being used.

Bound to a chair. Blood on my shirt. Proof of concept for a man who liked to own his enemies while they were still breathing.

Marco would play it smart. He always did.

Emil would come with a team. Or there would be negotiations. Leverage. Bloodless solutions wrapped in velvet language.

I wasn't sure I cared. Maybe this was my penance. Maybe this was what love cost men like me when we mistook obsession for control. I lifted my head just enough for the blood to drip faster.

If this was how it ended, then at least Alessio Rinaldi would understand one thing before the end—I had come for him willingly.

Pain dragged me back to consciousness.

A fist connected with my jaw, snapping my head sideways. Bone rang. My vision flashed white, then red. Blood spilled fresh into my mouth.

I laughed anyway.

Alessio Rinaldi stood in front of me, sleeves rolled, knuckles already bruising. He looked… pleased with himself. Like a man proud he'd finally done something with his own hands.

"That's it?" I rasped. "You fly me halfway across the world for a punch?"

He snarled, cursing me in Italian and hit me again. Harder this time. My head snapped back against the chair.

I swallowed blood and smiled.

"So this is you now," I said. "Finally dirtying your hands. Your son would be proud. You did always have him do the hard parts."

That did it.

He grabbed my face, fingers digging into my jaw, forcing me to look at him. His eyes were wild—angry, insecure, desperate to prove something.

"Like father, like son," I went on softly. "A coward hiding behind walls and men braver than him."

He struck me again, breath heaving. "You're the coward," he spat. "Hiding behind a woman. Sierra Blackwell. Using her like a shield."

Something in me snapped tight.

"You say her name again," I said quietly, the words vibrating with promise, "and I'll kill you with my teeth."

Alessio laughed, sharp and ugly. "I'm going to find her," he said. "I'm going to hurt her. Slowly. And I'm going to make sure she knows it's your fault."

I laughed. It surprised even me—low, cracked, unhinged.

"She's already gone," I said. "She disappeared from your control once. She'll do it again." I leaned forward as far as the restraints allowed, blood dripping from my chin.

"And this time," I added, "she'll have Moretti resources behind her. You won't even see her shadow."

His smile thinned. "Love blinded you," he sneered. "Obsession always ends the same way. With men like you bleeding on someone else's floor."

I laughed then—harder than before. I couldn't stop it. It ripped out of me like I'd finally let go of something fragile and useless.

"You still don't understand," I said. "That was never the risk."

Alessio scoffed, "Then what was?"

"The risk was me." The words cut through the room. It came from behind him.

Clear. Calm. Certain.

Alessio's expression changed—not fear yet, but calculation gone wrong. His gaze slid past mine, toward something over my shoulder. His mouth opened, then closed, like the thought refused to fit.

I followed his stare. For a moment, all I saw was red.

Blood blurred my vision, thick on my lashes, streaked the world into shadow and light. I blinked hard—once. Twice.

And then I saw her.

Sierra stood just inside the courtyard gate.

Black leggings. Worn Docs. An oversized black T-shirt hanging off one shoulder like she'd pulled it on without thinking. Her hair fell in wild waves around her face, untamed, like she hadn't slept — or stopped moving — since she left me.

She didn't look prepared. She looked *decided*.

My gun hung loose in her hand, her grip uncertain, not quite right — the way someone holds a thing they were never meant to use but will anyway. My knife was tucked into her boot, the leather strained where she'd shoved it there.

She hadn't come trained. She'd come to claim something.

Alessio turned fully now, dread blooming a second too late.

The courtyard was quiet. Too quiet. His men were gone — sent elsewhere, reassigned, confident the threat had already been neutralized. I smiled, something cracked and reverent pulling at my mouth.The chair didn't matter anymore. The pain faded to something distant, manageable.

Everything narrowed to the fact that she was here—that she had crossed an ocean and walked into hell without asking permission.

"You should have kept your security team," I told him softly. "You're fucked."

# Chapter 19



***Sierra***

I stood there, staring at the scene in front of me like it was a violent painting someone had decided not to look away from.

Bruises bloomed across Lorenzo's face, dark and angry, already settling into his skin. The cut above his eye still leaked, blood tracking down his temple and soaking into his collar. Alessio's knuckles were red. His sleeves were speckled with Lorenzo's blood like careless brushstrokes.

He looked caught between fear and intent — the moment where a man realizes he's miscalculated but hasn't decided yet whether to run or double down. I'd surprised him. He never thought I would answer his threat.

"Alessio," I said calmly, almost conversationally. "Do you remember the last time we were here together?"

His eyes flicked to me, sharp now, searching. I smiled when recognition crept in.

A week before the yacht party. A different night. A different version of me. Matteo had hit me here — in this very courtyard. Some Rinaldi gathering, expensive and indulgent. He'd been high, careless, cruel. He'd wanted me to play along. I'd said no.

A word they weren't used to hearing.

I'd thought Alessio had come outside to stop it. To help me. Instead, he'd leaned in close and told me to behave. To do what I was told and none of this would happen again. He'd threatened to end the engagement, to destroy my family quietly and efficiently if I didn't learn my place.

I'd swallowed it then. I'd let it go. Naive and cornered, trained to survive through polite society.

I wasn't that girl anymore.

Now, my future husband sat bound to a chair, bleeding in front of me, and the air felt different.

Alessio's hand drifted toward his pocket. A reflex. A mistake.

"Oh," I said lightly, lifting the gun and centering it on his chest. My grip wasn't perfect — I knew that — but my aim didn't waver. "I wouldn't."

He froze. The courtyard seemed to hold its breath. I tilted my head, studying him the way he used to study me — like a problem that needed correcting.

"You already tried taking something from me once," I continued softly. "You don't get to do it again."

Behind him, Lorenzo lifted his head just enough to look at me, blood and disbelief and something dangerously close to devotion in his eyes.

Alessio laughed—short, sharp, disbelieving.

"You think this ends with a gun?" he asked. "You think pointing it at me makes you dangerous?" He took a careful step closer, eyes never leaving mine. "You don't have it in you. You never did. You were always better at surviving than striking."

His gaze flicked to Lorenzo, bound and bleeding in the chair. "That's why you hid behind him," he said lightly. "Just like he hid behind you."

Something dark crossed his face, satisfied. "You let a woman become your armor," Alessio sneered. "And now look at you. Tied to a chair while she plays soldier."

"Stop." Lorenzo's voice cut through the courtyard—rough, wrecked, nothing controlled left in it.

"Don't," he said again, louder now, straining against the restraints. Blood slid from his jaw as he lifted his head. "Sierra, don't do this."

I didn't look at him. Not yet.

"You don't need this on your hands," he said, the words breaking in a way I had never heard from him. "You don't need his blood. This is on me. All of it."

Alessio smiled wider, delighted. "Hear that?" he murmured. "Even now, he's still trying to save you."

Lorenzo shook his head violently. "I used you," he said, the confession tearing out of him. "I watched when I should have stopped it. I let it happen. I turned you into bait and called it protection."

My fingers tightened around the gun.

"I deserve whatever comes next," he went on hoarsely. "But you don't. You don't have to become like us."

I finally turned then. Really looked at him.

Bloodied. Bound. Still trying to shoulder the weight of everyone's sins like it was his birthright. Still trying to save me from becoming something he already believed himself to be.

For a moment, the world narrowed to the three of us—the past, the present, and the violence waiting to be chosen.

Then I looked back at Alessio. His smile was sharp. Certain. "You don't have it in you," he said again. "You're a coward like your father."

"This isn't you," Lorenzo whispered, desperate. "Don't let him make it you."

I tilted my head, considering him. The gun felt heavy in my hand—unfamiliar, unbalanced. Not an extension of me. Just an object.

"I don't know," I said quietly. Lorenzo stilled. Alessio frowned.

I met Lorenzo's eyes over the barrel, something steady settling into my chest. Not rage. Not fear. Clarity.

"Maybe it is me." The words didn't echo. They didn't shake. They landed.

I squeezed the trigger.

The sound was wrong—too loud, too sharp, not the clean snap I'd imagined. It cracked through the courtyard like bone splitting.

Alessio flinched.

Then his head snapped back and his body collapsed—hard, boneless—slamming into the stone with a wet, final sound.

But the force hadn't come from my hand. The impact was wrong. The angle wrong. A gunshot thundered from behind me. For half a second, my brain refused to catch up.

Then everything detonated.

Gunfire ripped through the courtyard—deafening, overlapping, violent. Men shouted. Boots pounded stone.

Muzzle flashes tore the dark apart in jagged bursts of white. The gun slipped from my fingers and clattered uselessly to the ground.

Someone screamed. It took me a terrifying moment to realize it was me.

"SIERRA—MOVE."

Emil's voice cut through the chaos— commanding, controlled, already issuing orders I couldn't hear over the ringing in my ears.

I didn't move. I couldn't. My vision locked on the chair.

On Lorenzo. I ran.

I don't remember crossing the space. I remember dropping to my knees so hard pain shot up my legs. My hands were shaking so violently I nearly dropped the knife as I hacked at the restraints.

"Lorenzo—look at me—look at me—"

The blade sliced through plastic. The last tie snapped.

He collapsed forward immediately, dead weight, his forehead slamming into my shoulder as I caught him. He was heavier than I expected.

His blood was everywhere—slicking my hands, soaking into my sleeves, sticky and thick as I fumbled to keep him upright.

"I've got you," I sobbed. "I've got you—please—please—"

A gunshot cracked close.

Lorenzo's body jerked violently. A sound tore out of him—wet, broken—and then my hands were suddenly buried in blood. Too much blood. It poured between my fingers, hot and relentless, soaking my palms, my wrists, dripping onto the stone beneath us.

"No," I gasped. "No—no—no—"

He sagged fully against me, and we went down together, crashing to the ground. His weight knocked the breath from my lungs as we hit. Blood spread beneath us in a dark, shining pool.

I pressed my hands harder against his stomach, useless, frantic, smearing blood everywhere.

"Stay with me," I begged. "Lorenzo—stay with me—"

Someone was shouting my name. "Sierra—SIERRA—" Alexio. I barely heard him.

Pain exploded through my thigh. White-hot. Blinding. Like fire ripping straight through muscle. I screamed and looked down.

My leggings were torn open, fabric shredded. Blood pulsed out in thick, ugly bursts, soaking my hands the second I touched it.

I'd been shot. "No—no—no—"

Panic swallowed everything.

I clawed at my leg, sobbing, fingers slipping, digging blindly as adrenaline drowned out the pain and logic and reason.

"SIERRA—STOP—"

Hands grabbed at me. Marco and Emil. They were hauling Lorenzo up, shouting, moving fast, blood already coating their hands and suits.

I didn't care. I shoved my fingers into the wound and screamed as I felt metal. I hooked it and pulled. Something tore loose inside me. The bullet hit the stone with a sharp, metallic clink.

I felt feral.

My hands were shaking so badly I couldn't tell where my blood ended and Lorenzo's began. Alexio was in front of me now—face pale, eyes wild, shouting my name—but his voice sounded distant, warped, like it was coming through water.

I tried to say Lorenzo's name. I don't know if it came out.

My vision blurred as a dark object loomed closer.
A door slammed and my thoughts flatlined.

***

### *Lorenzo*

White. Not light. Not brightness. White like
pressure. Like being crushed from the inside out.

The smell hit first—bleach, alcohol, something
metallic that crawled up the back of my throat and settled
there. It made my stomach seize even though I couldn't
feel most of my body.

Beeping.

Slow. Too slow. Then faster. Urgent. Wrong.

I tried to breathe.

Fire bloomed in my gut when I did—deep,
internal, ripping. Not pain exactly. Damage. Something
torn that hadn't stopped tearing. My body existed in
fragments.

Weight on my chest.
Tightness around my arm.
Plastic in my mouth.
Pressure—hands—hard, efficient, unapologetic.

Voices drifted in and out, muffled like I was
underwater.

"…pressure dropping—"
"…keep him under—"
"…bullet track—"

My name surfaced. Distant. Bent out of shape.

*Moretti.*

Like it mattered. Something pulled at me—dragged me toward the surface. A violent tug, like being hauled up by the spine. Air forced into my lungs. My body arched without permission.

A sound tore out of me before I realized it was mine. Hands held me down. The world fractured.

Stone under my back.
Blood everywhere.
Sierra screaming my name.

My chest seized. I tried to say hers. It didn't make it past my throat. Darkness surged again, thick and merciful. And just before it took me—

Her. Not her face. Not her voice.

The *weight* of her.
The certainty that she had been there.
That she had crossed hell to get to me.

That whatever I had broken inside myself hadn't been enough to make her walk away. The monitors kept screaming.

And I let the dark take me, but it didn't come all at once. It seeped. Thick, heavy, viscous—like sinking into oil. Thought slowed first. Then sensation. Then time stopped behaving the way it should have.

I dreamed in pieces. Not scenes. Impressions.

Her laugh—unexpected, sharp, always a little disbelieving. Like she never quite trusted joy to stay. The sound echoed, warped, folding in on itself until it became something else.

A scream.

No—
My name.

I tried to turn toward it. I couldn't move.

I was standing behind glass, watching her on the other side. She didn't know I was there. She never looked back. She was smaller this way—softer. Hair pulled back, fingers worrying the hem of her sleeve the way she did when she was anxious but pretending not to be.

I hated this version of the memory. The one where I only watched. It shifted.

We were in the penthouse kitchen. Early morning light. She was barefoot, wearing one of my shirts like it was a mistake she hadn't noticed yet. Coffee forgotten on the counter. She was talking—rambling, really—about nothing important, hands moving, eyes bright.

She hadn't known I was watching then either.

I had memorized her like that. Not the moments she offered. The moments she forgot to guard. The dream lurched.

Blood on marble. Her hands—shaking—slick red to the wrists.

Not hers. Mine.

I tried to tell her to stop pressing so hard. Tried to tell her it wasn't her job to hold me together. That I'd made the choice to bleed for her long before that courtyard.

My mouth wouldn't open. The scene shattered.

She was laughing again—breathless this time, pinned beneath me, nails digging into my shoulders like she needed proof I was real. Her teeth caught my lower lip, not gentle, not careful.

"You're dangerous," she'd whispered. I'd smiled against her mouth. "So are you."

The memory burned warmer than the rest. Lingered longer. Then—The yacht.

Music too loud. Lights too bright. Her expression shuttered, distant, already gone somewhere she couldn't take me. I'd watched her that night too—from across the deck, from the edge of restraint I'd mistaken for control.

That one hurt. The dream twisted it cruelly.

She stood in the courtyard again—black clothes, wild hair, my gun hanging wrong in her hand. She looked at me the way she had right before everything exploded.

Not afraid. Certain. She said my name.

Or maybe she didn't. I couldn't hear anymore.

Pain rippled through the dark—deep, pulling, relentless. Something tugged at my middle, sharp and insistent, like a hook buried where it didn't belong.

I drifted.

I remembered her asleep against my chest, breath warm, trusting. The weight of her there had terrified me more than any enemy ever had.

Because I'd known. The moment I let myself keep her, this was always where it would end. Flashing lights cut through the dark.

Beeping. Voices. Hands again.

I fought them this time. Not because I wanted to wake—

But because I was afraid if I didn't, I'd lose her in the dark the way I always had in life.

Her face surfaced one last time—close now. Real. Tear tracks cutting clean lines down her cheeks. Blood smeared across her mouth, her hands, her clothes.

She was saying something. I strained toward it. Toward *her*.

And the dark swallowed me whole again.

***

I woke to light that hurt.

Not blinding—clinical. White and flat and wrong. The kind that didn't belong to a place where anything living was supposed to feel safe.

My body knew before my mind did.

Pain sat deep in my gut, heavy and pulling, stitched tight and unforgiving. Every breath dragged against it. Tubes tugged at my arm. Something beeped steadily near my head, too calm for how wrecked I felt.

I tried to move. Hands stopped me.

"Easy." Marco's voice. Hoarse. Older than it should have sounded.

I turned my head. Emil stood on the other side of the bed, arms crossed, shoulders slumped. They both looked like hell. Unshaven. Dark shadows carved under their eyes. Clothes wrinkled, slept in. Worn thin.

"How long," I croaked.

Marco exhaled slowly. "Five days."

The number hit wrong. Too big. Too much time stolen.

"You were hit clean through," Emil added. "They had to operate. Infection risk. You flatlined once."

I didn't care. My chest tightened—not with pain, but something sharper.

"Where is she?"

The room went still. Too still. Marco and Emil exchanged a glance. Not quick. Not subtle. Deliberate. Something inside me fractured.

"Where," I repeated, louder now. Ragged. Desperate. "Where the fuck is she?"

Emil looked away first.

Marco stayed. He always did the hard things himself.

"She lived," Marco said.

I sucked in a breath that tore at my stitches.

"She dug the bullet out of her own leg," he continued. "With her hands. Refused to let anyone touch her until you were stabilized. It was honestly something to watch."

My vision blurred.

"She slept here the first night," Emil said quietly. "On that chair. Wouldn't leave. Yelled at you while you were unconscious. Cried. Then yelled again."

I closed my eyes. I could see it too clearly. Her voice. Her hands. Furious and shaking and terrified all at once.

"She was discharged two days ago," Marco said. "Physically, she healed fast."

That wasn't what I needed to hear. "Why isn't she here," I whispered.

Marco hesitated. My stomach dropped.

"I put her on a plane," he said. "Personally." The word landed like a blade.

"No," I said. "No—she wouldn't leave. Not without—"

"She didn't leave without you," Emil cut in. "She left because of you."

I tried to sit up. Pain detonated. White-hot. I snarled, hands clawing at the sheets, breath tearing out of me in broken pieces.

Marco pressed me back down. "Stop. You'll rip something."

"Where," I demanded. "Where did you send her?"

Marco's jaw tightened.

"I won't tell you."

Rage flared—bright, reckless. "You don't get to decide that."

"I do," he said evenly. "Because I ended it." My heart stuttered.

"The contract," Marco continued. "The marriage. The protection clause. All of it. I absolved it."

"No," I said again, weaker now. "That wasn't yours to end."

"It was," Marco replied. "And it's done."

The room felt hollow. Like something vital had been removed and no one had bothered to stitch it closed.

"She went home," Emil said. Not our home. Not the penthouse. Not the place where she'd learned my shadows and still stayed.

"Home without me," I murmured.

Marco nodded once. "Yes."

I swallowed around the ache rising in my throat. "I'll find her," I said. It wasn't loud. It wasn't dramatic. It was certainty carved into bone. "I always do."

Marco shook his head. "No," he said. "You won't."

I turned to him, fury sharpening through the pain. "You think you can stop me?"

"I know I can," he replied. "Because if you go near her again, you'll destroy what little peace she has left."

Silence pressed in.

"She paid for our war," Marco continued. "In blood. In fear. In choices she never should have had to make."

I stared at the ceiling, chest rising unevenly.

"She crossed an ocean for you," Emil said softly. "But that doesn't mean she wants to live in one."

Marco's voice lowered. "You let her go. That's the cost."

Something inside me caved. Not shattered—collapsed. Slow and total. Let her go. The words didn't belong together. Didn't make sense in the same sentence as her name. I turned my face toward the window, blinking hard.

Marco rested a hand briefly on the edge of the bed. "If she wants you," he said, quieter now, "she'll come back on her own terms." He paused.

"But if you chase her?"

He didn't finish. He didn't have to.

I lay there, stitched and hollow and breathing because my body insisted on it, while the truth settled heavy and brutal in my chest.

She was alive. She was gone. And this time—I had been the thing she escaped.

# Chapter 20



Marco moved me without asking. Not roughly. Not cruelly. Just… decisively. Like a chess piece lifted from a board that had already claimed too much blood.

I woke up in Sicily with salt in the air and linen sheets and a dull, persistent ache in my leg that reminded me I was still alive. A private doctor came twice a day. A nurse checked the wound, the bruising, my vitals. Jenna arrived forty-eight hours later, eyes wild, arms tight around me, swearing and crying in equal measure.

Marco explained it once I had woken up in the hospital. Lorenzo had violated the contract. By every definition that mattered. He had acted without sanction, without protection, without strategy. He had gone alone.

The contract was over. I was free.

The word didn't feel like freedom at first. It felt like vertigo.

He told me I could stay as long as I needed. The property wasn't in the Moretti name—never had been. It belonged to their mother's family, tucked along the coast where the cliffs fell sharp into the sea and the mornings were impossibly quiet. He promised Lorenzo wouldn't find me. Swore it. Looked me in the eye when he said it as I boarded the plane.

I believed him. I had to. The days blurred into something almost gentle. Sun on my skin. Soft food. Slow walks once my leg allowed it. The sea visible from every room, changing color with the hour—steel in the morning, blue glass by afternoon, ink by night. I slept more than I talked. Thought more than I slept.

I healed. Not all the way. But enough. Enough that the adrenaline faded and left room for the other things to crawl in.

The memories.
The fear.
The want.

There were still twenty days until the wedding. Twenty days until the date that had already been announced, printed, mailed. Thick ivory invitations sitting on kitchen counters and entry tables all over the world. A future that had been decided publicly, formally, irrevocably—except it wasn't irrevocable anymore.

No one had mentioned it. Not Marco. Not Emil. Not even Jenna at first. It hovered between us like something fragile and sharp. Just because the contract was over, didn't mean all those public parts of our engagement were erased.

I brought it up one afternoon while we sat on the terrace, my leg propped on a cushion, Jenna picking at a bowl of fruit she wasn't really eating.

"So," I let my voice linger, "the wedding."

She froze. Then sighed. "Yeah. I was wondering when you'd say it."

"We should cancel it," I said automatically. The words came easily. Too easily.

Jenna studied my face. "Is that what you want?"

I opened my mouth and closed it. I didn't know.

That was the terrifying part.

I knew what I *should* want. I knew what made sense. I knew what everyone expected me to say now that the contract was over and the danger had passed and the man I was supposed to marry had nearly gotten himself killed for reasons that were tangled up in me.

But want wasn't logic. Want was quieter. Slower. Harder to pin down.

"I don't know yet," I admitted.

She didn't push. Bless her for that.

The truth was—I was enjoying the stillness. The anonymity. The way no one here knew my name or my history or what I'd been promised to whom. I was enjoying waking up without fear sitting heavy in my chest. Enjoying the way the sun warmed my skin without asking anything of me in return.

I was recovering. Mentally. Emotionally. Not just from the gunshot or the blood or the chaos—but from the constant vigilance. From being a bargaining chip dressed up as a bride.

The contract was gone. But Lorenzo wasn't.

He lingered in everything. In the quiet. In the moments just before sleep. In the way my hand still curled like it expected to find his.

Marco had promised he wouldn't find me. What he hadn't promised—what no one could promise—was that I wouldn't eventually go looking for myself.

Jenna healed me in the ways medicine couldn't.

She talked. Constantly. About nothing and everything. About how insane it was that I'd dug a bullet out of my own leg like a feral animal. About how she'd screamed at Marco in Italian she barely spoke when he tried to move me too soon. About how the sun here felt different, like it actually wanted you alive.

Eventually, she dragged me back into the world.

We went to a small beach gathering one night— locals and tourists tangled together under strings of lights, music drifting off someone's phone, cheap wine poured into plastic cups. I wore a loose linen dress that brushed my scars without clinging to them. My hair was still wild, still doing whatever it wanted, but I didn't fight it anymore.

For the first time in weeks, I laughed.

It surprised me. The sound of it. How easy it came once it started. We danced barefoot in the sand, the sea licking at our ankles. Someone lit sparklers. Someone else set off fireworks too close to shore. It was reckless and alive and beautifully unimportant.

I should have felt watched. I didn't.

And that was when Jenna noticed me scanning the crowd anyway. She leaned in, her voice gentle but firm. "He's not here, Si," she said. "You're safe. He's not watching you."

The words landed wrong. Because the truth rose up in me, sudden and sharp and undeniable. I wasn't looking because I was afraid. I was looking because I wanted him to be. The realization hollowed me out in the best and worst way.

Lorenzo had seen my pain—really seen it—and instead of turning away, he'd built his entire existence around containing it. He'd become obsessed not with owning me, but with keeping me untouched by men like Matteo. Like Alessio. When he failed, when the illusion shattered, he hadn't defended himself.

He'd knelt. He'd offered his life. Or his death. Whatever I chose.

And when there was still one man left who'd tried to use me, he'd crossed an ocean with nothing but his rage and his body, ready to break himself open if that was the price. Almost getting killed in the process.

I pressed my fingers into the cool glass of my cup, grounding myself as the music swelled around us. Twenty days.

That was all that remained until a wedding that no longer made sense. Invitations already sent. Seating charts probably finalized by some horrified planner back home. A future outlined in ink I wasn't sure I wanted to erase—or rewrite.

I told Jenna I didn't know what I wanted to do. She didn't push.

Later that night, back at the villa, I stood on the terrace alone, the sea stretching out endlessly below me. The air was soft. Forgiving. I should have felt peace. Instead, I felt the unmistakable absence of a man who had ruined me and saved me in the same breath.

I wasn't circling the wedding because I didn't know what I wanted. I was circling it because choosing it meant choosing him—and choosing him meant admitting the truth I'd been avoiding since the courtyard ran red. That what lived between us wasn't survival anymore. It was intention.

I woke before dawn the next morning with the sea still dark and breathing below the terrace. My leg throbbed softly, a reminder that I was still stitched together by consequences. I wrapped myself in a sweater and went outside barefoot, letting the stone chill my skin until my thoughts sharpened.

I thought about the way he watched me — not like a man waiting to strike, but like someone counting exits, calculating risks, memorizing the sound of my breath. Vigilance, not possession. Protection that could have so easily curdled into control.

And it almost had.

He had failed me once. But when it broke, when the truth was dragged into the open, he hadn't tightened his grip or rewritten the story to keep me. He had let it strip him down to nothing.

He had knelt. He had offered me his life or his death and waited — truly waited — to see which I chose. That was the difference.

I hadn't disappeared from him. I hadn't been hidden or erased or lost. I had stood in front of him and seen everything — the watching, the guilt, the obsession dressed up as protection — and he had still let me walk away.

So when I crossed an ocean with his gun shaking in my hand and his knife cutting into my boot, it wasn't fear that carried me. It was recognition. I wasn't running toward danger. I was meeting him where he stood. Ready to become something irreversible if that was what it took.

Jenna found me later with two coffees and a look she didn't bother softening. "You've decided," she said.

I nodded.

She exhaled slowly, then smiled—sad, proud, resigned. "Okay. Then we do it your way."

My phone felt heavier than it should have as I picked it up. Nineteen days. That was enough time to cancel a wedding. Or to claim it.

"I'm not calling it off," I said quietly. Saying it out loud locked it into place. "I'm choosing it. I'm choosing him."

Jenna studied me for a long moment, then reached out and squeezed my hand. "You know this isn't safe," she said.

"I know," I answered. "Neither is loving him."

Because love wasn't what frightened me anymore. Obsession did.

And I finally understood that mine didn't run from his—it ran alongside it, equal in depth, equal in danger. He had crossed the world to end a man for me. I had stood in blood and chaos and refused to leave him behind. We were already bound. The contract had just been the excuse.

The wedding wouldn't be a rescue or a performance.

It wouldn't be protection dressed up as love.

It would be a vow made without illusions, made in the blood we'd spilled. That I was choosing him — not because he was dangerous, but because I was.

And I would never survive quietly again.

***

### *Lorenzo*

Recovery didn't feel like healing. It felt like being dismantled somewhere quiet.

The vineyards stretched endlessly beyond the villa, neat rows carved into the Sicilian hills like discipline made visible. Morning light spilled gold over the leaves. The air smelled like soil and crushed grapes and salt from the distant sea. It should have been peaceful.

It wasn't.

My body obeyed on a delay. The stitches pulled when I breathed too deeply. My left side burned when I stood too fast. The doctors said I was lucky. Marco said I was reckless. Emil said nothing at all, which was worse. Dario had called a few times, but he was so tied up with the California opening, we'd decided it was best for him to stay there.

I spent my days walking short distances between stone walls and shade, relearning patience like it was a foreign language. I slept badly. Dreamed worse. Woke with her name lodged in my throat like something unfinished.

She was gone. Marco had made sure of it. I told myself that was mercy. I told myself it was what I deserved.

On the fifth morning, I was sitting on the terrace, coffee cooling untouched beside me, when the envelope arrived. Cream paper. Heavy stock. My name written in ink I recognized even before I opened it.

I didn't breathe. Inside was an invitation. My invitation.

*Sierra Blackwell*
&
*Lorenzo Moretti*

The date sat at the bottom like a challenge. Fifteen days from now.

The location was here. Sicily. The vineyards. For a moment, the world tilted. I thought maybe the pain medication had finally done its job and scrambled my head.

I stood too quickly, ignored the protest in my side, and walked straight inside. Marco was in the sitting room, on his phone, already irritated with someone. He looked up when I didn't knock. I held the invitation out. He went still.

"What the hell is this?" I asked.

He took it from me, scanned it once, then again more carefully. His mouth pressed into a line I knew well.

"So she did send them," he said. The words landed hard.

"You're sure."

Marco nodded. "Jenna handled the logistics. Vendors. Guest lists. But this?" He tapped the paper. "Only Sierra would've authorized printing. Distribution. Timing."

My heart started doing something dangerous.

"She could cancel it," Marco said carefully. "If this is confusion. Or impulse. We can stop everything."

"No." The word came out rough, immediate.

Marco studied me. "You don't even know what this means yet."

"I know exactly what it means," I said.

Because if she had wanted distance, there would've been silence. If she wanted safety, there would've been lawyers. If she wanted out, there would've been nothing at all. This was a choice. Deliberate. Public. Irrevocable.

Marco exhaled slowly. "If this goes forward, there's no pretending it's just business anymore. It becomes real."

"I know."

"And if she changes her mind—"

"She won't."

I didn't say it like a hope. I said it like a vow.

Marco watched me for a long moment, then nodded once. "Then we move."

And we did.

The days passed in a blur. Florists arrived first, moving through the vineyard like they already knew where everything belonged. White and black blooms appeared in vases, then disappeared again, replaced by different arrangements, different balances. Fabric samples were laid out across long stone tables. Tastings followed — wine poured and assessed, plates assembled and rejected, decisions made with the calm efficiency of people who understood deadlines.

The vineyard shifted from quiet to alive.It hummed with footsteps and voices, plans spoken quickly, confidently. Nothing tentative. Nothing uncertain. As if the choice had already been made and everyone else was simply catching up.

I watched most of it from a distance at first — from the terrace, from a chair pulled into the shade, from doorways I lingered in longer than necessary. Healing was slow. The doctors said I was progressing well. Marco said I looked like hell. Both were true. Every breath still pulled faintly at my ribs. Every step reminded me how close I'd come to not being here at all.

And yet the world kept moving around me. On the fourth day, a tailor arrived.

He was older, precise, quiet in the way men become when they're very good at what they do. He didn't waste words. He unpacked garment bags and laid them open with care, revealing a suit that made the air in my chest still.

Black. Not harsh — deep, matte, exacting. The cut was clean, architectural. Nothing ornamental. Nothing soft. It was restraint made visible.

"Your future wife selected everything," the tailor said casually as he measured my shoulders. "Sent notes, she's very precise."

I said nothing.

The fabric was heavier than I expected when I slipped my arms into it. It settled over me with weight and intention, the jacket fitting my frame as if it already understood it. When the tailor adjusted the lapel, I caught my reflection in the mirror.

I didn't look like a groom. I looked like a man who had survived something and chosen to stand anyway.

"She asked that it not make you look safe," the tailor murmured. "… inevitable."

Of course she did.

Over the next few days, fittings continued. Adjustments were made by millimeters. Sleeves shortened. The waist taken in slightly as my strength returned. Every change felt deliberate. Personal. Like a hand on my spine, guiding me upright.

Each night, the vineyard glowed later than it ever had before. Strings of lights were tested and retested. Tables were set beneath the open sky, then reset. Menus were finalized. Invitations were confirmed, arrivals coordinated.

Ten days passed like that — not slowly, not quickly.

I didn't ask where she was. I didn't ask if she was coming. I didn't ask because hope, in my experience, was a dangerous thing. But as I stood there one evening, watching workers somehow string more lights between the vines, the weight of the suit still fresh in my memory, something settled low and steady in my chest.

She hadn't canceled. She had chosen.

And for the first time since the gates had closed behind me in that courtyard, I let myself believe — not that I would be forgiven, not that I would be redeemed — but that she might be walking back toward me. On her own terms.

******

I stood at the front of the terrace with my hands clasped behind my back and tried not to think about the ways this could end.

The vineyard had been stripped down to its bones and rebuilt into something precise. Rows of chairs cut clean lines through the grass, black frames softened with sage linen, the fabric moving faintly in the coastal wind. Oxblood florals ran low and controlled along the aisle — not lush, not romantic. Intentional. Roses, calla lilies, dark ranunculus. Nothing wild. Nothing accidental.

It was beautiful. It was unforgiving.

The altar wasn't raised. There was no arch, no canopy, nothing to hide beneath. Just a slab of pale stone set against the open horizon, the sea visible beyond the vines like a blade laid flat under sunlight. No escape routes. No shadows. You stood there exposed or you didn't stand there at all.

She had designed it like this. Not for the guests — they murmured softly, impressed, charmed, unaware. To them it was elegant. Dramatic. A study in restraint.

To me, it was a test site.

Every line forced the eye forward. Every color choice sharpened contrast — dark against skin, green against blood-deep red. The space didn't soothe. It focused. It demanded attention the way a drawn weapon did.

I understood it immediately. If she walked down the aisle, it wouldn't be because she was being led.

It would be because she had decided — eyes open, spine straight — that this was the place she was willing to stand.

Marco shifted beside me, the movement minimal but deliberate. He wore the same suit as Emil and Dario — black, precisely cut, severe in its restraint. The three of them stood like an extension of my own shadow, identical lines, identical intent.

"If she doesn't come," Marco said quietly, his voice pitched for me alone, "we'll end this cleanly. No spectacle." A brother offering mercy without softening the truth.

Emil leaned in from the other side, mouth curving despite himself. "Or," he murmured, "this is her final move. Invite everyone. Make you wait. Let you feel it."

"Emil," Dario warned under his breath. Dario stood just behind us, posture steady, gaze fixed down the aisle like he could already see her there. "She'll come," he said simply.

Not hope. Certainty. I didn't answer any of them.t.

The breeze shifted, carrying salt and crushed greenery. Somewhere behind me, chairs stilled. Voices fell away. Time stretched thin.

This was the moment where men like me usually won — by endurance, by inevitability, by waiting long enough that the other party folded. But this wasn't that kind of power game.

If Sierra didn't come, this wouldn't be a humiliation. It would be a verdict.

It would mean I had crossed the line she'd drawn with her body and her blood and her choice. It would mean my obsession had tipped from devotion into something she refused to inherit.

I didn't pray. I didn't bargain.

I stood in the open and accepted that this — this waiting, this exposure — was the price of loving her the way I did.

Then the music began. Not swelling. Not soft. Controlled. Measured. Footsteps followed. And before I turned, before I allowed myself the relief or the ruin of seeing her, I understood the final cruelty of it.

She hadn't built a battlefield for us.

She'd built one for me alone.

Because only I knew what it would mean if she chose to walk toward me anyway.

# Chapter 21

***Sierra***

Jenna hovered in front of me, hands already fisted in my sleeves like if she let go, I might evaporate. Her fingers were cold. Mine were steady. That alone felt like a small miracle.

"Well," she said, blinking rapidly as she tried—and failed—to keep her smile in place. "Last chance to run. I can distract everyone. Trip a priest. Start a fire. Fake a medical emergency. I'm flexible."

Her voice wobbled on the last word.

I laughed. The sound surprised me—sharp and real, not hysterical. She laughed too, breathless and a little wild, until it tipped too far and cracked. Suddenly we were blinking too fast, the air between us tight with everything we weren't saying.

"I'm not doing this because I have to," I said quietly.

Jenna stilled. Not teasing. Not joking.

She searched my face the way she always had—carefully, thoroughly—like she was checking for fear hiding behind resolve. For old survival instincts wearing a prettier mask.

"I know exactly what I'm choosing," I continued. "And I'm choosing him."

The words settled. Not dramatic. Not fragile. True.

Something in Jenna's expression eased. Her shoulders dropped, the tension finally releasing.

"I know," she said softly. Then, firmer, like a vow of her own. "I'll go first. You come after. On your terms."

She squeezed my hands once—hard—then turned away before either of us could fracture completely. And I stood there alone, steady in the choice I was about to make.

The music shifted as she stepped out—measured, deliberate. I caught a glimpse of sage fabric moving through the light, dark florals gathered in her hands. Applause followed her, soft and controlled, like everyone instinctively understood this wasn't a moment to break.

I exhaled. And then I saw myself.

Not in a mirror—but in the tall window set into the stone wall beside me. Old glass, imperfect, fractured into narrow panes that bent the light and split my reflection into pieces. I stopped.

For a moment, there wasn't one Sierra looking back at me—there were many.

The girl who learned how to be quiet.
The woman who learned how to endure.
The one who crossed an ocean shaking, bleeding, ready to burn everything down if she had to.

The seams in the glass fractured me into layers, but none of them looked weak. None of them looked lost. I lifted my hand and pressed my fingers to the cool surface.

I wasn't broken. I was assembled.

The music deepened—lower now. Steadier. Not a summons. A signal.

No one was coming to walk me down the aisle. This wasn't about being given away. I turned from the window and stepped forward.

The aisle opened in front of me—black chairs, greenery woven through with sage and oxblood blooms, the whole space balanced on the edge between beauty and threat. It wasn't soft. It wasn't gentle. It was intentional.

Flower girls passed me, ivory dresses fluttering as they scattered dark petals across the stone. The contrast was stark. I liked that.

Then it was just me.

Almost a month had passed since I'd last seen him. My breath still caught.

Lorenzo stood at the far end of the aisle, dressed exactly as I'd imagined him—dark suit cut close to the body, no excess, no softness. The fabric drank the light, the lines sharp enough to suggest control without promising safety.

His brothers stood beside him, dressed the same, a united front of quiet violence and loyalty. Marco's jaw was tight. Emil's expression unreadable. Dario's gaze lifted to me with something like relief.

And Lorenzo—His eyes found mine.

It wasn't tears. It wasn't relief alone. It was raw.

Something stripped down and exposed, like he was holding himself perfectly still because any movement might shatter him. Fear lived there. Hope too. A reverence so sharp it bordered on pain.

He didn't smile. He just watched me. Like he didn't trust the world to keep me solid unless he saw me with his own eyes.

I walked slowly, every step deliberate. The petals crushed softly beneath my feet. The air smelled like salt and greenery and something metallic underneath it all.

This wasn't a rescue. This wasn't a trap. This wasn't a performance built to convince anyone. It was a choice.

And as I reached the end of the aisle, as his gaze never left my face, I knew with absolute clarity—

Whatever obsession had once bound us, whatever violence had tried to claim us— I was here because I wanted to be.

The priest stepped forward, hands folded, voice steady against the open air.

"We are gathered here today," he began, "not to witness a transaction, nor to bind two people by obligation—but to bear witness to a choice."

The breeze moved through the vineyard, stirring the sage and dark florals lining the aisle. Somewhere behind me, fabric whispered. No one spoke.

"Marriage," he continued, "is not the absence of danger. It is the presence of consent. It is not protection from consequence, but a promise made with full knowledge of it." His eyes lifted, moving between us.

"Lorenzo Moretti and Sierra Blackwell stand here having seen each other clearly. Not as ideals. Not as safe harbors. But as they are."

A pause. Intentional.

"If anyone present believes that these vows are being made under coercion, fear, or force, speak now."

Silence answered. The priest nodded once, as if satisfied.

"Then let us proceed." He turned to Lorenzo first.

"Lorenzo, will you speak your vows?"

***

### *Lorenzo*

I felt her before I fully saw her. The air shifted. The space tightened. Something in my chest went quiet in the way it only ever did when she was near—like my body had learned her gravity and adjusted without asking.

Then I looked up. She was walking toward me alone.

No arm to lean on. No one guiding her forward. Every step was her choice, measured and steady, like she was advancing into something she'd already decided to survive—or conquer.

She was dressed in ivory and black, the contrast stark against the vineyard's green. Not soft. Not ornamental. The lace cut across her like intent. The dress didn't hide her strength. It framed it. Claimed it.

Her eyes found mine halfway down the aisle. And held.

There were no tears. Not from her. Not from me. But something in my chest fractured anyway—quietly, irreversibly. A month apart had not dulled her. It had sharpened her. She looked like a woman who had walked through fire and come back carrying the flame.

When she reached me, the priest spoke—but the words barely registered.

All I could see were her hands. Still. Steady. I took them in mine.

Her fingers were warm. Real. Scarred in places I knew by memory now. I felt the faint tremor beneath her skin—not fear. Adrenaline. Choice. She squeezed once. Not reassurance. Permission.

The priest's voice settled into the background, a steady cadence about witness and consent and vows freely given. It felt distant. Like something happening around us instead of to us.

Then he turned to me.

"Lorenzo, will you speak your vows?"

I swallowed. Not because I didn't know what to say.

Because I knew exactly how much it would cost.

I tightened my grip on her hands—not to hold her in place. Never that. Just to remind myself that this was real. That she was here. That she had come back to me with her eyes open.

"I stand here having already lost you," I said quietly. "And having been forgiven for it."

Her thumb brushed against my knuckle. Barely there.

"I loved you before I knew what love cost," I continued. "And I obsessed when I should have protected. I watched when I should have stopped. I turned vigilance into penance and called it care."

The words burned on the way out. Necessary. Unavoidable.

"I will never pretend that I am safe," I said. "Or gentle. Or easy to love. But I will be honest. I will be present. And I will never again decide what you need without your consent."

I lifted our joined hands slightly, pressing my forehead to them for a single breath before looking at her again.

"You are not my shield," I said. "You are not my weakness. You are the truth I chose even when it could have destroyed me."

My voice roughened, just slightly.

"I will stand beside you without hiding behind you. I will let you leave if you must. And I will meet you again if you return—not with chains, but with open hands."

I paused. This was the line that mattered.

"I vow," I said, steady now, certain, "to choose you without ownership, to love you without erasing you, and to remain—no matter the cost—worthy of the woman who walked toward me today."

I squeezed her hands once more.

"I vow to choose you — ruthlessly, freely, and with my eyes open."

******

### Sierra

The priest let the silence settle. Then he turned to me.

"Sierra," he said gently, deliberately. "You have heard the vows offered to you. If you wish to respond, you may speak now."

I didn't hesitate.

I tightened my grip on Lorenzo's hands instead — felt the strength in them, the restraint. The man who had once tried to protect me by watching now stood still, letting me see everything.

"I stand here because I chose to," I said.

My voice didn't shake. It surprised me — how solid it felt leaving my chest.

"I wasn't brought here by obligation. Or fear. Or a contract written in someone else's blood."

I looked at him fully then. Let him see it — the knowing, the forgiveness, the line I would not let him cross again.

"I saw who you were when you thought you had already lost me," I said. "When you knelt instead of reaching for control. When you offered me your life or your death and waited to see which I would choose."

A breath.

"That mattered."

I swallowed, slow and steady.

"I won't pretend I don't know what you are capable of," I continued. "I won't ask you to be smaller, or safer, or something you're not. I have seen the violence in you. I have also seen the discipline it takes not to use it."

My thumb brushed over his knuckle — grounding, intentional.

"I am not afraid of your darkness," I said. "I am afraid only of a world where we lie to each other about it."

The vineyard was silent now. Even the breeze seemed to hold.

"I won't belong to you," I said. "And you won't belong to me. But I will stand with you — eyes open, hands clean, choices made out loud."

I leaned forward slightly, just enough that this part was only for him.

"If we burn," I said softly, "we burn together. Not because we had to. Because we chose it."

I straightened. Met his gaze.

"I vow," I said, certain now, unflinching, "to choose you without fear, to meet your devotion with my own, and to remain — no matter what we become — honest about the cost."

I squeezed his hands once.

"I vow to choose you — ruthlessly, freely, and with my eyes open."

******

### *Lorenzo*

Her words landed like truth does — not soft, not kind, but exact.

I didn't move. Didn't breathe. My hands closed around hers because they had to, because if I loosened even an inch I might betray what she had just given me.

She chose me.

Not the version of me I'd tried to sell her. Not the man behind the contracts or the watching or the blood. She chose the one who had knelt. The one who had been willing to be judged and found wanting.

I had crossed oceans prepared to die for her. She had crossed to find me— and stood here anyway. That was the difference.

Her vow wasn't forgiveness. It was something sharper. It was consent given with full knowledge of the weapon. I had always believed love was possession sharpened into permanence. She had rewritten it.

She didn't promise me safety. She didn't promise me forever. She promised me truth. And in doing so, she bound me more completely than any contract ever had.

I lowered my forehead until it brushed hers — not a kiss, not yet. A recognition. I would never deserve what she had just done.

The priest asked for the rings.

Marco stepped forward, precise as ever, and placed them into the priest's hands. Two bands. Dark. Unadorned. Honest. Sierra had chosen them, of course. Nothing ornamental. Nothing performative. Something that would endure.

"Lorenzo," the priest said quietly. "Place the ring on Sierra's hand."

My fingers closed around the band, and for the first time that day, they shook. Not because I doubted. Because I understood.

I took her hand like it was something alive — not fragile, but deliberate. Her skin was warm. Steady. She didn't look away as I slid the ring over her knuckle, slow enough to feel every fraction of resistance, every quiet inch of commitment until it settled at the base of her finger.

Mine. Not owned. Not claimed. Chosen.

The priest turned to her and offered the second ring.

"Sierra."

She took my hand without hesitation. Her thumb brushed once over my knuckles — not reassurance, not comfort. Recognition. Then she slid the ring onto my finger, firm and exact, like she expected me to carry its weight.

It fit. Of course it did.

The priest stepped back, giving us space without naming it.

"By the vows you have spoken," he said, voice even, "and by the choice you have made with full knowledge of its cost, I now pronounce you husband and wife."

The world narrowed.

"You may kiss."

I didn't move immediately.

I searched her face — not for permission, but for truth. For any sign that this had shifted, that she had softened or second-guessed or retreated.

She lifted her chin. That was all.

I kissed her with control sharpened into reverence, hunger held exactly where it belonged. Not desperate. Not hurried. My hands framed her face, thumbs warm against her jaw, grounding us both as if the ground itself might give way. The kiss was deep, controlled, reverent — hunger held carefully in check. Not conquest.

Meeting. She kissed me back without flinching. Without apology. Without fear.

The sound of the world returned — breath, movement, distant applause — but it didn't reach me. All I knew was the way she stayed. The way she chose to remain exactly where she was.

When we finally pulled apart, foreheads touching, breath shared, there was no triumph in me. Only certainty.

# Epilogue

*Sierra*

The vows were said not in a cathedral, but in the sun-drenched heart of our Sicilian vineyard, the rows of vines a silent, witness to our union. I chose him. I chose his chaos, his darkness, his all-consuming obsession. And in turn, he vowed to love me ruthlessly, to always choose me. It was a pact forged in blood and sealed with a kiss that tasted like forever.

Our honeymoon was a blur of sun and salt, a secluded villa on the Amalfi Coast where the only thing more intense than the Mediterranean heat was the fire between us. He didn't just fuck me; he worshipped me, memorizing every curve, every scar, every secret. He claimed me with a reverence that bordered on violence, and I met his fury with my own, our bodies a battleground where we fought our way to a blissful, exhausted peace.

We didn't return to the penthouse. On Dario's suggestion, we moved to the sprawling estate nestled in the rolling hills at the Californian vineyard. Lorenzo stepped back from the edge, his focus shifting from the blood-soaked business of vengeance to the intricate, cutthroat world of high-stakes wine. He was still lethal, his power a palpable force in every boardroom, but his hands, once stained with the blood of those who tried to hurt us, were now mostly clean, stained only with the rich earth of our land.

The vineyard became mine in ways no one could see. I curated desire—events, tastings, stories told just softly enough to feel exclusive. I turned our name into a promise people craved, while Lorenzo watched from the shadows, satisfied to let the world believe I was all softness and sun.

My parents, of course, came sniffing around, drawn by the scent of success and power. They found me on the terrace one afternoon, their smiles as practiced and hollow as ever. "Darling," my mother began, "we were so worried. You owe us a call, at least."

I'd felt him before I saw him, a familiar, comforting presence at my back. He didn't speak, didn't move. He just stood there, my silent, deadly shadow, a constant reminder of the world I had chosen.

I looked at the woman who had sold me, at the man who had offered me up to a monster. "I don't owe you anything," I said, my voice calm, clear. "You traded my future for your safety. The price was paid. The contract is closed." I turned my back on them, dismissing them as easily as they had dismissed me, and walked into Lorenzo's waiting arms. Security escorted them out and they haven't been heard from since.

The cameras are still there. They are hidden throughout our home, silent sentinels in the corners of every room. But it's not about control anymore. It's about presence. It's his way of being with me, even when he's thousands of miles away. It's a constant, unwavering vigilance that has become the most twisted form of intimacy I've ever known.

And I've learned to use it.

Sometimes, when I know he's watching from his office, I'll let my fingers trail along the neckline of my dress. I'll catch my own reflection in a darkened screen and offer a slow, secret smile. I'll send him a text, *Are you watching?*

Because I know he is. And in the quiet sanctuary of our vineyard, under the vast, star-dusted sky, I have finally found my truth. He is my obsession, and I am his. And I wouldn't have it any other way.

He is the blade, and I am the hand that holds him steady.

# Acknowledgement

Thank you for joining me on this adventure! I've always been an avid reader, and for as long as I can remember, I dreamed of writing a book of my own. This story has been a true labor of love, and I'm incredibly proud and grateful to finally share it with you.

To my amazing husband, Mike – thank you for giving me the confidence to sit down and write this story. I'm not sure I would have found the courage to begin, let alone finish, without you.

To our sweet daughter, thank you for inspiring me to do the things we love. Right now, you are six 'writing' your own story about a girl who lost her unicorn horn. I love watching you grow.

Thank you to my family – my mother, grandmother, and aunt for being my biggest supporters throughout this journey. Your feedback and confidence has kept me going.

And, of course, thank you dear reader. Your time, trust, and heart mean more than you know.

# About the Author

I write dark contemporary romance filled with power plays, dangerous loyalty, and love that refuses to stay in the shadows. My stories explore morally gray heroes, fiercely resilient heroines, and the complicated legacy of family, identity, and choice.

I first fell in love with storytelling as a child, finding grounding and escape in the pages of well-worn books. Reading became both refuge and anchor, a place where complicated emotions made sense and love always fought its way to the surface. Once, I was even grounded from reading as a kid.

When I'm not writing about ruthless men and the women strong enough to love them, I is spending time with my husband and daughter, soaking up the outdoors, playing video games, or enjoying quiet moments with my pets, friends, and extended family.

I believe the best stories, on the page and in life, are built on loyalty, resilience, and love that endures.

# Also by Sutton Kay

**The Ruthless Love Series**

*Ruthless Vows*

*Ruthless Temptations*

*Ruthless Devotion* - Coming Fall 2026

# *Ruthless Temptations*

**Spring 2026**

Jax Vitelli has spent his life walking the line between shadow and legitimacy—loyal to the man who gave him a second chance, determined to outrun a past soaked in violence.

Jenna Cole has been groomed for a gilded future she never chose, her every move orchestrated by powerful parents who see her as leverage in a high-stakes game of status and control.

When their worlds collide at the center of Chicago's elite social scene, the attraction between them is immediate—and impossible. She belongs to a world of silk dresses and whispered alliances. He belongs to one of inked knuckles and unspoken debts. But beneath the glamour and polished smiles lies a darker truth: both of their lives are already entangled in a web of legacy, obligation, and blood.

As old loyalties resurface and new power shifts threaten the fragile balance around them, Jax must decide whether staying in the shadows will protect Jenna—or leave her exposed to men who believe everything has a price. And Jenna must confront a terrifying possibility: the only man strong enough to shield her from the fire may be the one willing to burn the world down.

In a story where love is both a sanctuary and a weapon, *Ruthless Temptation* asks one question—how far would you go to protect the person who feels like home?

9 798995 361701